FACING JUSTICE

Recent Titles by Nick Oldham from Severn House

FACING JUSTICE

A Henry Christie Novel

Nick Oldham

This first world edition published 2011
in Great Britain and in the USA by
SEVERN HOUSE PUBLISHERS LTD of
9–15 High Street, Sutton, Surrey, England, SM1 1DF.
Trade paperback edition first published
in Great Britain and the USA 2012 by
SEVERN HOUSE PUBLISHERS LTD.

British Library Cataloguing in Publication Data

Oldham, Nick, 1956–
  Facing justice. – (A Detective Superintendent Henry
  Christie novel)
  1. Christie, Henry (Fictitious character) – Fiction.
  2. Police – England – Blackpool – Fiction. 3. Intelligence
  Officers – United States – Fiction. 4. Detective and
  mystery stories.
  I. Title II. Series
  823.9'2-dc22

ISBN-13: 978-0-7278-8075-8 (cased)
ISBN-13: 978-1-84751-374-8 (trade paper)

All Severn House titles are printed on acid-free paper.

Severn House Publishers support The Forest Stewardship Council [FSC],
the leading international forest certification organisation. All our titles that
are printed on Greenpeace-approved FSC-certified paper carry the FSC logo.

MIX
Paper from
responsible sources
FSC
www.fsc.org FSC® C018575

Typeset by Palimpsest Book Production Ltd.,
Falkirk, Stirlingshire, Scotland.
Printed and bound in Great Britain by
MPG Books Ltd., Bodmin, Cornwall.

To Belinda, my love

ONE

Massey was amazed to wake up alive. He was certain he'd be dead, that the horrific beating he'd endured – the fists, boots, sticks and bats – would have, *should have*, killed him. He'd obviously been lucid at the start of it, expecting to get a good hammering, basically what he deserved. But, only a short way into the assault, he realized this was much more than a punishment beating. He could tell by their faces and their eyes and their determination. And he knew this would be the last time he would ever be assaulted by anyone. But there had been nothing he could do about it. He couldn't protect himself or fight back in any way. Being securely gaffer-taped to a chair ensured that.

Then the pain took over, followed by the distortion of sight, sound and thought. Next the in-and-out of consciousness, vision blurring as though he'd opened his eyes deep under murky water, unable to see, then unable to feel, then unable to breathe. And then the merciful blackness of what he assumed was his death.

As consciousness returned, his eyelids fluttered but he didn't open them. Just lay there on the cold, gritty surface and explored how his body was feeling. He wasn't stupid enough to believe he would have fooled his captors into thinking he was still out of it. He knew he'd moved, knew he'd groaned, knew his breathing was in a different rhythm, but he didn't care. If they wanted to start on him again after they'd realized they hadn't killed him – which must have been their intention – eyes open or closed would not make one bit of difference.

Searing pain arced through his cranium, starting at a place just behind his eyeballs and radiating out in agonizing pulses, like a migraine times a thousand. Did this mean he had a fractured skull? He recalled the vicious stomp on the head that must have been the origin of the pain. That was when they'd got really carried away and lost it, after the chair had toppled over and one of them had jumped on him. His whole face had been forced out of kilter, distorted like a kid standing on a balloon.

Massey ground his teeth and moved the tip of his tongue along the back of them. Many were loose, hanging there in the gums, barely connected any more. There were two big gaps and he recalled spitting out fragments of crushed teeth when the men had heaved the chair back upright. He'd spat out the broken teeth and blood and squinted at the men through his pus-swollen eyes, then seen the baseball bat arcing towards him.

Now he did open his eyes. At least as far as they would open in the liquid-filled sacs of swellings now encasing them. He coughed, swallowed blood, and pain tore at his chest. Broken ribs? He moved a fraction, convulsing at the pain in his knees from the blows delivered by the bat.

He tried to control his breathing as a deep, long shudder passed like a ghostly shockwave through the entire length and breadth of his body.

He was in darkness, unable to work out where he was. So he lay still, moving his ankles and wrists slightly, realizing he was no longer taped to a chair, nor was there any duct tape binding his arms or ankles. He was lying on a hard floor now. He wondered if they thought they had succeeded in killing him, whether they had ripped the tape off and dragged him to this place that was like a basement of some sort. Somewhere to stash the body before disposing of it?

Massey brought up his legs, a movement that made him gasp. Then he eased himself very slowly and painfully up until he was sitting on his backside, still trying to control his breathing as if by doing so he could control the agony. He swayed a little, not wanting to move. What he wanted were painkillers and then to close his eyes and reawaken in a week's time, having healed.

Keeping his body as still as possible, he squinted at his location, and saw that he was definitely alone. They were not waiting for him to sit up just so they could begin again.

From what little light there was, it seemed as though he was in a basement room of some sort. A square room, not much bigger than a police cell – and he'd been in plenty of those in his time – with rough-hewn concrete flooring and inner walls constructed of breeze block. There was a tiny window, maybe a foot square, high up on one wall. Massey could see it was made from opaque, reinforced glass with three iron bars set into the window ledge.

And yes, he was definitely alone.

And there was a door.

Massey inched his head around and slowly tried to focus on it. It was steel-reinforced – another reminder of a cell, even down to the inspection hatch just below eye level. At ground level there was also a flap in the floor through which a food tray could be slid, something which puzzled Massey faintly. His eyes, though watery and swollen, were starting to work better now, seeing things more sharply even though he could not open them any wider than slits. The door had no handle on this side, so its locking was controlled from the outside. Again, just like a cell door, not a basement door.

He groaned involuntarily, spat something out that dribbled messily down his chin and on to his chest. He rocked, his head feeling as though lots of sharp stone chips were inside it.

But he was definitely alive. Of that he was certain.

Death, he now knew, had no feeling. Being alive meant sheer agony.

He wiped the back of his hand across his mouth. Then, closing one nostril with a finger, he blew down the open one, clearing it of blood and phlegm. He repeated the process with the other nostril.

His nasal passages clear, he smelled something other than his own blood and gagged at the odour. Something . . . a combination of heavy urine and dead flesh. Very strong and almost overpowering. A smell he could not place even though it was familiar and he had smelled it before. Sometime in his past, many years before. Or was it somewhere else in his memory, deep-rooted and primeval?

He shivered in fear.

'Fuck it,' he said and slowly curled his body around and eased himself up to his knees. He didn't stay in that position for long because his kneecaps had been hit by the baseball bat – but, as painful as they were, they had not been shattered. Then he recalled something else that puzzled him a little.

The man hitting his knees with the bat. And the other one holding him back. What had been said?

'No . . . don't break 'em. He needs to be able to . . .'

Massey tried to remember. Couldn't quite put the piece there.

'*Able to what?*'

'Fuck it,' he said again and pushed himself slowly up to his feet, then lost balance as everything inside his skull rolled loosely around. He staggered to the wall for support before he fell again, the palms of his hands holding him upright, his face just inches away from the breeze block.

He cursed and rested his forehead on the wall, then, puzzled, he drew back a few inches and made his eyes focus on a sign spray-painted on the wall. It was a diamond shape, basically an orange-coloured square tilted on to one of its corners. The word 'EXPLOSIVES' was written across it in thick black capitals. There was a graphic image above the word representing an actual explosion. Massey realized he was looking at a health and safety sign.

'What the . . .?' he started to say, thinking, *explosives in a basement?* But he could not be bothered continuing with the thought thread.

He inhaled another stuttering, painful breath, wincing as he felt the jagged end of a broken rib touching a lung. He turned, leaned on the wall, again exploring his current situation.

Despite the sign, the place did remind him of a basement, maybe situated under the main house. The ceiling seemed to be made of thick concrete and a light bulb dangled, unlit, on a foot-long thread of wire.

Then that smell. That odour. Where had he smelled it before? There was something horrible about it. Animal.

Using one hand on the wall for support he took an uncertain step towards the metallic door and stood in something soft. He looked down. It was shit. Despite his physical condition, Massey pulled a face and dragged his shoe across the floor to get it off his sole. He heard a click as the foot connected with and moved something.

This time it was a thick steel chain, one end sunk deeply and concreted into the wall. Massey reached for it and pulled it up. The links were heavy and strong. He ran them through his hands until he came to the end, attached to which was a leather collar two inches thick, one that would have fitted around the neck of the world's biggest dog.

Massey inspected the collar. It was made of thick but softly pliable leather with a big steel buckle. He held it to his bloodied nose and sniffed it cautiously. Then he dropped it as his guts spun over and he suddenly remembered where he had smelled that reek before – and realized that the stupid rumours he'd heard were true.

A very basic terror gripped him. Every hair on his body rose as adrenalin rushed into his system and drew blood away from the surface capillaries.

He moved quickly to the door. Fully expecting it to be locked, he ran his fingertips down the edge opposite the hinges and pulled at it. It creaked open an inch.

Massey paused. His senses tingled, heart pounded. He half expected them to burst in now, having realized their mistake in that they hadn't actually killed him. No one came. A cold, biting wind hissed through the gap, hitting his face with its iciness, and its freshness took away the odour of the room for a moment.

He opened the door a few more inches. Cautiously he peered out, still uncertain as to his whereabouts, but definitely not in the location in which he'd been assaulted. He edged out into a bright, moonlit, but excruciatingly cold night and seemed to be standing in the middle of nowhere. The world was completely silent, other than the sound of the wind. Not even distant traffic. And the room he had woken up in, thinking it had been a cellar under the main house, was nothing of the sort. It was the inside of a complete little building, about the size of a detached single garage. It was a sort of fortified hut, with one door, the high barred window and nothing else, with an outer perimeter twelve by twelve, maybe eight feet high and flat-roofed. The outer walls were thick stone. A sign on the door reiterated the inner warning: 'DANGER – EXPLOSIVES!'

His beaten, befuddled brain then realized where he'd been dragged to and dumped, and what the building was, or used to be.

He waited, listened for a few seconds, hearing nothing but the crash of his heartbeat. All he could feel now, even above the pain that wracked his injured body, was complete and utter fear.

He moved away from the building, limping, dragging himself along, knowing he had no time at all to worry about his wounds, what might be broken, damaged or bruised. Somehow he had to get away from this place. He forced himself to walk as quickly as he could across the barren, rocky ground, stumbling but managing to stay upright. He scrambled up an incline to the top of a mound of earth and stood squinting across a vast, open expanse in front of him, a huge black hole on the face of the world. But he did not pause for long. He moved on, hoping he had regained consciousness sooner than they thought he would.

He caught his foot, stumbled, fell, smacked down on to his sore knees, jarring his whole being. He cried out involuntarily and tried to muffle the noise, turning it from a scream of agony into a moan. But a noise nevertheless.

Then he was on his feet again, half sliding down a rubble-strewn slope and skidding into a wheel rut, cut deep into the clay.

Which way?

He started to follow the ruts, hoping there was some logic to this plan. Surely they would lead somewhere.

Once more he kicked a big stone and lurched. His body jarred and the broken rib touched his lung again, making him hiss with pain. He crumbled to the ground, waiting for the pain to ebb. Slowly it receded. He took a few more seconds for complete recovery.

Then, somewhere behind him, a slight scuffing sound. And another noise to accompany this: a rough, sawing cough.

The fear he felt intensified.

He rose slowly to his full height. Turned and looked into the darkness behind him. All his senses prickled. He was ready to flee.

Now he recalled what the man had said about his knees: 'Don't break 'em. He needs to be able to run.' Run! That was the word and Massey now knew why his knees hadn't been smashed and broken. It was always the intention that he would wake up. That he would live through the beating, as savage as it was. Intended that he had some ability to run, or at least hobble, on two feet. So he could take part in a dangerous race for his life.

He could not see or hear anything now. 'So it's true,' he said to himself. Then shouted, 'Come on you bastard,' into the dark.

And then he remembered that other thing. The stench. Now he placed it and he knew what was out there in the dark just beyond the periphery of his vision.

The moon had been covered by cloud which now peeled away and cast light across the rutted ground.

There were two short coughs.

Massey spun. He had been looking in the wrong direction. For a moment he was fixed to the spot, anchored by injury and terror, paralysed. Then he moved, but too late. His ankle twisted in a tyre rut, he screamed and went down. The last thing he saw were the two almond-shaped eyes reflecting silver in the moonlight.

TWO

F lynn immediately didn't like the guy. Smelled the stale alcohol on his breath, instinctively knew there would be trouble to come.

Had times been less harsh economically, Flynn would have told him the boat was fully booked and pointed him in the direction of one of the other charter fishing boats moored along the quay. But any charter is a good charter, Flynn's boss had told him, especially in this day and age. The fishing business had gone pretty limp over the last few months and there had been a rumour about mothballing some of the boats next month – January – if things didn't pick up. That meant no income from fishing and, for Flynn, a long, unpleasant spell as a doorman at one of his boss's clubs up in Puerto Rico's Commercial Centre.

So, quoting a vastly inflated price for the day that did not even cause the man to bat an eyelid, and separating him from 800 euros, Flynn said, please step aboard, sir. The only good side of it was that trailing behind the guy like a petulant teenager was his scantily clad lady friend, who looked as though she would rather be anywhere else in the world than climbing aboard a sportfishing boat in Gran Canaria. Her continually rolling eyeballs and accompanying body language told their own sorry story.

Flynn introduced the customer to Jose, his Spanish crewman, who extended his bear-paw of a hand to be shaken and was completely ignored by the man. Jose, undaunted, maintained his professional attitude and kept his broad grin in place as he withdrew his hand and redirected his attention to the even less receptive girlfriend.

She teetered up the gangplank on to the deck, losing one of her flip-flops into the water, and demanded, 'I want to be inside, I want food and booze . . . ugh, I feel sick already.'

'Your wish is my command,' Jose said and ushered her into the stateroom, passing within earshot of Flynn, mouthing a Spanish obscenity to him.

'Nah then, mate,' the customer said to Flynn, who hooked the floating flip-flop out of the water with a gaff, 'I'm told you're the best skip in the Canaries. Let's see, shall we?' He rubbed his hands and raised his face challengingly. 'If I don't come back having caught a blue marlin, I'll be really pissed off.'

'The marlin run ended late September,' Flynn told him. 'Won't be much chance of catching one, I'm afraid.'

'So what will we catch?'

'Maybe nothing, but there's plenty of thornbacks, stingrays and congers out there. Maybe lock into a shoal of tuna if we're lucky. Shark are always out there, too.'

'Don't want luck to be a part of it. You got fish finding equipment, haven't you? Sonar, y'know?'

'The most sophisticated and up to date,' Flynn confirmed. 'But even that doesn't guarantee fish.'

'Good job I know my stuff then, isn't it?'

'You're an experienced sport fisher?' Flynn asked as though he was interested.

'Oh yeah.'

Flynn waited, but there was no elaboration. 'I'll do my very best for you, then,' he assured the customer and began to prepare the boat – named *Faye 2* – for the day ahead.

The fishing turned out to be pretty good. No great monsters of the deep, but a fine array of specimens including a very meaty red snapper that Flynn kept and gutted, and would be his supper that night. The customer, whose name turned out to be Hugo, was kept reasonably happy and busy, though none of his claimed skills were either evident or tested much.

It was a different matter for his girlfriend, Janey. As the charter went on, she became progressively more seasick until she was begging Hugo to have the boat turned back to dry land. She had gone the colour of the decks, pure white, from an original golden brown tan, had spent some time with her head down the chemical toilet and even more hanging pathetically over the side of the boat, all sense of modesty having vanished as she hollered dreadfully at the sea gods.

Eventually she could bear it no longer. She dragged herself across the deck like a wounded animal to Hugo. He was strapped regally into the fighting chair with a rod rising majestically from his lower belly area. She begged him to end her misery.

Flynn watched the exchange from his lofty position in the flying bridge. It ended with Hugo roughly pushing Janey away. She fell flat on her backside and looked up appealingly at Flynn, as did Jose whose expression was a dark scowl of anger. Flynn sighed and slid down the ladder on to the deck. He helped Janey to her feet and back into the stateroom where she flopped on to the sofa and closed her eyes, gulping.

Then he spun back on to the deck and approached Hugo, who was still in the fighting chair.

'That's the end of the charter, sir,' Flynn told him.

Hugo's good-looking face turned towards him. 'Why would that be?'

'You want me to spell it out?'

'I think you'd better.'

'I don't tolerate your sort of behaviour on board.'

'What sort of behaviour is that?'

Flynn's chest tightened. He gestured to Jose. 'Bring in the rods, we're heading back.'

Jose nodded and grabbed one of the outriggers.

'I paid good money for this charter,' Hugo whined.

'You can have it back, less what it's cost so far.'

'Does that include this?' On his last word, Hugo pulled the rod butt out of the gimbal that was fixed to the leather pad worn around his waist and jettisoned the rod, reel and line out of his hands and into the churning sea behind the boat.

Flynn's mouth drooped in astonishment. Words began to form on his twisted lips, but before he could say anything, Hugo rose from the fighting chair, elbowed past him and stomped into the stateroom. Still not having said anything, Flynn watched him, utterly dumbfounded by his action.

Jose had witnessed the whole thing. He said, 'He threw that into the sea deliberately,' his Spanish tongue struggling slightly on the last word.

'I know,' Flynn said, turning desperately to the water to see if the rod was still there. It had disappeared instantly. Flynn's expression changed to anger and he took one step towards the entrance to the stateroom. Jose saw the alteration on Flynn's face – something he had seen too often recently, and invariably it meant trouble – and stepped in front of him, holding up one of his big hands.

'No boss, *nada stupido.*'

'I'm gonna launch that son of a—'

'NO,' Jose said firmly, looking into Flynn's eyes, holding his gaze.

Flynn ground his teeth, did a mental back-count from ten and took a deep breath. 'I'm OK.'

He went into the cockpit and grabbed the radio handset, pressed the transmit button, thinking he would call the coastguard and have them get the police to await their arrival back at port. Then he decided on a different approach. He ducked into the stateroom where a still sick Janey was laid out dramatically on the couch, eyes closed, a forearm covering her eyes. Hugo lounged in a chair, legs splayed, a bottle of San Miguel resting on his stomach. He glowered belligerently at Flynn.

'That gear's worth fifteen hundred euros.'

'And?' Hugo shrugged. 'Accident. Claim on the insurance.'

'Listen, bud, when we get back it can go one way or the other. First way, we go along to our quayside kiosk, you present your credit card and pay up. Second way – my preferred way – cops're waiting for you.'

'On what charge?'

'Criminal damage. Whatever way – no refund.'

'Do what you want.'

'Oh, just pay him,' Janey piped up from her sick bed. 'This whole holiday sucks.'

'Tell you what, Hugo, I'll have the cops waiting either way, eh?'

Hugo took a long, noisy draw from the bottle and scowled at Flynn. People seem to do that a lot, Flynn thought: glare at me.

'You're a big, hard man, aren't you, Mr Flynn?'

Flynn shook his head and sighed. He pivoted away, could not be bothered. 'Cops it is,' he murmured – but loud enough for Hugo to hear.

What he didn't expect was for Hugo to jump him.

Flynn patted Hugo's cheeks. 'C'mon, c'mon, wakey, wakey.'

Hugo had been placed in the recovery position – after Flynn had roared like a bear and thrown Hugo over his shoulder – and that was as long as the fight had lasted. Hugo smashed the back of his head on the corner of the door frame as he landed awkwardly and was knocked out instantly. Flynn had looked down at him in disbelief.

'The stupid . . .'

'Oh, what have you done?' Jose demanded, seeing the towering, muscled frame of Flynn standing over the unmoving body. Of a customer.

Flynn looked at him pointedly.

'He didn't do a thing,' Janey piped up despondently. 'Hugo went for him. He's like that, only he usually wins.' She propped herself up on one elbow, no colour whatsoever in her complexion.

Flynn gasped in exasperation and bent over to check Hugo's vital signs, which were fine. Even so, he hadn't recovered full consciousness by the time Flynn edged *Faye 2* back into her berth in the marina at Puerto Rico half an hour later. An ambulance was waiting on the quayside, as was Adam Castle, Flynn's boss and owner of the boat, as well as other boats and businesses. Castle slid the gangplank across to the stern and stood aside as two paramedics trotted aboard to tend to Hugo. Castle waited on the quayside, a stony, serious expression on his face.

Flynn briefed the medics and they carted a groggy, cross-eyed Hugo off into the ambulance.

Janey, having miraculously recovered from seasickness simply by standing on terra firma, made no attempt to join Hugo in the ambulance. She looked fine now.

'You not going with him?' Flynn asked.

'I don't think so. I'll catch up with him later.' She produced a wallet from the back pocket of her minute shorts. 'I'll pay for the fishing tackle. Hugo's credit card's in here and I know the PIN.'

'Thanks,' Flynn said.

The ambulance pulled away and Janey started to walk towards the booking kiosk, but paused, turned and looked meaningfully over her shoulder at Flynn. 'If you're interested . . . I'll be in the Irish bar in the Commercial Centre at eight tonight.'

'What about Hugo?'

'He won't be there, whatever.' She smiled. All her colour had returned and she was a completely different character to the one Flynn had been introduced to originally. 'Your choice, Flynn. One thing though – try not to bump into Hugo again. He bears grudges.'

He nodded graciously and then Adam Castle stepped into his line of sight. 'Words,' his boss said. 'Now.'

Castle led Flynn along the quayside, saying a great deal with just his body language. Flynn, big man that he was, followed meekly and they went all the way around the harbour into one of the first-floor cafés in the mini commercial centre overlooking the marina. Flynn sat glumly whilst Castle ordered a couple of Cruzcampos and set the chilled beers down on the table.

'Here, you're going to need this.'

Flynn was parched but he took the bottle cautiously and sipped the wonderful brew, rather than pouring it all down his throat in one, which was his instinct.

'Look boss,' he said, 'the guy went for me and I just reacted in self-defence. He'd been an arsehole all the charter; even his girlfriend was up to here with him.' Hell, his throat was dry and he spoke croakily, but necking the beer still seemed a little inappropriate to the circumstances. He was shocked by what Castle had to say next.

'I don't really give a monkey's about him, and I believe you, Steve – so as far as I'm concerned, there's no problem there.'

'Oh?' Flynn's eyebrows furrowed. 'So what's this about – the face and everything?' He wrapped his right hand around the bottle and lifted it to his cracked lips, deciding that a long slurp – not too long to be rude – was now OK. The ice-cold beer spread gratify-ingly down into his chest.

Castle looked very troubled. He was chewing his bottom lip and shaking his head sadly.

'What is it, boss?' Flynn liked the guy. He had been very good to Flynn when he'd landed penniless on the island almost five years before. Had given Flynn a job on a boat, and Flynn had repaid him by becoming the best sportfishing skip on the islands. Flynn had grafted, learned his trade and applied his instinctual knowledge of hunting down the big fish, something that was innate and something most of the other charter skippers didn't have. Flynn also took out day safaris inland up into the mountains in the centre of the island and worked the doors of Castle's two night clubs when necessary. He had a lot to be grateful for to Castle.

'Don't know how to say this, pal . . . credit crunch and all that.'

Flynn ingested the words and his insides went even icier than the beer.

He went on, 'I'm a bit over-extended and I need to pull in the reins a bit, so I'll be mothballing the boats for two months because we haven't got one firm booking for that period and I can't rely on walk-ons.' He was referring to the ad-hoc customers who simply appeared at the boat, such as Hugo had done. 'Especially if you knock them all out,' he added lightly, but there was sadness in his voice. Castle had diverse business interests but particularly loved sportfishing. Flynn felt sorry for him.

'Every boat?' Flynn asked. There were half a dozen of them dotted around the Canaries.

'I won't lie to you – all but Orlando's in Tenerife. Business isn't quite as bad there, but everyone else will be out of the water.'

Flynn went hollow.

'I know you're ten times better than him, but Tenerife isn't suffering as much as Gran Canaria and you're here, not there. If it was the other way around . . .' Castle left the words unsaid. 'I'll review the position at the end of January.'

'So I'm out of a job?'

'For the time being. If you want to try and find work with any of the other charters, I'll understand.'

Flynn scrunched up his face. 'What about Jose? He has a wife and kid to look after.'

Castle shrugged. Not as if to say 'Whatever,' but as though the whole thing was tearing him apart. 'I'm closing down two of the bars, too. It's like a ghost town on the Centre, but I'll keep the Irish-themed bar ticking over. You can do the door there, if you like. And if I get any bookings for the jeep safaris you can take them out. I'm keeping the travel agency open.'

Flynn inhaled deeply and rubbed the back of his neck. 'You going to tell Jose?'

Castle nodded, finished his beer and rose from the table. Flynn watched him wend his way back to the quayside, shoulders slumped, then head towards *Faye 2*. Flynn ordered another beer, this time in a glass, and sipped it slowly, his mind working the angles. So for at least the best part of two months he would be ashore and effectively out of work. Chances were the Irish wouldn't open every day of the week and the money from doing the door would be spasmodic at best.

He mulled over the possibility of approaching another charter boat but could not convince himself it was a good idea. They were all struggling with a shortage of demand. Even the annual regulars weren't re-booking. And he'd feel uncomfortable on another boat. He had a history with *Faye 2*. She had been his choice of vessel when the original *Lady Faye* went up in a ball of flame and exploding gas bottles. He had worked with the replacement and knew her intimately, her foibles, her strengths, her weaknesses. And he worked well with the Spanish curmudgeon that was Jose, even though their relationship was often fraught. So even if he could, he probably wouldn't go to another boat.

The ice in the beer glass rose languidly to the surface. Flynn watched it as he also mulled over the financial aspects of the situation. He had very little money stashed, had recently moved to a small apartment which required him to fork out a nominal rent. Probably had about four months before he needed to start looking seriously for work, six before times would become desperate.

He uttered a short internal laugh and took a long draught of the beer. In spite of the circumstances he felt in reasonable spirits. Things weren't half as bad as they had been five years earlier when he'd been effectively drummed out of the cops with a very black rain cloud hovering over his head, been thrown out by his wife who afterwards had shacked up with his best friend and prevented him from making any contact with their son Craig, then ten years old. Those had been bleak times and he had come through them, more or less, even if his past had managed to creep up on him in a most unpleasant way about a year ago.

Flynn wondered if the bleached bones of the two men would ever be discovered in that inaccessible gully near the Roque Nublo up in the mountains. He doubted it. He smiled grimly at the memory, then shrugged it off and thought that something would turn up.

He fished his mobile phone out of his pocket, switched it on and waited for it to find a signal. It bleeped, telling him he had received a voice message whilst the phone had been switched off. There was no number or name recorded but it did state it had come from an international number.

Flynn grinned with pleasure. He expected it would be a message from Craig. Following the events of the previous year, contact between the two had been re-established with the consent of Flynn's ex-wife. Craig had even been allowed to come out to the island for two weeks over the summer holiday when they'd worked together on the boat. It had been a wonderful fortnight and he'd re-bonded with Craig. When the lad had returned to the UK, both had been heartbroken.

He dialled the answerphone service and waited for the connection, fully expecting to hear Craig's still childlike voice.

But the voice he heard was not that of his son.

It was a thin, desperate-sounding female voice, one that Flynn recognized immediately.

'Flynnie? Flynnie? It's me . . . Cathy . . . hi, hope you're OK, big guy.' Flynn heard what he thought was a sob. 'Sorry, sorry . . . look, Flynnie, can you give me a call? I'm . . . I don't know what to do or who to turn to . . . God, it sounds so pathetic, but' – another sob – 'it's just going all wrong, everything, please . . . gimme a bell . . . I know you're two thousand miles away . . . need someone to talk to, to talk it out . . .'

The robotic voice of the answerphone lady came on. 'End of messages. To play this message again, press one . . .'

Flynn pressed one and listened hard to the message again. The phone then beeped and the screen display told him another voice message had landed from the ether. He listened to the new one.

This time the voice was even more fraught. 'Flynnie, it's me again, Cathy, you're probably getting sick of hearing me by now. God, this must be the eighth time of trying . . . need to see you, talk to you, mate . . . please, please call me.'

The message ended but before Flynn could do anything more, four more landed in quick succession.

THREE

Preston Crown Court. Court Number One. Shell-shocked and evidence weary, the jury of eight men and four women shuffled back into the court room for the last time, having reached their verdict after four days of heated deliberation. They sat meekly, avoiding eye contact with the accused.

Detective Superintendent Henry Christie noted the body language and as usual, when he became excited at the possibility of a result, his bottom clenched tightly. He exchanged a very quick glance with the detective inspector sitting next to him, Rik Dean. A glance of triumph. Both men could smell it. Surely this had to be a guilty verdict.

The investigation had been long and difficult, understaffed and fairly low-key, even though the police were hunting a professional killer who had executed a gangland lord by the name of Felix Deakin. Having escaped from custody, Deakin himself had been on the run from the police; tracked by the cops to an isolated rural farmhouse, he had been re-taken into police custody but before the police had even managed to put him in the back of a van, the hit man had struck. From his hiding place up on the moors, almost a mile away, he had expertly blown Deakin's head apart with a high-powered rifle. He had escaped before the stunned police could react.

Henry was convinced the killer had been hired by one of Deakin's rivals, a man called Jonny Cain, because Deakin had volunteered to give crucial evidence against Cain in a murder trial. Although Henry was certain of this, certainty didn't mean evidence, but it was a starting point for what was only part of a complex investigation with many threads.

Setting a small team to work consisting of experienced detectives, intelligence and financial analysts and firearms officers, Henry let them get on with the job. Five months down the line they had a name. From the name came various aliases. From the aliases, bank accounts across the world, complex travel arrangements, forensic tie-ins – and then the location of the individual.

Working with Interpol and the Cypriot police, an armed raid was carried out on a secluded villa near Paphos and a man arrested without any bloodshed or drama.

Three months later, after much solid detective work assisted by a forensic team that managed to link the man in custody to the position he'd laid up in with his rifle (not recovered) on the bleak moors of Rossendale, he was in crown court facing a murder charge, even though he had not said one word whilst in custody. But that didn't matter.

And now the jury was back.

Henry held his breath as the clerk of the court asked the jury foreman if they had reached their verdict.

The man stood nervously, as though his back was killing him. His eyes did not look into the steel-grey impassive eyes of the killer in the dock. He said, 'Yes we have, Your Honour,' addressing his reply to the judge.

Henry glanced at the defendant. He was ex-army, had been a sniper in Kuwait, Iraq and Afghanistan – a superb one – and had left the services and offered his killing skills to the highest bidder. He had an exemplary service record and no previous convictions, facts referred to many times by the smooth defence barrister. But Henry knew he had carried out at least four other assassinations in African republics that had netted him about a million and a half pounds, probably foreign aid money. The killing of Felix Deakin had brought him two hundred thousand, money that was still being tracked by the financial experts, but it was proving tricky to find the source.

The man, who was called Mike Calcutt, allowed his gaze to take in the jury foreman and Henry – pausing just a little too long for comfort on the detective – before looking back at the jury.

The clerk asked if the verdict reached was unanimous or by a majority.

'Unanimous.'

A whisper of amazement flitted around the public galleries, which were packed with gawping public and greedy media.

The clerk then read out the murder charge against Calcutt and asked if the jury found him guilty or not guilty.

For a brief moment, as the foreman paused, Henry thought he was witnessing some reality TV show, where contestants were voted off.

'Guilty.'

Henry's eyes swept to Calcutt. He did not flinch. Cool, cool bastard, he thought. But we got you in the end. If only we could get the bastard who hired you in the first place.

Henry, Rik Dean and four other detectives involved in the case had gathered in a loose congratulatory circle in the public waiting area outside the court-room doors. They all beamed wide smiles and there were lots of handshakes and high-fives amongst them. The kind of euphoria that comes after a protracted, successful investigation that nails a killer.

'Well done everyone,' Henry said, checking his watch. He meant what he said, because he'd very much taken a back seat and had only put his twopenn'orth into the machine when asked. Now that he was a detective superintendent he was trying to delegate more and not get involved in day-to-day investigating. It went against his natural instinct, as was the case with most high-ranking detectives who loved to get down and dirty with the lads. Problem was that it was easy to lose sight of the overview and at his rank, as he was learning, that was not something he could afford to do. He had now become a professional plate spinner and this major inquiry was just one of many he had to manage.

'Drinks?' Rik Dean suggested. There was an eager gaggle of yeses from his colleagues, who wanted to celebrate in the traditional way.

This was although the defendant had yet to be sentenced by the judge. Once the jury had informed the court of the verdict, the defence had immediately leapt up with a desire to make submissions, so the judge had adjourned proceedings when he would hear further bleating from Calcutt's defence. Then he would sentence him to life imprisonment, the only available option in the case of murder.

'You guys go ahead.' Henry delved into his jacket, extracted his wallet and pulled out fifty pounds, which he gave to one of the jacks. 'Have a round on me. I need to—' He was interrupted by the arrival of a court usher.

'Detective Superintendent Christie?'

'That's me.'

'Message from the holding cells . . . Mr Calcutt wishes to speak to the senior investigating officer before he's taken on remand.'

Henry looked blankly at the black-smocked man. 'You mean the defendant, Calcutt?' The other detectives had become silent.

'Yes sir, his brief asked me to pass on the message.'

Henry squinted, then looked at Rik Dean. 'You're the man,' he said. 'Take one of the other guys with you. Your job, I'll leave it with you.'

Henry strode out of the court and stood on the mezzanine. It had become brutally cold outside and he shivered as he slid himself into his Crombie. His first impulse had been to grab Rik and head down to the cells and see what was behind this turn-up for the books. But he would have been butting in. It was effectively Rik's investigation and Henry was happy to leave it to him. He had been angling to get Rik on to the Force Major Investigation Team (FMIT), which he jointly headed, and it had taken some persuading to get the nod for Rik to run this investigation. Now that it had proved to be successful, Henry hoped he would be able to convince the chief constable that Rik should have a permanent position on the team. If something came out of speaking to Calcutt, then all the better.

He pulled out his mobile phone, switched it on, called home. 'Has Karl landed yet?' he asked Kate, his wife.

'Just this minute pulled up outside.'

'Great. Hey – see you soon. And we got a result here, by the way.'

'Ooh, you are such a good detective,' Kate cooed mockingly. Henry didn't pick up on the lack of sincerity and said, 'I am, aren't I?' without a trace of irony.

Flynn took the decision to avoid the Irish bar when he turned out late that afternoon, suspecting that an encounter with Janey might lead to complications he could well do to avoid. After showering and dressing in the tiny terraced villa he rented, he wandered back down to the harbour and trotted down the steps into one of the bars in the complex at the back of the beach itself, wearing his beloved Keith Richards T-shirt and three-quarter length pants. It was still early and quiet, but Flynn knew it was unlikely to get any busier. Many bars were struggling to survive in the economic downturn as tourists kept their own heads down and shied away from foreign holidays. This was one of Flynn's regular haunts and had managed to keep going by providing bargain booze and inexpensive but good food. The manager smiled at Flynn's arrival and immediately filled a half-litre glass with Estrella Damm, placing it in front of Flynn, together with a small plate of olives, as he nestled up to the bar. Flynn nodded and sipped the ice-cold beer.

'You eating, Señor?'

Flynn had intended cooking the red snapper caught earlier by Hugo, but couldn't be bothered. It was in the fridge, would keep until the day after.

'I think so, Manny.'

A menu appeared in front of him as if by magic. Flynn chose paella for one, which he knew would take about twenty minutes to prepare. He slid off the bar stool and said, 'I'll eat outside.' He took his beer and olives and walked to one of the tables on the decking erected over the sand.

It was still warm, twenty-eight degrees, and Flynn settled into one of the big, comfy chairs and soaked in the heat. He loved it. He had been out on the island for almost five years now and the pace of life, the people and the lifestyle had really taken a grip of him.

He took out his phone and tried, not for the first time, to return the call from Cathy James.

He waited patiently for the connection, but when it went through, the answering service cut in. His mouth warped with frustration. He placed the phone on the table, pulled his baseball cap down over his eyes and reached for the beer, wondering what the hell she could want.

She had sounded troubled and unhappy. Totally different to the last time Flynn had seen her.

That had been in October last year when she and her new husband, Tom James, had come out to the island for their honeymoon. Flynn had been unable to get to the UK for the wedding, so he had tried to make amends by finding a villa for them – for free – and picking them up from the airport. He had also arranged a fishing trip and a jeep safari, both at no cost, and they seemed to have had a great time.

Flynn and Cathy went way back. He had met her when he joined Lancashire Constabulary after leaving the Marines over twenty years ago. They had been new recruits at the same intake, he being a bit older than her at twenty-three, she nineteen, shiny, straight out of the box, a bit naive, but extremely beautiful.

At the time she had been single and he'd been married. This hadn't stopped them from becoming lovers for a very brief time, though ultimately they became just very good friends. As their careers moved off in separate directions, they kept in contact but hardly saw anything of each other in the years that followed. Flynn knew she got married and then divorced, while he had remained spliced until both his job and relationship went south and he ended up quitting the cops and taking up residence in Gran Canaria.

It was during the period he was under investigation that he re-established contact with Cathy. By then she was seriously into a relationship with a detective from Lancaster, who she married a few years later – hence the provision of a honeymoon by Flynn.

Flynn raised his eyes and looked across the beach, watching holiday-makers trudge through the gentle surf at the water's edge.

He wondered if something had gone wrong with the marriage, Cathy's second. Was that why she was calling him, wanting to talk? He hoped it was something much less complicated, but couldn't guess what. He wasn't a good counsellor, but a man of action who wasn't anywhere near in touch with his feminine, touchy-feely listening side.

Cathy and Tom had seemed a perfect couple, but wasn't that what honeymoon couples usually appeared to be? Flynn remembered discreetly watching her on the day he took them out fishing. She had been all goo-goo eyes for Tom, the new hubby. Couldn't stop watching him, hanging on his every word. Flynn had actually felt some mixed emotions at that point.

First and foremost he was happy for Cathy. She had been through a bad time, had had a terrible first marriage, really been through the mangle. Then she'd found Tom, who on the face of it came across as a caring, generous guy, and she was head over heels in love with him. On the flip side, Flynn had felt a pang of envy. Not many months before he thought he had been on the verge of finding the love of his life, but had lost her tragically. The third side of the coin, if there was such a thing, was that Flynn also thought about what *could* have been with him and Cathy, had the timing been right. They had probably been in love, he thought, way back when – whatever love meant, he thought cynically. Maybe things would have been very different if both had been free to pursue their relationship beyond a fling at a police training centre. Instead, they had accepted that their only future was as mates.

Cathy – maybe, it seemed – had also harboured the same wistful idea. She had caught Flynn looking at her and sidled up to him, out of sight and earshot of Tom. She was down to a skimpy bikini and her body was still slim, yet plump in all the right places – just as Flynn remembered it all those years before. She gave him a loving hug and whispered into his ear, 'Oh, what could have been.'

'I reckon you've got a good man,' Flynn said, trying to hide the rush of blood her proximity had given him.

'Yeah, I have. He's a good man, you're right.' She glanced over at Tom who was harnessed in the fighting chair, being attended to by Jose. Then her face turned to Flynn. 'Thanks for this,' she said.

'It's what friends are for.'

'I just wish you were as happy.'

Flynn chortled. 'One day I will be.'

'Good. I hope so, Flynnie.' She touched his face gently with her fingertips. 'Always be there for you, y'know, y' big lug.'

'And me for you,' he promised.

But then that little moment of tenderness was shattered by Jose's booming Spanish-accented voice. 'Big one, boss!'

Flynn looked up. Two hundred metres off the stern of the boat was almost certainly the biggest, and the last, blue marlin of the season, rolling magnificently through the waves. Flynn jumped into action and with his skill as the best skipper in the Canaries – something he rarely let Jose forget – took the bait to the fish and brought in a seven hundred pounder that had the newly married Tom fighting a battle that lasted almost two hours.

Halfway though the contest, Flynn had said to Cathy, 'I hope you weren't planning any conjugals tonight. After this I don't think he'll be able to lift a pint, let alone . . . you know.'

'In that case he'll have to lie there and take it – just like you used to do.' Cathy laughed lustily and screamed with glee as the magnificent fish leapt a dozen feet out of the blue sea in an effort to shake loose the steel hook. Its muscular body writhed and twisted before it fell back into the water and dived deep into the ocean.

Flynn blinked himself back to the present day as his seafood paella arrived, decorated with pink langoustines, still in the shell. Flynn took one, burning his fingers, cracked open the hinged body to access the lovely white flesh within. With the assistance of another beer, he wolfed down the dish, then sat back to let it settle.

It was slightly cooler now, a breeze getting up, but still plenty warm to sit out, something rare in the UK, he thought, even in summer.

His mobile rang.

'Steve Flynn.'

'Flynnie . . . Flynnie . . . oh, thank God I got you.'

'Cathy? What the heck's going on? I tried to call you back loads of times. Are you all right, love?'

He heard her choke. 'No, no, not really.'

'What's up then?'

'Steve, can you come back? I know it's a big ask . . . but I need to talk to you. I need a friend I can trust.'

'Cathy, what is it?'

'Look, I can't talk over the phone. Steve, it's Tom.'

'Is he OK?'

'Flynnie, I don't know who to turn to.'

'Cathy, what's happening?' he asked firmly.

'I think . . . I know . . . oh, God . . .'

'What do you know?'

'Flynnie, I think Tom's on the take.' She paused. 'I mean big style. He's a bent cop.'

FOUR

I t was one of those slightly potty middle-aged-man ideas that usually don't get anywhere. A product of a conversation loosened by alcohol which no one took seriously at the time but which planted a seed and was remembered.

The main problems were of logistics, workload and opportunity.

Both men were horrendously busy.

Henry Christie, as joint head of FMIT, had many serious enquiries to oversee, committees and working parties to attend nationally and locally. All that in itself would have been fine if the world stood still, but it didn't, it continued to revolve relentlessly. People did not stop murdering others; long-running investigations didn't suddenly get cleared up and there was always some new initiative that needed the presence of someone at Henry's rank to make it happen.

Karl Donaldson, Henry's American friend, worked as an FBI legal attaché at the US embassy in London. He, too, was overwhelmed with work. Fundamentally he was an analyst and liaison officer, making and forging links between law enforcement agencies across Europe, from the UK to Russia. At the same time he often made forays into the field, sometimes finding himself in dangerous situations, whether coming face to face with a wanted terrorist or dealing with corrupt factions in his own organization.

The two men had first met over a dozen years before. Their paths had crossed when Donaldson, then a full-time FBI field agent, was investigating American mob activity in the north-west of England. Henry, then a detective sergeant, had encountered the Yank when an investigation he was pursuing became explosively intertwined with Donaldson's. They had made friends hesitantly at first, but as their personal and professional lives continued to criss-cross over the years, they became good pals.

It also helped that Donaldson had met, fallen in love with and subsequently married a Lancashire policewoman. Even though she had subsequently transferred to the Metropolitan Police to be near Donaldson's work in London, her northern connections often brought the both of them up past Watford regularly. His wife, Karen, also became good friends with Henry's on-off-and-on wife, Kate.

A couple of months earlier, Donaldson had been in Lancashire on business – something hush-hush he could not even begin to reveal to Henry – and when it was completed he had stayed on at Henry's for a couple of nights. On one of those nights, they had hit Henry's local, the recently refurbished Tram & Tower.

They'd reminisced over a few pints, Donaldson becoming increasingly garrulous after his intake: he was a big man, six-four, as broad as a bear, but he couldn't hold his drink. Anything over two pints and he started to lose control. Henry, on the other hand, raised in the seventies and eighties culture of the cops, always remained steady, although he didn't actually drink much these days as he grew older.

'Y'know, man,' Donaldson slur-drawled in his soft American accent, 'I love ya, man.'

They were seated in one of the newly constructed alcoves of the pub, chatting and paying passing attention to the newly introduced 'Kwiz Nite' hosted by the landlord, Ken Clayson.

Henry squinted at Donaldson's revelation.

'No, I mean, you're a guy who's always on the edge, but I kinda like that.'

'Right.' Henry drew out the word.

'Hey! You thought about having any more kids?'

Now Henry screwed up his face. 'That's a resounding no.'

'God, I can't wait,' Donaldson said, misty-eyed. He had – accidentally – made Karen pregnant but now he couldn't wait to be a father again, even though they already had two kids who were just into their teens.

'I'm too old, and so is Kate,' Henry said. 'We've only just got rid of the two daughters as it is – and they keep bouncing back like they're on elastic bands. It's chill time, pal.'

'Karen's no spring chicken,' Donaldson pointed out.

'How gentlemanly,' Henry remarked. 'Is everything going OK?'

'Aw, hell yeah. Child-bearing hips, y'know. She's blooming – and the pregnant sex is awesome.'

'Whoa.' Henry made the number one stop sign. 'Too much. Anyway, glad to hear things are fine, but it'll put the brakes on everything else,' he warned his companion.

Donaldson sipped his third lager ruminatively. 'Guess so.' His voice was wistful. Then, 'Hey! I have an idea.'

'Go on.'

'Before she gives birth, how about you and me sneaking away for a night or two of debauchery? Wet the baby's head before it arrives.'

'If I recall, the last time you were off the leash, you debauched a little too much.'

Donaldson looked sheepishly at Henry, his mind full of the one and only time he had been unfaithful to Karen. In a hotel room in Malta with a Scandinavian lady who had subsequently bombarded and terrified him with obscene e-mails with photographic attachments. 'I was thinkin' more of a guy thing. Not sure what, though.'

'Whatever, it would have to be short and sweet, I guess. How about a walk and an overnighter?'

'A walk? Do you walk?'

'I've been known to put one foot in front of the other occasionally. We could set off over the hills one day, overnight in a village pub somewhere, then walk on. Park a car at either end, something like that.'

Donaldson thought about it. 'Lake District, you mean?'

'Possibly,' Henry shrugged.

'And now for round two of our Krazee Kwiz Nite.' Their conversation was interrupted as the voice of Ken, the landlord, boomed out over the PA system. 'Pens and answer sheets at the ready. Next ten questions are on the hits of the sixties.'

'Ahh,' Donaldson said, 'your era.'

'You ain't far behind, pal.'

There was no more talk that night of a boys' break, but it was a thought that remained with them, nagging away at the back of their minds.

Jack Vincent sat in the battered chair at the battered desk inside the stolen mobile cabin that doubled as his office and a refreshment area for the workers in the quarry that deeply scarred the hillside a quarter of a mile away. Vincent's cruel face set hard as he shivered and hunched himself deeper into his thick donkey jacket. The gas heater was on, but fighting a losing battle against the harsh north-easterly wind that swooped down from the moors above the village of Kendleton in north Lancashire. Keeping any warmth in the cabin was a constant battle as the outside temperatures continued to tumble with the approach of evening.

From Vincent's position, looking out from the cabin, he could monitor any traffic approaching the quarry up the steep winding lane from the main road. He could watch his heavy lorries as they reached another cabin where they booked in and then were sent on the right-hand fork through the gates into a steel-walled compound. Here any 'necessary changes' were attended to by Vincent's fitter, before they were sent on towards the loading area, where the crushing and filtering machines smashed the rock that had been blown out of the quarry face, then graded it to customer requirements. The lorries were then refilled and sent back out on the road.

At the moment, Vincent's main customer was a huge multinational road-building company subcontracted by the Department of Transport to widen a stretch of the M6 near Stafford. It was a government contract worth several million pounds and Vincent had manoeuvred brutally to get his piece of it. There had been the necessary payoffs, a bit of very heavy intimidation against his rivals – because a well-paid contract like this was always hard fought for by the minnows – and one particularly nasty incident where Vincent and his silent partner had been forced to resort to whacking the edge of a shovel into a man's head. There was now nothing left of that man. He had been fed limb by limb into a crusher, mixed in with a few tons of hardcore, and was buried underneath a bridge pillar on the stretch of motorway he had, ironically, been so keen to build.

Vincent checked his watch, a Rolex, incongruous against the sleeve of his grubby donkey jacket, then peered down the twisting track.

Two empty lorries were expected. Their fourth run of the day. And, like clockwork, they appeared. They were huge monsters, but even they were overshadowed by the giant machines that worked the quarry itself.

Vincent smiled and his face softened with triumph. There would be something extra for each of these vehicles when they left the quarry with the many tons of ground rock in them. He stood up.

The first of the lorries drew up at the reception cabin. The driver dropped out of the cab. He went in and did some paperwork with the woman who dealt with admin, the dispatch and return of orders. Then he clambered back and drove through to the compound, pulling up with a hiss of airbrakes under a drive-through awning constructed of corrugated metal. He got out of the cab again and turned to Vincent, who had walked in behind.

'The Department of Transport and the cops have set up a couple of stop-checks on north and southbound at Charnock services on the M6,' he told Vincent.

'Make sure you don't stop there for a brew, then,' Vincent replied to the driver, who was called Larry Callard.

'Just saying – they're out and about and me and Bert have already exceeded our hours today. If we get pulled, we're screwed.'

As they were talking, a man clad in overalls, rubbing his hands with an oily cloth, strolled across to them. He was big and broad, early forties, with deep-set eyes and a ruddy complexion. This was 'Ox' Henderson, Jack Vincent's vehicle fitter.

'What's up, boss?'

'Department's out and about.'

'And my hours are way over,' Callard whined.

'Can you fix it?' Vincent asked Henderson.

'Fix anything.' He heaved himself into the cab of Callard's lorry, lay across the seat and reached down to the tachograph, the device fitted underneath the dashboard that recorded drivers' hours on a plastic-coated disc. It was supposed to be tamper-proof. Many people, however, had found ways and Henderson was a bit of an expert with them. He had once been the transport manager of a small, criminally run haulage business, but when the company had been investigated by the ministry and the police, Henderson's way with a tachograph had been uncovered. He had been hung out to dry by the company owners, found himself behind bars for fraud for three months and then completely unemployable. Until Jack Vincent took him on.

'Go grab a brew,' Henderson shouted from the cab. 'Be about ten minutes here, then no one'll even know you've ever been out on the road today.' He laughed.

Callard turned to leave. Jack Vincent's spidery hand grasped his arm. 'You having problems, Larry? I'm picking up a vibe, mate.'

'What do you mean?' He looked nervously at Vincent.

'I mean you do what I say and you get paid well for it – yeah? I don't want no moaning, otherwise . . .'

'I wasn't moaning.'

Vincent held Callard's eyes meaningfully for a long second. Then he nodded as an understanding passed between them.

'There'll be something extra in the next run. I'll give you details on the way out, OK? Usual bonus.'

'Yuh, whatever, boss.'

Vincent's fingers uncurled from Callard's forearm and he nodded curtly. The second of the returning, empty lorries pulled into the awning. As the driver climbed out, Vincent said to him, 'See Ox.' He jerked his thumb in the direction of the first lorry, and Henderson's booted feet sticking out of the cab as he worked on the tachograph. 'Then grab yourself a brew – but I want you back on the road in half an hour.'

'No probs, boss,' the second driver said. His name was Bert Pinner.

Yeah, Vincent thought as he walked back towards the cabin, his head tilted against the biting wind, never is a problem with you, Bert. But I'm starting to get mighty concerned about Callard.

Whatever, this would be the last run of the day for the two lorries. By the time they'd had their tachographs fixed, then reloaded with hardcore and been sent on their way, done the delivery down the M6 – plus the extra side-bits – it would be almost ten at night.

No other traffic was due to be coming up to the quarry, so Vincent jarred to a halt when he saw a pair of headlights bouncing up the track. He stood by the door of the cabin, collar pulled up, and waited for the vehicle to arrive, which it did a few moments later, skidding to a grit-crunching stop on the stony ground.

It was a big four-wheel drive Land Cruiser, with greyed-out windows, similar to the kind of thing Vincent drove whilst on quarry business. Difference was this one was newer, cleaner and a better model. The doors opened and two men got out.

And Jack Vincent cursed himself. He wondered how quickly he could get into the cabin and reach the sawn-off shotgun he kept Velcroed under the desk, always fully loaded, usually within hand's reach.

Instead, he affixed a tight smile and approached the men, hand outstretched, the very model of welcome.

Henry and Donaldson decided to try the new menu at the Tram & Tower, which was mostly based around chicken: roast chicken, fried chicken, piri-piri chicken – and chips with either peas, carrots or salad. It was not terribly inspired and when this was delicately pointed out to the proud landlord, Ken, he looked crestfallen and pouted from underneath his beard.

'All the products are sourced locally,' he defended his menu at the newly created 'Food Ordering Point' at one end of the shiny new bar. He glared at Henry and Donaldson, daring them to challenge his statement. They hid their eyes behind the huge laminated menus and exchanged a look of fear. They did not want to upset a tame landlord. 'And,' Ken declared, 'I've got new chef. He's brill.'

'OK, OK,' Henry said to pacify him. 'I'm sure it'll be great. I'll have the piri-piri and Karl will have the roast breast wrapped in bacon . . . both with chips, obviously.'

Clayson entered the order into the new till with a flourish, then extended his hand for payment. 'Twenty-seven pounds and fifty pence.'

'Sheesh,' Henry muttered. 'It's not cut price then?'

'You can't cut corners with quality. And that does include your drinks and a free trip – once only, mind – to the salad bar.'

Henry inserted his debit card into the machine and tapped in his PIN. Clayson tore off the receipt and handed it over, together with a wooden spoon with a number painted on it.

'What's this for?' Henry asked. 'Don't we get cutlery any more?'

Clayson gave him an expressionless stare. 'Stick it in the empty wine bottle on your table and the waitress will find you. Enjoy your meals,' he added smarmily.

The two men turned away from the bar with their drinks and found a table in an alcove. After clearing a space amongst the salt, pepper and cutlery containers that seemed to take up most of the table, Henry laid out an Ordnance Survey map, easing out the folds. Then he raised his pint of Stella Artois and clinked glasses with Donaldson, who was drinking the same.

'To a bit of a lads' adventure, eh?'

Vincent knew one of the men, but not the other. The Land Cruiser's driver was the one he hadn't come across before and he could tell, pretty much, that he'd simply come along to help provide some intimidatory support for the passenger.

Not that he needed any help. Because the rangy black guy, who was called H. Diller, had a fearsome reputation as a torturer, enforcer and killer, and he rarely needed any help from anyone. Which meant that the message was loud and clear to Vincent. He would have been wary enough if H. Diller had turned up alone; to be accompanied by someone who looked just as hard meant that feathers had been ruffled and this was real business. Patience had worn out.

'H. Diller,' Vincent said, offering his hand to the black man and addressing him in the way Diller demanded. Everyone was obliged to call him H. Diller – with the exception of one man. Few people knew what the H stood for, and his insistence on it being used was nothing more than an affectation, but it was one everybody respected.

Diller smiled warmly, a smile that often lured in unsuspecting mortals. He took Vincent's hand and they shook simply, no fancy fist-banging, finger-wrapping, high-fiving, just a simple manly hand-shake. 'Jack, my son.'

There was an uncertain hesitation before Vincent spoke. 'So what brings you to these parts – these cold parts?'

'Hey, really is cold up here. Any chance of a warm?' Diller
gestured to the cabin. 'We can talk in there.'

'You've come to talk?'

'You bet your soul,' Diller winked.

'Not much warmer inside.'

'Yeah, but more convivial.'

'Who's the running partner?' Vincent asked, nodding at the
unsmiling man lounging by the four-wheel drive.

'That's Haltenorth. He's new, but useful.' Diller clicked his
tongue.

Vincent shrugged. 'OK. There's a kettle inside we can fire up.
But only got tea. That OK?'

'Magic.'

Vincent turned and led the way. His forced smile disintegrated,
knowing this was no social call. This, he knew, was purely business.
Dirty business. In fact he had been expecting it, nay had engineered
it, but he hadn't foreseen Diller would be the lead soldier. But then
again, maybe he should have. The time for games had long since gone.
Problem was, he was just slightly off balance and would have felt
better if his partner had been with him. It would have made the
equation much more even-handed.

'Fuck,' Vincent uttered under his breath, half expecting Diller to
step up behind him and stick the barrel of a pistol against his hind-
brain and blow his head off. Things really had got that far, but the
fact that Diller didn't kill him was the first of his mistakes. Vincent's
smile returned as he opened the cabin door and allowed Diller and
Haltenorth to enter ahead of him.

'You guys want to grab a chair at the far end?' Vincent said
amicably, his mind manipulating angles and possibilities because
he was certain this would not end prettily.

Steve Flynn smiled winningly as he passed the two pretty female
cabin crew members and boarded the flight. He had managed to
book a very last minute ticket, via Adam Castle's travel agency, for
a flight that would take him back to Manchester from Las Palmas.
He'd had a quick discussion with Castle about leaving the island
for a short period. There would be nothing lost because of the lack
of work. Castle also told him that a short-term disappearance might
be a good thing anyway. Rumours were already circulating that the
petulant charter boat customer who Flynn had accidentally knocked

unconscious was after blood – or a payoff. Flynn's absence from
the island might be a good thing, Castle had suggested.

Flynn heaved his only baggage into the overhead locker and
edged sideways into the middle of three seats. He looked at both
his travelling companions and they studiously avoided eye contact.
With a sardonic twist of his mouth, he leaned forward, struggling
to take off his windjammer, which he stuffed under the seat in front
of him after he'd taken out the paperback thriller he was halfway
through. He found his place and continued reading about a tough
guy walking into town with no ID, just the clothes he stood up in,
and then kicking the crap out of the 'ornery yokels'. Completely
unreal, but highly exciting. Only four and a half hours to go, he
thought. Then he smiled at the prospect of seeing Cathy. Her
predicament sounded iffy, even though she hadn't said very much
on the phone, but he was looking forward to being with her again.
She promised that somehow she would pick him up from the airport.

They walked past the desk and sat on the plastic chairs at the far
end of the cabin, which were positioned in the vicinity of the tiny
gas-powered heater. Vincent, too, walked past the desk, and reached
for the kettle – but Diller placed a hand on his forearm and glanced
up at him.

'We don't need a drink, actually.'

Vincent's fingers unravelled slowly from the kettle handle.

'Mr Cain wants his money. He's tired of waiting.'

'H,' Vincent began, his voice reasonable.

'H. Diller,' he was corrected.

'H. Diller . . . look, pal, one of my donkeys got away with it. It
can't be found, but I took care of him – you can't really ask for
anything more than that.'

'Mr Cain wants payment.' Diller flexed his large black fingers.
To his left, Haltenorth sat forward in his chair, his fingers interlocked.
His eyes were angled up at Vincent.

'I don't have payment. We were ripped off by my donkey.'

'Mule, you mean?'

'I call 'em donkeys. Thicko lowlifes. Who else would take the
chance, but doombrains, i.e. donkeys?'

'I see.' Diller's eyes hadn't left Vincent's face. 'In that case, Mr
Cain would like goods in exchange – at double the value.'

'Twenty grand's worth?'

'Plus interest. Make it twenty-two. Round it up to twenty-five for my inconvenience, and that of Mr Haltenorth, too.'

Vincent shook his head.

'You have that amount here. This is where the distribution starts.'

'I have no stock. The vehicles took the last of it on their last run.' Vincent sighed. 'This won't go away will it, H. Diller?'

'Be like an elephant in your brain until it's settled.'

Vincent ran a hand over his unshaven face. 'I've got a grand in the petty cash drawer.' He jerked his head in the direction of the desk. Then he bent forward, placed his hands on his knees like he was going to play pat-a-cake, and looked directly into Diller's eyes. He spoke tauntingly. 'And that's all the fucker is having. That's the bill paid. It's just one of those write-offs you occasionally have to make in this business. People get greedy. That greedy person has been dealt with and that's the end of the matter – you tell him that.' Vincent rose to his full height. He wasn't a tall man, five-nine, but he was lean, with power behind his shoulders. 'I'll get you the money.'

He stepped to the desk and, as he expected, Diller moved – quickly. He shot up from the plastic chair and manoeuvred himself into a position between Vincent and the desk. At the same time, a handgun appeared in his right hand, a 9mm pistol of Chinese origin. Even with the gun jammed in the soft part underneath the cleft of his chin, Vincent recognized the weapon as part of a consignment he'd brought in and distributed two years before, one of his other sidelines. He wondered how many jobs it had been used on, how many lives it had taken, how much cash it had generated.

'N-no, back away, pal,' Diller said.

Vincent tried to swallow, his throat rising and falling against the 'O' of the muzzle. He moved as requested.

'Check the drawers,' Diller said out of the corner of his mouth. Haltenorth was already on his feet. Diller pushed Vincent further back as the other man swooped to the desk and yanked open the drawers. He rifled through them, found nothing but papers and a money tin with a piece of paper taped to it that said 'Petty Cash'.

He took it out and showed Diller.

'What did you expect, a shooter?' Vincent asked.

Diller removed the muzzle from Vincent's neck, but couldn't resist dragging the barrel up to his temple and pressing it hard against his skull, before withdrawing.

'How much in tin?' Diller asked.

'Twelve hundred, give, take,' Vincent shrugged, his face taut with tension.

'Unlock it.'

Vincent edged out of Diller's proximity and sat down on the office chair. Diller and Haltenorth stood back to watch him. He fished a key out of his jeans pocket and inserted it into the lock of the box, which measured about six inches by nine, maybe four inches deep. As he did this, his knee touched the shotgun strapped underneath the desk. His mind whirled as he worked out his moves. The flaw in it all was the time it would take him to free it from the Velcro straps, turn, rise, aim it – the weapon was ready to fire, loaded with two twelve-bore cartridges – and take out two very streetwise individuals, one of whom already had a gun in his hand. No doubt the other was also armed but hadn't yet shown his fire-power. But they had expected to find a gun in the desk drawer, and hadn't. Vincent could tell they'd dropped their guard. They'd relaxed. And that was all to his advantage. Plus they hadn't killed him yet.

'Why don't you two guys sit back down?'

'Nah, we'll stand, because it won't be enough. We had specific instructions, Jack. Oh yeah, don't get me wrong, we'll take the money – but you're still gonna die. You had your chances, y'see. That was the last one and you didn't come good.'

Vincent slowly unlocked the money box, opened the hinged lid. It was stuffed with cash, many notes, all tightly rolled up. He removed the money from the tin, a bitter expression on his face, and bounced it on the palm of his hand. 'How much to pay you guys off?' he asked, playing the game.

'What you mean?' Diller demanded.

'How much for you to go back to Cain and tell him I wasn't here, you couldn't find me? Eh?' His eyebrows arched.

Haltenorth checked out Diller, but the latter kept his eyes on Vincent, who continued with his subterfuge, because there was no way he would think about paying these guys off. 'Follow me back down to my house. I got a couple more grand stashed away. You guys take this' – he held up the money roll in his fist – 'as a show of my good will, and I'll give you the cash down at my house. Three grand, plus, in total. Not bad for a ride out to the back of beyond. It'll give me more time to get stuff together. Do me now and Cain won't be getting anything. How about it? Take the cash,' he pleaded. 'No one will be any the wiser.'

His eyes darted between the two men. He could sense Haltenorth was up for it, but Diller wasn't even wavering.

'Mr Cain will still get his dues, man,' Diller said, 'even with you dead. We'll just move on to your partner in crime. I'm given a job to do, I do it.'

Haltenorth's bottom lip dropped with disappointment. Clearly he wasn't being paid anything like the money Vincent was offering now. Haltenorth had no loyalty in his bones. Vincent had placed doubt in his mind.

'What about it, man?' Haltenorth hissed to Diller.

Diller turned slowly to him, unable to believe his ears. His gun drooped to one side and his face showed complete surprise.

'I'll tell you why, dumb-ass. You do not double cross Mr Cain. He don't do double crossing. That's why!'

'But man, all that cali.'

'I thought you were cool, man.' Diller crashed his gun across the side of Haltenorth's head, sending him spinning backwards.

Vincent watched the short verbal exchange intently, saw the minute change in Diller's body language that reflected his disbelief in what he was hearing, then saw the gun arc across his dim partner's head. Even as the gun started to move, Vincent reached under the desk and slid the hanging shotgun out swiftly and neatly. It was a movement he had practised time and again whilst sitting at the desk. He spun on the chair just as Haltenorth stumbled backwards, holding the side of his bloodied head. Diller was angled slightly away from him, the gun in his hand pointing upwards and away from Vincent.

It was a side-by-side double-barrelled sawn-off shotgun. A simple weapon. Vincent liked simplicity, because it rarely went wrong. Revolvers rarely went wrong, but sometimes pistols did. Sometimes pump-action shotguns that needed racking went wrong because their mechanisms jammed. But a simple, old-fashioned, pre-loaded one, safety catch off, never went wrong. The only drawback was that there were only two cartridges in it and he had to get this right first time. He would not be allowed the privilege of reloading.

But here, in the confines of the cabin, with two targets less than six feet away from him, he had absolute confidence that he would be successful. He couldn't miss. The trick was to ensure that he brought the two men down. There was the possibility they wouldn't be killed straight away, but if they weren't dead they would be severely injured enough that he would have time to reload.

As he spun on the chair, he held the shotgun at the base of his belly, just above the groin, angled upwards.

Diller's face turned, a scream coming to his wide mouth as he tried to spin back and bring his gun around on Vincent.

Vincent released the first barrel, the recoil thumping his tensed stomach muscles. The pellets exploded out with a huge bang and splattered across Diller's upper torso, chest, neck and head. The cartridge wad hit his throat, punching a hole in it the side of a ten pence piece. The impact hurled him against the cabin wall like a stunt man on a rope.

Vincent rose, aimed the shotgun again. Haltenorth, already stunned from the pistol whip across his head, held out his left hand beseechingly. 'No, man, no,' he cried.

Callously, Vincent shot him too.

FIVE

Henry dropped unsteadily from the bar stool but kept his balance. Donaldson emerged from the gents' toilet, wiping his mouth and walking towards Henry in a less than straight line across the pub. Henry watched him with a slightly warped grin.

'You OK, pal?'

'Yup.'

The pub had closed an hour ago and all the customers, barring Henry and Donaldson, had left. The pair had been invited up to the bar by Clayson, the landlord, where he plied them with a couple of extra pints each and a few chasers.

That meant they had each downed five pints plus numerous spirits. Henry held it quite well, whereas the American did not. He had allowed himself too many that night and it was taking its toll.

There had been times during the evening when Henry's little voice of reason told him that any over-indulgence was not a great idea. In the morning they planned to get out into the hills and do their walking trip and a skinful the night before was not the greatest of ideas. But his little devil was seduced by the ambience of the pub, the excellent taste of the beer – Clayson was proud to bursting over his clean pipes – and, of course, the offer of free drink. Their defences were well and truly weakened. They had planned to be in bed at Henry's house by eleven, but by the time they bade farewell to the landlord, who was even drunker than they were, it was quarter past midnight.

As the extremely cold night hit them, Henry staggered back a pace and Donaldson almost fell over.

'Just whoa there,' the American said as though he was steadying a stallion.

'You OK?' Henry asked him again.

'Yup . . . nope.' He walked unsteadily over to a low wall by the car park and was copiously sick.

At the same time as Karl Donaldson was emptying the contents of his stomach, Steve Flynn's flight from Las Palmas touched down at Manchester Airport. It had been uneventful. He had read his book, nodded off a few times, visited the loo and not spoken to the people either side of him. A fairly typical flight.

Although the plane docked right up to the airport terminal, Flynn could instantly feel the biting cold British night air as he stepped off the plane and entered the building via the walkway.

With no luggage to collect, he went straight out through the green channel, nothing to declare. On the flight he'd bought a bottle of Glenfiddich but had nothing customs would be interested in. He sauntered into the arrivals hall and made his way to the overhead meeting board, expecting to see Cathy.

She wasn't there.

Using his height he scanned around, but couldn't spot her. Frowning, he wandered around the terminal for a few minutes and even stepped out into the night to check outside. He knew she liked an occasional cigarette and thought she may have sneaked out for a drag.

There was no sign of her.

He resisted the temptation to have her paged. Instead he switched on his mobile phone and waited for the signal to be picked up, expecting a text or voice message from her. Nothing landed.

After fifteen further minutes, still nothing.

After half an hour the arrivals lounge was virtually empty. Flynn stood alone, looking slightly forlorn under the sign, like he'd been stood up. Thinking he had given her enough time either to call him and explain why she was late, or actually turn up flustered and apologetic, he called her. It went straight through to the answering service. Then he called the landline number she had given him. After half a dozen rings, that too clicked on to answerphone.

Cathy's pre-recorded voice came on the line. 'Hello, this is the police office at Kendleton, Lancashire. I'm PC Cathy James, your rural beat officer. I'm sorry I can't take your call right now, but if you leave a message after the tone, I promise I'll get back to you as soon as possible. If you're calling with an emergency, please hang up and redial 999.'

The tone beeped. Flynn hesitated, but hung up without saying anything. He thumbed his end-call button, a very strange, uneasy sensation in his gut. He knew Cathy well enough to be sure that if she said she would be here to pick him up, she would be. And if she wasn't, there would be one hell of a reason why not.

One hell of a bad reason, Flynn thought.

He spun on his heels and trotted over to a car rental desk, just in time to catch the booking clerk who was just about to pack up for the night. He gave the tired-looking woman his best smile and said, 'I need to hire a car, please.'

SIX

Squinting unsurely at Donaldson, Henry pursed his lips. The big American looked pale and ill. Henry knew he had spent some time both on and over the toilet overnight.

'You sure you're OK?'

'Yeah, I'm fine,' he said shortly. He hitched a medium-sized rucksack on to his back and stamped his feet. He didn't look fine, certainly not up to a five to six hour hike across the moors of Lancashire.

'We can do this another day, if you wish,' Henry persisted.

'Said I'm fine. Just had too much to drink, that's all. Once I get walking, I'll get it out of my system.'

Henry backed off and swung his own rucksack over his shoulders, securing the straps comfortably. He squatted slightly and leaned into the driver's window of his Mondeo, in which sat his wife, Kate. Behind Henry's Ford was Donaldson's excessively large four-by-four Jeep driven by Karen, his heavily pregnant wife. The two women had kindly consented to drive the men up to the starting point of their proposed hike, then take one of the cars to the finishing point at Kirkby Lonsdale, park it up and leave it for them to pick up when they finally got to their destination after two days of walking.

'Thanks for this, babe,' Henry cooed. He realized he would never have been able to do this 'guy thing' with Donaldson without Kate's – or come to that, Karen's – blessing. He had only managed to convince her by taking her away on a delayed holiday to Venice, which he had secretly extended to include four days in Tuscany, supplemented by the subtle use of flowers, the completion of chores and a lot of lurv. He knew she wasn't fooled by the sudden surge of attention, but it seemed to work. He leaned in and kissed her.

At the Jeep, Donaldson was doing much the same thing. 'You gonna be OK, baby-doll?' he said, leaning through the driver's window. He reached in and lovingly patted the ever-expanding bulge that was her third, unexpected but eagerly awaited child. 'And you too, blob.'

'We'll be fine,' she assured him. 'But you look really pale.'

'I'm OK. You know me and alcohol don't mix.' They kissed lingeringly, tongues and all. As a couple they'd had a rocky road to travel over the last few years, but that was now behind them. They were as passionately in love with each other as they had ever been.

The men stood back and the women gave waves and kisses before the cars pulled away from the side of the road, leaving primitive man to his own devices. They waved until the cars disappeared over the hill.

'Good,' Donaldson said. 'Now they're gone, let's end this charade and call a cab to take us to Blackpool for a night of debauchery.'

Henry chuckled. 'I think they would have seen through that ruse.'

'Mm, maybe.'

They surveyed their surroundings. They had been dropped off slap-bang in the centre of the Trough of Bowland, that remarkable chunk of wild countryside that forms the part of Lancashire between Lancaster and the Yorkshire Dales National Park. The intention was to walk across the Forest of Bowland, keeping due north until they reached the town of Kirkby Lonsdale. Henry estimated that, taking it reasonably easy, the journey would take two days with an overnight stop in the pretty village of Kendleton where they had booked a couple of rooms in the only pub in the village, the Tawny Owl. Henry, who had pored over maps and footpaths, estimated they would need to spend about six hours on foot each day, crossing terrain that varied from easy to difficult, but he knew both of them were well capable of completing the walk.

Henry had got back to keeping himself fit by doing a three-mile run each lunchtime with a couple of weekly bouts of circuit training. He'd lost some poundage, down to about thirteen and a half stone, and was feeling pretty fit. He knew Donaldson was a bit of a fitness freak anyway, often pounding the London pavements as well as doing a lot of weights in the state-of-the-art gym at the American embassy where he was based.

The only thing that might cause them problems was the weather. Initially it had been their intention to do the walk in autumn but because neither of them could marry up their diaries, it had dragged on until early December. Henry had made the unilateral decision that the walk would go ahead, even when Kate had warned him of the possibility of rotten weather. Henry had checked records and pooh-poohed her concerns. Winters had been mild for a long time now – 'Global warming,' he'd said knowledgeably. The worst that might happen was that they would get wet.

As the two vehicles disappeared towards Dunsop Bridge, Henry made a quick mental checklist and was happy he'd brought along everything he needed for the walk, including a change of clothing and spare trainers for the evening in the pub, which was supposed to be a great, old-fashioned hostelry. He adjusted the strap on his rucksack again, pulled his bob cap down over his ears, then set off across the road to the opening of a public footpath. The sign at the stile pointed to Brennand Tarn. Henry climbed over, flexing his toes in his recently acquired, but worn in, walking boots. As he dropped on to the other side he turned, expecting Donaldson to be right behind him, but he was still on the opposite side of the road – and had just been sick again on the grass verge.

'Bloody hell, you sure you can do this?' Henry called. 'We can get the ladies back if you want.' He held up his mobile phone and waggled it enticingly.

Donaldson wiped his mouth. 'Nahh, fine now. That was the last of it,' he said as he jogged across the road and vaulted the stile spectacularly.

Henry slid the phone back into his jacket pocket, but not before he noticed it wasn't picking up any signal.

*   *   *

'Thanks, I owe you one.' Steve Flynn rubbed his tired eyes as at 8.15 that morning he padded into the kitchen where his ex-wife, Faye, was swilling dishes at the sink. She glanced over her shoulder and gave him the up-curved smile that once, years before, had melted his heart.

He'd had a bit of a panic at the airport when Cathy had failed to show or respond to any of his calls and he was at a bit of a loss as to where he could bed down for the night. Having had to pay for car hire, his money had immediately dwindled and to get a room at an airport hotel was out of the question. Based on the flimsy fact that relations with Faye had thawed over the last few months, he took a chance and called her.

She had been groggy with sleep and part of him thought that most of the conversation he'd had with her didn't register. But when he arrived at her house – formerly *their* house – in a decent part of South Shore in Blackpool, the front door had been left unlocked and a pillow and some bedding dumped on the settee in the front room. He'd helped himself to a cheeky smidgen of whisky before settling down and dropping off to sleep almost immediately.

'No problem,' Faye said. 'Good job I wasn't entertaining a man friend, though.' As the words came out, her contrite expression told Flynn that the words were instantly regretted. Yet a pang of annoyance still shot through him. A big part of their past marital problems had been the fact that she entertained a man friend, namely Flynn's best mate and cop partner, an affair carried on behind his back for a long time.

Faye saw the cloud pass over his face and went on quickly, 'Anyway, what's going on? How come you're over here?'

He settled himself at the kitchen table. 'You remember Cathy Turnbull? Became Cathy James when she married a jack up in Lancaster?'

Faye frowned, then said, 'Oh, yeah.' She had no idea that Flynn and Cathy had had a brief fling all those years ago at the training centre. Flynn wasn't about to enlighten her.

'She was a mate, wasn't she?' Faye said, no hidden knowledge behind the words.

'Yep.' Flynn then explained Cathy's strange phone calls, but before he could finish his story, a deep male voice behind him said, 'I thought I heard you talking.'

Flynn spun. It was his son, Craig. Now fifteen years old, broadening out, shooting up, voice deepening, and on his way to becoming a bloody good-looking young man.

'Pal!' Flynn stood up and opened his arms, embracing the lad tenderly. 'Jeepers, you've grown.' They hadn't seen each other in a few months and the teenager had noticeably expanded, but in a good, healthy way.

'What are you doing here, Dad?'

'Flying visit – and your mum was good enough to let me crash out here at short notice.'

Faye watched the two of them with a proud, sad smile. Flynn caught her eye, grinned back. 'Can I take him to school?' he asked.

'Be my guest. What do you want for breakfast?'

'Has the menu changed?' Flynn knew that the kitchen wasn't Faye's most comfortable environment. She shook her head, again with that slightly crooked, heart-melting grin, taking no offence from Flynn's slight mockery. 'I'll have toast then.'

'Toast it is.'

Craig watched the exchange between the adults, his eyes narrowing. 'You guys getting back together?' he asked with cautious hope.

'Only when hell freezes over,' Faye declared and popped two slices of bread into the toaster.

Although extremely cold, the day had started bright and free of cloud, even though the wind was biting in its intensity. The two men trudged up into the Forest of Bowland, their faces into the wind, their bodies angled against it. Had this really been a forest there would have been some protection against the elements, but Bowland was only called a forest because it was once a royal hunting estate. Now it was wide open grouse moors and outcrops of millstone grit, and was designated an area of outstanding beauty.

The walk they had chosen to undertake wasn't too foolhardy, though. In his younger days Henry had roamed these moors frequently, as well as the Lake District, and the route he and Donaldson had plumped for was one Henry had walked a few times many years before. Walking was something he'd grown out of, but he still had vivid memories of crossing an unspoilt area and seeing some of the wildest scenery in the UK.

Henry was a few yards ahead of Donaldson, walking on nothing

more than a narrow sheep trail, in places quite boggy. Henry's leg
had sunk to mid-shin at one point and Donaldson had helped him
slurp it out. Fortunately he was wearing gaiters and his foot stayed
dry.

Henry stopped, his cheeks red with effort and the chill, waited
for his friend to catch up. They had made slow but reasonable
progress, had passed Brennand Tarn and were now making their
way to Whitendale Hanging Stones.

'You OK, bud?' Henry asked, feeling it was a question he had
posed many times that morning.

Donaldson still looked ill and Henry felt a little bit guilty, but,
he reasoned, he had given Donaldson the opportunity to withdraw
from the walk a couple of times and he'd refused.

'Yeah, yeah.'

'Fit to go on?'

'Yes,' he said firmly.

'Thing is, once we reach the stones, that's about halfway, then
it's as broad as it is long.'

'I get you.' Donaldson took a mouthful from a bottle of water
and wiped his lips. Henry watched him. Donaldson winced.

'Sure you're OK?'

'Yeah, just a bit of wind, I guess. I'll fart it out.'

'Let's push on.' It was 8.45 a.m., and the day had only just started.

The last time Flynn had taken Craig to school was over five years
before, when the lad had been nine or ten and at junior school. He
had always enjoyed the experience, watching Craig run through the
school gates. Now, though, Craig was no longer a kid and when
Flynn dropped him off, there was just a fleeting wave as he went
to stand with a group of his pals at the school gates. Flynn watched
him for a few moments, bursting with pride, before pulling away
into the four-wheel-drive traffic outside the school. At least his union
with Faye had produced one good thing.

He drove back to Faye's house. She had gone to work and had
told him he could use the place if he needed a shower, which he
did. He wandered slowly through the rooms, seeing how little had
actually changed in the years he'd been excluded from the place.
The dining room was still how he had decorated it, and so was the
master bedroom. Craig's room had been repainted and the main
bathroom completely refitted. Flynn recalled that was an insurance

job after a leak had caused a lot of damage when Faye had been away.

He undressed, showered and shaved in the en suite shower room off the main bedroom. He sat on the edge of the unmade bed after, drying himself off, when a surge of tiredness pulsed through him. He lay back and closed his eyes, thinking he would rest for a few minutes.

Half an hour later he jumped awake, cursing. He dressed quickly, using the underwear he had brought along in the flight bag, keeping on the jeans and shirt he'd worn the day before. Then he called Cathy on her mobile. It went directly to answerphone, frustratingly, as did the landline number she had given him.

He stood by the kitchen window overlooking the compact, overgrown back garden, a mug of tea in his hand. His mouth crimped in thought. He looked down at his mobile phone, weighing it all up, then decided to make another call, just on the off chance. He tabbed through the contacts menu, found the name he was after, pressed the green dial button with his thumb and put the phone to his ear.

'Can I help you?'

'I take it you don't introduce yourself and your department for the sake of secrecy?' Flynn said.

'As I said, can I help you?'

'Jerry, my old cocker, how the hell've you been, matey?'

For a moment it was as if the line had gone dead. Then, 'What the hell do you want?'

'You sound cautious, maybe not even pleased to hear from me,' Flynn chuckled.

'Last time I spoke to you, I ended up telling you things I shouldn't have. Got me in the shit with my boss,' DC Jerry Tope whined.

'Ahh, Henry Christie? How is the twat?'

There was another pause. 'What do you want, Steve?'

'First of all, for you not to worry. What I need to know won't compromise you this time.' Flynn smiled to himself. 'Unless of course you don't tell me, in which case I'll have to make a very delicate phone call . . . if you get my drift? How is the lovely Marina, by the way?'

'Flynn, you're the twat.'

Flynn cackled wickedly. He had known Jerry Tope for a very long time and they had been good friends when Flynn had been a cop in Lancashire Constabulary. So good that Flynn had done Tope a great favour once, lying to save Tope's marriage. Ever since, Tope had been in Flynn's debt. Flynn had never expected to become a debt collector but he had tapped into Tope's role as an intelligence analyst the previous year when he was after some details of a couple of very bad men who were out to get him. Their friendship had not survived Flynn's ignominious departure from the cops, but Flynn had found it useful to have someone on the inside who could search databases.

'It's different this time,' Flynn said.

'I seriously doubt it.'

'Honest – Cathy James? You remember her. Cathy Turnbull as was?'

'Yeah, we were all at training school together. Everybody wanted to get into her panties. Rumour had it that someone did . . .'

'Yeah, lucky sod, whoever it was.'

'You did, didn't you!' Tope exclaimed. 'Jeez, you did. Now it all fits into place. Christ, if I'd known that,' he said wistfully.

'I didn't, actually,' Flynn lied. 'But, yeah, Cathy James, née Turnbull.'

'Mm, haven't come across her for years. Do know she's working a rural beat up in Northern Division. She married a jack from Lancaster. Tom James, good lad.'

'Know much about him?'

'No, just of him. Good thief-taker by all accounts. Used to be a traffic cop, of all things, but seems to have found his niche. I think Henry's used him a few times on murders. And he recently got a chief cons commendation for busting a prostitution racket. Probably go far . . . Look, why?'

'Oh, nothing. It's just that I'm here on a flying visit and thought I'd drop in on Cathy.'

'You're back in Lancashire?' Tope said it as though Flynn's presence was something akin to a deadly virus.

'Affirmative.'

'Ugh. Why don't you just call her up?'

'Done – no reply.'

Jerry Tope sighed. 'Hold on, I'll check the duty states.' Flynn heard the tap of his fingers on a keyboard, Tope accessing the computerized system that recorded the working hours of every officer on duty within Lancashire. 'You back for good?' Tope asked.

'As I said, flying visit.'

'Good . . . here we are . . . she's down as being on a rest day today. Maybe she's gone out for the day.'

'What about Tom?'

More key-tapping. 'Nine-five,' which Flynn knew meant nothing as far as detectives were concerned. They tended to be loose about what hours they actually worked and the official system was often wrong. 'Oh, what about yesterday?'

'Yesterday? Um, Cathy, rest day, Tom, nine-five.'

'Thanks, Jerry.'

'That it?'

'Uh-huh.'

'Thank God for small mercies.'

Flynn hung up feeling ever so slightly guilty, but not so much that he wouldn't use Tope's knowledge and position again if necessary. Because there was no statute of limitations on adultery, Flynn's knowledge of Tope's one and only infidelity was something he would hold over him for the rest of his life.

He scribbled a note to Faye, thanking her for letting him crash out and use her facilities, left twenty pounds he could ill afford for Craig, collected his gear and locked the house, then jumped into his hire car. He hoped that he would be done with whatever problem was ailing Cathy by tomorrow and was already looking forward to going home to Gran Canaria, even if he was going to be sued for assault by the jumped-up Hugo. He was missing the feel of the boat under his feet and even though *Faye 2* was going to be in dry dock for a couple of months, he wanted to be there, tending her, carrying out any necessary repairs and in general looking after his baby. Survival money would come from somewhere.

'This is the centre of the known world,' Henry Christie said grandly as he swung his rucksack off his shoulder and sat down on the ugly rocky boulders busting out of the heathland that were known as Whitendale Hanging Stones. 'Well,' he said, amending the claim as he delved into the rucksack for his steel flask and sandwiches, 'the middle of Britain, anyway.'

He unscrewed the flask and poured himself a welcome coffee, sipping it as he admired the view from a vantage point that made him feel on top of the world.

'Whaddya mean?' Donaldson said indifferently. He dropped his rucksack beside Henry, sat down miserably and pulled his anorak hood over his head.

Henry looked at him, realizing what the term 'green at the gills' meant. Donaldson was not improving healthwise. If anything, he looked more unwell than earlier and it had been his excellent physical condition that had kept him going up to this point. They had been walking for three hours and when the sheep tracks had petered out, it had been tough going. The bogs were unforgiving and possibly treacherous to the unwary.

'I mean that this position here is the geographical centre of the British Isles – if the four hundred and one outlying islands are included in the calculation.'

'Oh.' Donaldson sounded unimpressed. He had food and drink in his rucksack, but did not open up and get any, just sat there glumly.

It was very windy at this location, 496 metres above sea level, and icy blasts seared through their layers of clothing.

Henry sipped his hot coffee and bit into a Lancashire cheese sandwich, laced with piccalilli, as he surveyed the countryside. It was a truly magnificent vista, the hills of Bowland and Pendle lying like huge sleeping dinosaurs. He looked at the sky. To the south it was fairly clear, and across to the west he could still make out the pinprick that was Blackpool Tower on the coast. He swivelled around, then his eye caught a bird zooming across the moorland just below him. A frisson of joy shot through him.

'Would you look at that?'

In his not misspent youth, Henry had been a bit of a birdwatcher and could still recognize most of the common species, as well as many birds of prey, which were always a favourite. And what he saw made his heart beat faster with excitement. An adult male hen harrier, grey plumage above, white underneath, showing its dark wing-tips as it shot past. It was a rare bird and still persecuted by ruthless gamekeepers.

Donaldson didn't even look up, but said, 'What?'

'Nothing.'

'Ooh.' Donaldson hissed and doubled up, gripping his stomach. He scrambled to his feet, gave Henry a desperate look, and ran behind a rocky outcrop.

Henry looked to the north-east. The sight he saw filled him with some dread. Maybe thirty miles distant, the clouds were black, rolling and heavy. 'Not good,' he said.

A few moments later, Donaldson reappeared, his complexion grey.

'You OK?' Henry asked him again.

'I've just had the shits on the middle of Britain,' he said.

Flynn had driven out of Blackpool and dropped on to the M55, heading east across Lancashire. At the junction with the M6, he bore left and north, eventually passing Lancaster on his left, then the young offenders' institution, exiting the motorway at junction 34. Then he'd gone right, heading in a vague north-easterly direction along the A683, following the Lune valley, the River Lune being Lancashire's second river after the Ribble. He passed through the village of Caton, past the police house on the left, but before he reached the next settlement, Hornby, he took a right turn, picking up the signs for Low and High Bentham, then took another right following the sign for Kendleton.

The tight meandering roads rose steadily and at one point on the brow of a hill, he got a superb view of the hills across the Yorkshire Dales National Park in the next county.

The view was marred only by the approaching black sky – and if he wasn't mistaken, Flynn was certain that flecks of snow were in the air. He cursed and thought of the magnificent weather he'd left behind, two thousand miles to the south.

SEVEN

The black Range Rover with smoked-out windows loomed large in Flynn's rear view mirror. His hire car, a tiny Peugeot, had been the only vehicle on the road for the last four miles in any direction, but the big four-wheel drive had come up behind quickly and unexpectedly and almost attached itself to Flynn's rear bumper. The road was narrow, widening very occasionally, but virtually impossible for overtaking, which is what the driver of the Range Rover obviously wanted to do.

The headlights flashed repeatedly but Flynn had nowhere to go, nowhere to pull off. On both sides of the road were either very spongy looking grass verges or deep drainage channels. Maybe if he pulled in tight and slowed right down, the Range Rover might be able to pass carefully.

Flynn's eyes constantly checked the mirror, which was now completely filled with the front radiator grille of the following car. He gritted his teeth and began to seethe as the driver kept up the pressure on him. He had been just tootling up to that point, but the harrying from behind made him increase speed involuntarily.

And then reduce it. He wasn't going to be intimidated by some clown in a fancy motor. If the guy wanted to pass so badly, go ahead, welcome, and don't blame me if you end up in a field. But Flynn wasn't going to accommodate him by sinking his own wheels into a muddy verge, or worse running into a ditch.

'Wanker,' he breathed.

The guy didn't let up, kept pushing.

Flynn's hands gripped the wheel white-knuckle tight, still nowhere to pull in and let the car pass.

And then the inevitable happened.

Coming out of a right-hand corner, Flynn saw another car coming towards him, a Jeep or something, a similar size to the one clinging to his rear end. Whatever happened, this was going to be a squeeze.

Flynn had to jam on the brakes on the narrow road, which was just about wide enough for two standard-sized cars to pass carefully. He slowed right down, as did the approaching Jeep. Two cars approaching each other on a country road, the drivers showing courtesy towards each other. And behind him the impatient Range Rover.

Flynn signalled his intention to pull in.

But then the Range Rover swerved out and accelerated past, taking off his driver's door mirror with a loud crack. Flynn jumped.

The Range Rover powered ahead, its offside wheels leaving tracks in the opposite bank and forcing the oncoming Jeep to veer left and on to that same bank with its nearside wheels. The Range Rover sped past, this time taking the driver's door mirror of the Jeep and avoiding a scraping collision by what seemed only millimetres to Flynn.

And then, with a gush of exhaust smoke, it was gone, leaving him and the Jeep stationary, facing each other.

Flynn could see a woman at the wheel, another in the passenger seat. Leaving his engine running, he climbed out of the Peugeot and examined the door and the remnants of the damaged mirror which had been jaggedly snapped off. Broken bits of it, including shattered glass, were scattered on the road. He picked up the biggest piece, kicked a few other scraps of plastic and metal off the road and walked to the Jeep, seeing the debris of that vehicle's door mirror strewn down the road.

Flynn had taken off his jacket to drive and was in short sleeves. The brutally cold wind pierced his bones as he reached the Jeep. The driver's door window opened slowly, revealing the woman at the wheel.

'Are you all right?' he asked.

'Yeah, yeah, reckless sod. Are you?'

'Yeah. He'd been up my chuffer for a mile or two but I couldn't find anywhere to pull in.' He bent his knees and looked into the Jeep across at the woman in the passenger seat. 'Are you unhurt?'

She nodded. 'Thanks.'

Both were very attractive and neither seemed unduly frightened by their experience. Cool women, he thought.

'Did you get his number?' the woman at the wheel asked.

He nodded and tapped his head. 'Up here.'

'Don't suppose there'll be much point in pursuing it,' she said.

'Probably not. Mine's a hire car, so I'll have to pass on details to the company and report it to the police. It was a hit and run after all. Anyway, if I give you my details and you give me yours, maybe we could be witnesses for each other if it comes to it? Whether you want to tell your insurance company or the cops is up to you, but I don't want to get saddled with a bill I can't afford to pay. What d'you say?'

'Good idea.' She fished out a pad and pen, handed it to Flynn. He jotted down his details and the registered number of the Range Rover. He gave Faye's address as his own. Didn't want to get too complicated by bringing Gran Canaria into the equation. He handed the pad back and she wrote down her name and a mobile number. Moments later both vehicles were back on the road.

Flynn discovered that Kendleton was actually not much more than a hamlet. As he drove into it he guessed there was probably no word to describe something that fell between a village and a hamlet. 'A hamage?' he mused. Whatever, it was a picturesque little place. To its credit, it had a nice-looking pub called the Tawny Owl which advertised en suite rooms, but as he drove past, he saw a 'No

Vacancies' sign propped up in a window. There was a shop-cum-post office, a few houses scattered around a tiny village green and a babbling brook fed by water coming down off Great Harlow, the hill that dominated the village to the south. There was also a butcher's shop and amazingly, a red telephone box that looked as though it had not been vandalized.

Within seconds he had driven through, then the road rose steeply again and after about half a mile, he came to the red-brick detached police house/office in which Cathy James lived and from which she performed her role as rural beat officer for the area.

Flynn remembered a conversation he'd had with Cathy years before in which she had declared her undying passion for animals and nature. Her ambition was either to be a dog handler or a member of the mounted branch, or a wildlife officer, or, failing all of them, a rural beat officer. She had become a dog handler quite early in her service but it had been her failed marriage to another dog handler that put paid to her career in that department. His mates on the branch had given her an underhanded hard time and eventually she'd had enough and managed to move on to the mounted branch, where she had a few good, enjoyable years with a massive piece of sweaty flesh trapped between her legs. Lucky horse, Flynn thought dreamily, pulling up outside the house.

Following mounted she had got the job as rural beat officer here in Kendleton, the biggest beat in Lancashire, covering a wild, sparsely populated area. Her job included a lot of wildlife conservation and enforcement. Poachers, she'd once told Flynn, were a dangerous menace.

Flynn opened the car door a crack. The harsh wind from the upper moors rushed in and almost ripped it out of his hand with its strength. There was more snow in the air now, beginning to fall thickly with the possibility of sticking. Flynn put his jacket on and was about to open the door again, but a sixth sense made him check over his shoulder just in time and slam it shut again as the same black Range Rover that had ripped off his door mirror shot past less than three feet away. It carried on up the hill and disappeared over the crest into the encroaching weather.

'Gonna get you,' Flynn promised grimly. This time he made sure nothing was coming before getting out and walking up the driveway, past a selection of bushes and trees, to the front door of Cathy's house. From inside he heard the sound of a barking dog.

'Like I said before, it's as broad as it's long,' Henry apprised Donaldson. 'Now it'll take us just as long to get back to where we started from as it will to where we're going.'

'Basically we're in the middle of nowhere,' Donaldson concluded morosely.

'Pretty much,' Henry agreed. He looked to the north-east again. The view was quickly disappearing as the black, snow-laden clouds moved quickly towards them, a bit like the devil in the film *Night of the Demon*, Henry thought. The film had scared the living daylights out of him whilst watching it on TV once, when he was a home-alone teenager. He swallowed nervously and cursed the weather forecast. There had been the possibility of snow, but it had definitely shown just a light dusting down the Northumberland coast, at least a hundred miles away from his present location. Something had gone seriously wrong in the stratosphere, he thought bleakly. A north-easterly which had probably begun life somewhere over the steppes of Russia was now blowing bitterly, and was bringing a huge blanket of snow with it.

He saw Donaldson wince again as a severe griping pain creased his guts. He had been to the toilet again – 'Shitting a fountain' had been his wonderfully evocative description of the act – and it was now apparent he was suffering from something far worse than a hangover. Diagnosis: food poisoning. Something he laid well and truly at the door of the landlord of the Tram & Tower, and its chicken-based menu to be precise.

'Musta been that chicken,' Donaldson said.

'I had chicken too,' Henry said. 'I think I'm OK.'

'Not the same dish,' Donaldson pointed out. 'Sorry pal, I need to go again.' He shot behind a rocky outcrop, out of sight, and yanked his trousers down with a long groan.

Henry's jaw rotated thoughtfully as he glanced at his mobile phone. Still no signal, which seemed ironic being at such a height above sea level. If it was food poisoning, the journey ahead was going to be tough. Henry knew how debilitating it could be, even the mildest dose. To have been stuck out here even on a sunny day would be bad enough, but, as his eyes took in the approaching weather front, this was going to be extra, extra difficult.

The snow, which had started as a sprinkle, had become much heavier, something Henry hadn't seen the likes of for twenty years.

He glanced down at his map and compass, the only items he'd
thought he would need for the walk, and cursed. He had a GPS at
home, thought it would be unnecessary, now wished he'd brought
it along.

Donaldson emerged from cover, gave Henry a sheepish smile.
'Feel slightly better.'

'OK to push on?'

'No choice, is there? Can hardly stay up here.'

A sudden gust of wind caught the two men, almost knocking
them over with its ferocity. It carried sleet with it, slashing across
Henry's exposed face as though he was being pebble-dashed. It hurt.
He tugged his bob cap down over his ears and pulled his jacket
hood over too. He turned so his back was against the wind. Ahead
was a sheep track, heading due north.

'Need to be going in that direction.' He pointed.

'Yeah, let's go, pal.'

Flynn knocked. The dog barked louder. He knocked again, bent
down to the letter box and flipped it open to peer through. The
whole of the rectangular gap was filled by the snout and menacing,
bared, snarling teeth of a very large German shepherd dog. Flynn
jumped back with a little squeal as the dog snapped nastily at him.

'Nice doggy,' he said. He took a couple of steps backwards and
checked the front of the house. It had probably been built in the
1960s and was of typical design for a police house of that era, with
the exception that it had been extended on one side for the office
and on the other by a double garage with a bedroom above. Flynn
knew that the force had done its best to get rid of all the rural beats
covering far-flung countryside areas where nothing much seemed
to happen and the cost of policing was disproportionate to the results
achieved. The powers that be had managed to close a lot of the
rural stations, but Kendleton had remained open because of vocif-
erous public and parish council pressure. And the fact that Cathy
did a fantastic job. She had been single – newly divorced – when
she took up the post before the cost-cutting started. Within a year she
had wormed her way into the heart of the community and got
quantitative results as well as the touchy-feely stuff. When the force
tried to close the beat down, there had been severe ructions from
the tribal elders and they had to back down.

She had also done a deal to buy the house, with the promise she

would continue to stay on as local beat officer. The house, considered
prime real estate, had cost a fortune, but marriage to Tom, a DC in
Lancaster, had eased the pain of purchase.

Flynn thought about this as he walked along the front of the
house, past the huge bay window of the lounge, down the side then
through the unlocked gate into the back garden. It was a massive,
unkempt chunk of land. Flynn walked along the back of the house,
peering into the windows, seeing no one. However, by going on
tiptoe he could see into the garage and there was a car parked inside,
a VW Golf. For some reason, he thought this was likely to be Tom's
car. When he got back around to the front, he started knocking
again, clattering the letter box and generally driving the dog bonkers.

Jack Vincent had a pen in his hands, a cheap ball-point, holding it
between the thumb and first finger of both hands.

The cabin door opened and the lorry driver called Callard stepped
in. He had just returned from his third delivery of aggregate of the
day. His vehicle was now going through the power wash. He had
done his last run.

Vincent's eyes refocused from the pen to Callard's nervous figure.
'What?'

'I want out,' Callard spluttered.

Vincent's lips twisted into a cruel grin. 'You want out? Out of
what?'

'This.' He made a sweeping gesture with his hands. 'This whole
fucking thing.'

Vincent looked at him for a few moments, licked his lips, then
placed the pen down slowly on the desk without a sound.

'I can't do it,' Callard admitted. He'd been taking a big chance
that day, knowing the cops and the ministry were out and about.
The evening before he had got seriously drunk down at the village
pub and had continued drinking once he got home, only flopping
into bed at 4 a.m., horrendously pissed. His alarm had gone off at
six, but a shower, shave and copious amounts of coffee had done
nothing to alleviate his condition. So he had driven drunk and had
continued to sip from a bottle of whisky throughout the day, main-
taining the level.

Drinking had been Callard's problem before, the reason why no
one else would touch him with a barge pole. Since Vincent had
taken him on, he'd kept himself sober for the driving, but last night

had tipped him over the edge again. And the reason he got drunk wasn't connected in any way to the demons that haunted his past: the divorces, the depression, money troubles, the deaths.

The reason for last night's bender was helping to clear up a blood-soaked crime scene.

Two dead black guys. One with his throat blasted out, the other with half the side of his face missing. And the fibreglass walls of the cabin splattered with blood, gore and brains.

And the shotgun had still been in Jack Vincent's hands, literally still smoking.

Callard had just been under the crusher at the quarry, refilling his lorry with hardcore, had driven to the weighbridge and was ready to get back on the road when Henderson swung up on to the footplate and leaned in the driver's window.

'We need some assistance.'

'What d'you mean?'

'Switch off, come with me.'

Callard shrugged. He got out, followed the big fitter to the cabin. Vincent was standing at the door, talking to the woman who did the admin at the other cabin. She was a wiry woman in late middle age called Penny. They stopped talking as the two men approached and Penny took a step back, angling herself to one side to let the men stand in front of Vincent. It was then that Callard noticed the shotgun hanging loosely in Vincent's right hand, at his thigh, a wisp of smoke coming from the barrel.

'Been some bother,' Vincent said. A major understatement. He stood aside. Henderson went past him, looked down the cabin, then glanced at Vincent and sniffed up.

'Crusher?' he asked efficiently.

'One of 'em, the other's cat food.'

Callard had no idea what they were talking about. 'What's going on?'

'Take a look,' Vincent gestured in a 'be my guest' kind of way.

And from Callard's reaction, Vincent knew that he was going to be a problem. Drunks always were. Untrustworthy, self-absorbed and pathetic.

Vincent now looked at his driver, having expected something like this. He wouldn't have minded, but he knew of Callard's past. There was violence in it, he'd once been a minder for a low-level drug dealer, had broken fingers in his younger days, made people squeal for mercy.

Now he was an alcohol-riddled wimp. He said, 'It's gone beyond that, Larry. You're too much a part of it now. All that drug transporting, now helping me to dispose of two bodies, one of which you took in the aggregate this morning.' He smiled at Callard, his eyes hooded. 'Accessory to murder at the very least. You're locked in, pal.'

'Jack, I won't say anything . . . I just . . .'

'Look, come in proper, don't stand there. Let's chat. This'll be OK. Seriously. No worries.'

Callard hesitated, then stepped into the cabin, his eyes quickly moving to the far back wall on which most of the flesh and blood of the dead men had been splattered. Now you couldn't tell. Once the bodies had been dragged out and disposed of, Vincent had set Callard to work with a power washer inside the cabin. As the furniture in that section was all cheap plastic, it hadn't mattered about it getting soaked. Callard had covered his wooden desk with a plastic sheet, pulled open the drain plug in the cabin floor and got to work, hosing it all away. He'd gagged at first, then gone on to autopilot. Dazed, shocked and simply doing what he'd been told to do, terrified of the consequences of refusal. The washer had done a good job and Callard had spent extra time spraying the water jets into the nooks and crannies, transfixed as the resultant liquid mix gurgled away down the plughole.

And that was after he'd helped to get rid of the bodies.

He and Henderson, who had been completely unaffected by the task, had dragged the first body all the way to the stone crusher. Henderson adjusted the machine to spew out the finest grade of rock and then they'd hauled the body on to the conveyor belt, switched it on and watched it feed in.

The second body was more of a conundrum as far as Callard was concerned. He could see the reasoning in getting rid of a body through a crusher. It was pounded to nothing. Spat out on to a pile of hardcore, then tipped into a lorry and would eventually be part of the foundations underneath the stretch of motorway the hardcore was dumped at.

No body. No evidence. A very good way of disposing of it. Even Callard could see that.

But the second body?

He and Henderson had heaved it on to the back of Vincent's Toyota four-wheel drive. Henderson drove up beyond the working quarry, on rough, deeply gouged tracks, up on to the rim of the

disused quarry that Vincent also owned on the hillside behind his
house. This was fenced off by a high, thick chain-link fence with
many 'Danger – No Entry' signs posted on it. Henderson stopped
at a gate, unlocked it and drove through, then around various tracks
until they came to the old single-storey explosives store on the far
edge of the quarry. Under Henderson's instructions they dragged
the dead body off the flat-back and dumped it inside the store, which
was about the size of a small garage.

Henderson drove back to the cabin. Callard was told it was his
job to clean up the mess, then power wash the back of the Toyota
too, which was smeared with blood as though they'd had the carcass
of a deer in it.

All these awful memories were still vivid in Callard's brain as
Vincent sat him down.

'You owe me big style,' Vincent said. 'No one else would take
you on, but I did. It's not as though you didn't know what you were
getting into, is it?'

Callard stared numbly at his boss. Then blurted, 'The drugs, yeah
– but killing! Fuck me, Jack! You in a turf war or something?'

'Sometimes the shit hits the fan. Bad things happen and they
have to be dealt with – and that's what happened here.' Vincent slid
open a desk drawer, took out the money box and opened it. His
hand came out with a big roll of notes crushed in his palm, the
same ones he had shown the now deceased H. Diller and his equally
dead backup, Haltenorth. 'But we always get good money for what
we do, don't we?' He looked at the cash. 'I don't know how much
there is here, but it's yours for what you did yesterday.' His hand
stretched out to Callard, offering it.

'Don't want it,' he said stubbornly. 'Just want out. I can't take
what's going on.'

Vincent's mouth tightened. Slowly he slid the money back into
the cash tin and locked it. He pocketed the small key and rested
his right hand, fingers slightly outstretched, across the box, which
was just small enough for him to pick up with the one hand, like
a brick. He picked it up as though he was going to replace it in
the drawer.

Then he smashed it across Callard's head.

The tin wasn't particularly heavy. But it was sturdy and well
constructed. It was a secure money box, after all, made of quite
thick metal. The force of the blow deformed Callard's whole face

for a moment and he crashed off the chair on to his hands and knees. Vincent discarded the box and reverted to his fists, pounding Callard's head until, finished, he stood up slowly and breathless. Callard scuttled away across the cabin, whimpering and groaning. Vincent stood over him.

'I decide,' he gasped, 'who comes, who stays, who goes and what you do. I own you. I decide. And you'll do everything I tell you.'

EIGHT

During his time as a cop, Flynn had hammered on many doors, especially when he'd been on the drugs branch. Somehow an instinct was acquired as to whether anyone was at home, but on this occasion it didn't take the greatest detective in the world to work out there was a reasonable chance someone was inside. The car in the garage was a bit of a clue, as was the presence of the dog. Maybe. Or maybe Tom was at work, had got a lift in, and no one was inside.

Flynn shrugged mentally. He thumped the side of his fist on the door, rattled the letter box and stuck his finger on the door bell, making enough noise to raise the dead.

They pushed against the worsening weather, heads bowed, for as they trudged northwards, the north-easterly came in at them from forty-five degrees to the right, continually buffeting them and making walking along some stretches of the narrow paths quite dangerous.

Henry led, Donaldson bringing up the rear, trapped in his own world. To the American it had all become a bit unreal and he was focused on nothing more than the function of putting one foot in front of the other and the huge effort that it took. What he wanted to do was succumb to the awful way he was feeling, the nausea that enveloped him, the pain that weakened him every time it shot across his lower guts, and the fact that he dared not even fart. He even chuckled at that thought – and then the pain wracked him again and sapped more energy. His knees were weakening all the time, his muscles beginning to feel soft and pudgy. He pushed on, hoping his physical fitness and his mental attitude would be his saviour.

Henry was maybe ten feet ahead of him, but as the sleet turned to proper snow and the wind whipped it around, it became a series of interplaying curtains in front of his eyes, making it hard to keep Henry in view.

A sudden panic came over Donaldson. He was a tough guy and had been in many life-and-death situations, but they had always been on level playing fields or, more usually, Donaldson had had the advantage. And with the exception of one major blip – when he'd come face to face with one of the world's most wanted terrorists and almost lost his life – he had always come out on top. Because he was fit, healthy, strong and hadn't eaten bad chicken the night before. He could hardly believe how terribly it was affecting him, how vulnerable it was making him feel.

Henry disappeared in a snow flurry. Donaldson shouted his name desperately.

And then he was back in sight, had turned and was waiting for him to catch up. 'Jeez, man, I thought you'd gone.'

'No mate, still here,' Henry reassured him. 'How's it going?'

Donaldson shook his head. Not good.

Persistence paid off. Flynn saw the twitch of the curtain at the bedroom window and knew for certain. He waited patiently but when the door was still not opened he began banging again, using his knuckles for a short *rat-a-tat*, often more irritating than the bass drum knock with the side of the fist.

The dog continued to bark.

There was a shout from inside the house and the dog fell silent. Flynn heard a movement, a door closing, footsteps. Then behind the frosted glass inlaid in the UPVC door he saw a shadowy figure, heard the key turn in the lock and the door opened a couple of inches on the security chain.

Tom James's face appeared at the crack, but not the clean-cut face Flynn remembered from last year's honeymoon. The eyes were sunk deep in their sockets, bleary and shot with blood. He was unshaven and even from where he stood, Flynn could smell the body odour. At knee level, the dog's long nose poked through the gap, sniffing, growling.

Tom didn't even look directly at Flynn, just said, 'What the hell d'you want?' A whiff of stale booze came to Flynn's nostrils.

Flynn hesitated. 'Tom, it's me, Steve Flynn.'

The detective's eyes rose wearily. A glint of recognition came to them, but not friendliness. He did not unlatch the chain, simply said, 'What're you doing here?' There was suspicion and challenge in the voice.

'I was over here visiting family,' Flynn fibbed. 'Just had the chance to pop over and catch up with you and Cathy. On the off chance, y'know?'

'Oh, very nice.' Tom did not budge.

'Is she about?'

Tom shook his head. 'No.'

'Right,' Flynn said, expanding the syllable to indicate disbelief. 'Er, any chance of getting a brew?' he suggested. 'It's brass out here.' He wrapped his arms around himself to prove his point and exhaled a steamy breath.

Tom considered him, put the door to and slid the chain free. 'Come in,' he said reluctantly.

'The weather's turning real nasty,' Flynn observed.

The door opened. Tom was dressed in a dressing gown over a T-shirt and shorts, slippers on his feet. He fastened the gown, grabbed the dog by its thick collar. 'He won't do you any harm once you're in,' Tom said.

Flynn edged around the dog. It eyed him malevolently. It was a massive beast and he guessed it was the one Cathy had handled whilst she'd been on the dog section. The dogs were usually allowed to stay with their handlers when they left the department if they had a long-standing partnership, for in such cases it would be too problematic to re-establish an old dog with a new handler. Always better to start afresh. The dog did look quite old, greying like a human being, and Flynn guessed it would be around the nine year mark, if he did his maths correctly. However, its eyes remained sharp and keen, watching him enter the house and turn right into the lounge.

'Nice doggy,' he said.

'His nickname was Lancon Bastard,' Tom said. 'But he's a doddering old softy now, on his last legs, literally. He's called Roger, of all things,' he added tiredly and Flynn picked up that he wasn't keen on the beast. 'Grab a seat. I'll put the kettle on.'

'Great.' Flynn sat on the settee, glancing around at the furniture and fittings in the bay-fronted room. Everything looked expensive. The soft leather three-piece suite, the forty-two-inch TV mounted on the wall over the fireplace, the surround sound to go with it, a Bang and Olufsen sound system and a series of watercolours that looked original. Through the front window he saw that the snow had thickened and stuck, already some depth to it, and he worried if he was going to be able to get out of the village today. Whilst he was thinking this, Roger was framed in the doorway, observing him.

Flynn turned his head slowly and smiled cautiously. 'Hello, Roger,' he said quietly. He could hear Tom in the kitchen, mugs being placed on work surfaces, the tap filling the kettle.

'Where's your mum, then?' Flynn asked the dog. The ears twitched, so did the tail – in a friendly way, Flynn hoped. He held out his hand warily, hoping it wouldn't be seen as a piece of meat to be chewed on. 'You going to say hello?' The dog didn't move, but the tail wagged and the ears flickered uncertainly.

Tom appeared behind the dog, placed the sole of his slipper against its back hip joint and pushed the animal roughly away. 'Shift, dimwit,' he said and came into the living room bearing two mugs. He handed one to Flynn, then sat in an armchair. The dog, cowed by the push, stayed in the hallway, looking in.

'So, Tom, how's it going? How's married life?' Flynn asked brightly.

Tom's mug had almost reached his mouth and stopped under his bottom lip as he considered the question. He looked through slitted eyes at Flynn and said, 'OK,' non-committal.

'Good, good,' Flynn said. He sipped his coppery-tasting brew. 'Where is the lass, then? Out working?'

Tom shrugged. 'Yeah, probably . . . haven't actually seen her in a couple of days . . . shifts and that . . . ships that pass in the night.'

'So you don't know where she is?' Flynn tried to phrase the question as unthreateningly as possible.

'No, I don't. I've been working a big case in Lancaster, so I've been doing all the hours that God sends. We'll collide eventually, then we'll be in each other's hair for days,' he laughed. 'That's how it is – cops who get married. Not easy.'

'Yeah, guess you're right.'

Tom looked across the room at Flynn, waiting. Flynn sipped his tea, feeling extremely uneasy. 'Look, as a friend,' he said, now trying not to sound too patronizing, 'you sure everything's OK between you?'

'Has she phoned you? Is that why you're here?' Tom snapped. Before Flynn could answer, he went on, 'Everything's fine, OK? So, nice to see you and all that, but I need to get ready to get back to work. Need a shit, shave and a shower. You finish off your tea, let yourself out. Sorry you had a wasted journey.' He rose to his feet and swept past Flynn, then up the stairs. Flynn watched him open-mouthed, then clamped his lips shut with a clash of his teeth.

The dog sat at the open door, ears back, tail swatting sideways, back and forth across the carpet behind him.

'Some people, eh?' Flynn laughed, and thought, *Definitely not the same Tom James I met last year on holiday. Maybe that's what marriage does to a person . . . hm, it did to me.*

Flynn stood up and went into the kitchen, passing within inches of Roger's big wet nose, hoping he wasn't one of those sly dogs that let you in, then refused to let you out. He swilled his mug, then came back into the hallway. Ahead of him was the front door, to the left the lounge and to the right a door marked 'Office', leading through to the police station bit of the house. He glanced upstairs. He could hear Tom moving around and the sound of a shower being turned on. He looked at the dog, still sitting in the hallway, but having swivelled around ninety degrees to keep an eye on the stranger.

'What d'you think?' he said. The dog wagged its tail. Flynn took that as a yes, so he tried the office door and found it open.

'What gets me,' Henry moaned, 'is that no matter how good and advanced technology gets, nature always has the last laugh.' He shook his mobile phone and considered lobbing the useless thing into the snow. He didn't, but was finding it increasingly frustrating that there was no signal to be had on his, or Donaldson's, phone. They were sheltering under the lee of a rocky outcrop, out of the winds that had continued to strengthen and bring thick curtains of snow with them. Donaldson was huddled beside him, unable to even mouth a response as his illness became progressively worse.

Henry had drunk the last of his coffee and taken some from Donaldson's flask, swapping the hot drink for a bottle of water, basing the transaction on the belief that it was important for Donaldson to keep his pure liquid intake up to compensate for the stuff leaving his body. Coffee wouldn't be much good for him, even though they were entering a phase that Henry thought would be a balancing act. Donaldson needed to keep up his fluids, yes, and water was the best, yes, but he also needed to keep warm as the temperature dropped, and a few mouthfuls of coffee could help that. Maybe. Coffee, though, didn't always have a beneficial effect on the bowels.

Henry finished his high-energy cereal bar that tasted of card, then stood up. The harsh wind blew into his face, so he dropped back down again, unfolded his Ordnance Survey map and tried to plot their current position using that and the woefully inadequate compass.

'Where are we?'

Henry blew out his cheeks and placed a gloved finger on the map. 'Here,' he said confidently.

Donaldson did not even glance. 'Let's push on.' He got up unsteadily, swung his rucksack on to his back, then doubled over in agony.

The office was pretty sparse. Desk, two chairs and a sturdy, old-fashioned filing cabinet. There was a cordless phone on a base on the desk, next to a charger for police radios. Pretty dull, even as offices go. Flynn glanced one more time up the stairs before putting his finger to his mouth, saying 'Shush' to the dog, and stepping through the door.

Items of female uniform, including a hat, were hung on a series of hooks on the wall. There was a message log on the desk, a ring binder in which every call-out was recorded by hand, whether it came from a member of the public ringing in directly, calling into the office in person, or a telephone or radio message received from the divisional comms room at Lancaster, the main station covering. Flynn knew it was procedure to log everything. He opened the binder with his fingertip, noticing there were two batteries in the charger, both with the green 'fully charged' lights glowing, and an actual radio next to this. Personal radios were issued to each individual officer now and Flynn assumed this was Cathy's own radio, although it could have been Tom's.

'Mm,' he said at the back of his throat. So wherever she was, he thought, she wasn't in uniform and didn't have her PR with her . . . maybe. Flynn wondered if she and Tom had argued and she had stormed out and was now holed up with a relative or in a hotel somewhere, licking her wounds. It was only speculation, nothing more, Flynn admitted to himself. He could be wrong on all counts. Perhaps Tom simply didn't want to discuss a deeply personal situation. Flynn could empathize with that.

A blank block of message pads was crocodile-clipped to the left side of the message log binder, with several days' worth of messages inserted on to the steel rings on the right-hand side. Flynn started to peek at the top message, which was handwritten – he assumed, by Cathy.

'I thought you were leaving.'

Flynn jerked around to see Tom standing at the office door. He had been able to come silently down the stairs, his approach masked by the sound of the shower. He was still in his dressing gown. 'And you've no right to be in here.'

'Have you two had a fight?' Flynn asked, unperturbed.

'None of your business,' Tom stated.

'Fair do's.' Flynn raised his hands in defeat. 'But I take it you do know where Cathy is?'

Tom pointed towards the front door of the house, saying nothing.

Flynn took the hint and sidled past Tom, who was almost as big as he was. He patted the dog on the way out and as he stepped out into the cold afternoon, the door was slammed behind him. Without a backward glance he walked through the sticking snow to his hire car, spun it around and drove back to the village, stopping outside the pub called the Tawny Owl. A free house, it proclaimed on the sign.

They edged carefully along a tight shale track that clung to the edge of the steep hillside, stumbling occasionally and travelling, according to Henry's compass, slightly north-north-west. Being on the exposed eastern side of the hill, they were completely at the mercy of the weather. The wind had increased forcefully, driving hard sleet-ice remorselessly into their sides as though they were being pelted by gravel.

As much as he was cursing himself for getting them into this mess, Henry was pretty sure they were on the right track. They were just starting the descent down Mallowdale Fell into the valley cut

by the River Raeburn. When they got down to that level, Henry
knew they should be able to find a good track that would lead them
to the civilization that was Kendleton, their stop for the night and
now, of course, the end of their journey. He knew that Donaldson
could not possibly go on, that his friend was in embarrassing and
continual agony. He might even need medical help, although Henry
knew that doctors only dealt with extreme cases of food poisoning
these days. You literally had to excrete it all out of your system, all
by yourself. Probably all that Donaldson needed was TLC, immediate
access to a toilet and a bed to crash on.

Henry stopped. Donaldson had lagged behind. As he waited for
him to catch up, he turned his back to the wind and took out his
mobile phone. Still no signal, but even so he typed out a text message
with a frozen thumb and pressed send, hoping it would wing its
way into the ether anyway. The screen said 'Unable to send message',
so he tried again, pressed the send button, gave a flick of his wrist
as though this would help, and hoped it would somehow land on
Kate's phone.

Donaldson stood miserably behind him. His eyes had sunk into
his face. He looked drawn and exhausted.

'We start going down now.' Henry had to shout above the howling
wind. 'Then there'll be more cover and it should be easier, OK?'
His friend nodded. 'Push on?' Henry asked. Another nod. Henry
turned and started to walk, imagined he heard something – a thud?
– but wasn't certain. Something that wasn't part of the weather
noise. He glanced over his shoulder, expecting to have Donaldson
right behind him.

He wasn't there.

Flynn climbed out of the Peugeot and walked to the front door of
the pub. The snow was now horrendously heavy, falling in a way
he hadn't seen since he'd been a teenager, when winters were much
more severe in this part of the world. It was thick and was definitely
now sticking – almost as soon as he walked through it, leaving
footprints, his tracks were instantly filled in as though he hadn't
been there. He knew at that point that if he was going to get out
of Kendleton that day, now was the time to do it. The weather
looked set and bleak and it wouldn't take long to cut off a village
like this one, set deep in a valley, one road in, one road out.

He decided to do what he needed to do first, then make a

decision about leaving. If he got snowed in, he would just have to throw himself on the mercy of the innkeeper. If necessary he would sleep in the bar, something he'd done on many occasions in the past. The good old days.

He glanced up at the name plate over the door as he went in and saw the licensee's name was displayed as Alison Marsh. He found himself in a very pleasant country pub, low beamed, dark wood, nicely decorated and with a huge fire roaring in a grate. He approached the bar, noticing only a couple of other people in the snug. One was a youngish woman who seemed slightly out of place, sitting alone in an alcove, the other was a grizzled old-timer on a corner seat at the bar who looked as though he'd been rooted there, growing old, for many years. He had a pint of Guinness in front of him, and a whisky chaser. The young woman watched him but the man didn't even raise his eyes from the newspaper he was scanning. Behind the bar was a nice-looking lady, maybe early forties, who smiled at Flynn.

'Hi,' he said, 'Er . . . do you do coffee?'

'You name it.'

'Latte with an extra shot?'

'No problem. Small, medium or large?'

'Medium.'

She nodded and turned to the complex-looking coffee-making contraption at the back of the bar. Flynn eased one cheek of his arse over a bar stool and surveyed the room again. He gave the lone woman a quick smile – she looked away – and the man continued to ignore him.

'Weather not good,' he said to the back of the woman behind the bar.

'No.' The coffee maker gurgled, hissed and steamed. 'It's caught us by surprise and it looks like it could be a bad one.' She turned to him with his foamy drink and placed it carefully on the bar. 'Passing through?'

'Just visiting – but they weren't at home.'

'Ah.' She leaned on the bar and he couldn't help but notice her figure, which was very nice. She caught his look and smiled. 'Two twenty-five, please.'

He paid her, counting out the exact change. When she turned to the till, he pulled a crumpled piece of paper from his pocket and ironed it out on the bar top. Headed 'Lancashire Constabulary

– Message Log', it was a pro-forma document that ensured nothing could be missed when taking a message of any sort from anyone. The top message that Flynn had seen on the pad in Cathy James's office, he had managed to snaffle it in the instant before Tom had appeared at the office door and thrown him out. It was the most recent message she had taken.

Flynn read it, then got out his phone, waited for a few moments for a signal to be indicated on the screen. One didn't. He tutted. He raised his head to the woman behind the bar, who had turned to watch him.

'We struggle out here at the best of times,' she told him. 'They're always on about putting boosters in, or whatever, but they never seem to get round to it. Probably not worth it. This weather will make certain there's no signal at all, I reckon.'

'I take it the landline works?'

'There's a public phone in the toilet corridor.'

Flynn had noticed a phone behind the bar. 'Any chance of using that one?' he asked sweetly. 'Don't want my coffee to go cold.'

She weighed him up, then said, 'OK,' and gave him the cordless handset.

'Thanks. I'm Steve Flynn, by the way.'

'Alison Marsh.'

'Ah, the landlady. Pleased to meet you,' Flynn smiled. He got Cathy James's mobile number from the contacts menu on his own phone and thumbed it into the handset, put it to his ear and waited. A connection was made – then went straight through to voice mail. He tutted and hung up, realizing he was doing a lot of tutting recently.

'No joy?'

'Nah.' He handed the phone back to Alison.

Reading from his stolen message pad, Flynn asked, 'You wouldn't know where Mallowdale House is, would you?'

Flynn saw the woman's instant reaction. 'Why?' she said sharply, and it took him back slightly.

'Is it local?' he asked, carrying on as though nothing had happened.

'Yes.'

'And it's . . . where?'

'Two miles up the road, past the police house.'

'And that's it?'

'Big house, behind a big fence, big grounds.'

'When you say big grounds, what do you mean?'

'Well, the house itself is in big, fenced-in grounds, but the land surrounding that all belongs to Mallowdale.'

'What, like moorland or forest, kind of thing?'

'Yeah – why?'

'Er, nothing,' he said. He picked up his coffee and took a sip. It was a good brew and the extra shot had an instant effect. He was puzzled by Alison's strange reaction as he re-read the message again, written down and recorded by Cathy James, who still remained uncontactable.

In the 'From' section, she had written, '*Anon.*'

In the body of the message she'd written, '*Poachers on Mallowdale House land again.*'

And that was it, very bare bones. Flynn could only imagine the conversation. He guessed the phone must have rung in Cathy's office and she'd answered it: 'Hello, police at Kendleton. PC James speaking. Can I help?' It would have started something like that. Professional, courteous. Then, whoever it was had said, 'There's poachers on Mallowdale House land.' The phone call would have ended abruptly, or she would have quizzed the caller further, asking who was calling, asking for a description of the poacher or poachers, any vehicle, any accompanying animals – such as a dog. But the message was from Mr Anon. It was dated yesterday, timed at 16.30 hours. The words *PC James attending* were scribbled on the bottom of the form.

But Flynn was only guessing. All he had was a sketchy message about poachers from an anonymous source, and no doubt Cathy would have seen it as her duty to investigate, even though yesterday was actually her rest day. What it did was tell Flynn that Cathy had taken a message yesterday afternoon and that Tom was possibly telling lies about having seen her at home. How true was his claim that he hadn't seen her for a couple of days? Or perhaps he wasn't fibbing and they'd just had a big spat that wasn't any business of Flynn's, perhaps everything she'd told Flynn over the phone was just a woman's scorn? Perhaps she was just making things up to get at Tom for something else. What Flynn didn't like, though, was Tom's attitude.

Flynn scratched his head, not really knowing what to think, but he did know that policemen had occasionally come a cropper investigating reports of poachers. He remembered a PC even being murdered. These days poachers weren't jolly characters feeding their families, they were often organized, ruthless gangs and big money was involved, depending on what they were hunting.

He sighed, thinking he should just get the hell out of here before he got trapped.

'I'm curious . . . sorry . . .' Alison interrupted his jagged train of thought. 'Hope you don't mind.'

'About what?'

'Mallowdale House . . . you're not the first person to ask about it today.'

Flynn pouted. 'And?'

'Like I said, I'm curious.' She leaned on the bar again, pushing her breasts tightly against her jumper in a move with obvious consequences for the male of the species, a fact Flynn was certain she was fully aware of.

'To be honest I'd never heard of Mallowdale House until about twenty minutes ago,' Flynn said. His eyes registered the fact that the third finger of her left hand bore no ring of any sort.

'Well, you wanna keep away.'

Flynn blinked. 'You said that without moving your lips,' he said, and he and Alison grinned briefly as both of them turned to the origin of the voice – the old-timer sitting on the stool at the end of the bar, apparently engrossed in his newspaper but actually earwigging. 'What do you mean?'

The man, bearded, dressed in ancient tweeds, raised his chin and said, 'Just an observation, is all.'

Flynn waited for more. Nothing came. He glanced back at Alison and arched his eyebrows.

'They're not that friendly, that's all,' she said, ending the subject.

'Do they have a poaching problem?'

She guffawed. 'Anyone who goes on to Mallowdale land does so at their own risk. The poachers have a problem with the owners, I'd say.'

'Is that a long way of saying no?'

'You work it out.' Clearly the tone of her voice implied that she'd said enough.

Flynn exhaled and thought, 'Bloody villagers.' He was

half-expecting to hear banjos being plucked in the background. 'I see the "No Vacancies" sign is up.'

'Yeah, sorry. I've only got two rooms, both booked for the night. I have actually got six, but the rest are all being renovated and are uninhabitable.'

'Have the guests landed yet?'

'Not so far.'

'Think they will?' He gestured at the weather through the window.

'Why, do you need a room?'

'Considering.'

'I have to give them time to arrive. If they're not here by eight and I haven't heard from them, I'll assume they won't be coming and maybe re-let – if that's any good to you?'

'Sounds half promising.' He threw back the remainder of his coffee and wiped his lips with the paper napkin. 'Nice brew. Maybe see you later.'

Alison leaned on the bar again in the way that stretched her jumper tight. 'Maybe . . . ooh, speak of the devil.' She looked past Flynn's shoulder through the window. 'These are the people who asked about Mallowdale House.'

The blood drained from Flynn's face. Outside, a black Range Rover that Flynn immediately recognized had pulled up in the car park. The one with the impatient driver that had taken off his and another car's wing mirrors. Two men got out. Flynn slid off the bar stool and walked to the door, zipping up his jacket, then stepped back into an alcove as the two men came in through the pub door with a crash and headed to the bar without apparently noticing him.

Flynn noticed Alison's eyes had become wary. The men unzipped their top coats and stomped their feet on the floor to dislodge the snow they'd picked up.

Flynn's mouth went dry as his inner sluice gates opened and adrenalin gushed through his body. In the five years since he'd been a cop, his memory had not dimmed with the passage of time. He recognized that two dangerous men had just entered this out-of-the-way country pub.

Before his departure from the organization he loved, he had spent a good number of years hunting down professional criminals who made their grubby but lucrative living from dealing drugs and causing misery. Not the gofers or the toe-rags on the streets, but those who organized the importation and distribution of the substances had been Flynn's targets. Flynn, as a detective sergeant on the drugs branch with Lancashire Constabulary's Serious and Organized Crime Unit, had successfully targeted some of the leading crime lords in this genre.

Sometimes, of course, he'd been unsuccessful. Often cases built up meticulously over months or years came crashing apart for a variety of reasons.

One such case that he'd been involved in was against a very high-ranking villain called Jonny Cain, maybe one of the richest dealers Flynn had ever encountered. His wealth had been estimated to be somewhere in the region of twenty million. But Cain, a sly, devious man, had eluded the clutches of the law by surrounding himself with layers of protection and operating his business on a cell-by-cell basis. Above all, though, his ruthless approach to anyone who might be a threat to him ensured that few people had the courage to testify against him.

Flynn knew that about a year ago, the police had got Cain as far as a crown court trial for murder, but that had collapsed. Flynn also knew that an unlikely potential witness against Cain – another gangster – had ended up with his brains blown out by a professional assassin. As far as he knew, it had been impossible for the police to prove a definite link between Cain and that killing (although everyone knew it to be the case).

Flynn recalled all this in the moments standing in that alcove because the two men who had just walked into the Tawny Owl, and changed the atmosphere completely, were two of Jonny Cain's most trusted minders.

Flynn had a quick flashback to the Range Rover incident – the slicing off of his door mirror – and bored into his recall of it. Even though the vehicle's windows had been smoked out, he was sure there had been four shapes within and it didn't take a rocket scientist to guess that one of those shapes could well have been Jonny Cain.

Had Cain and the other guy been dropped off at Mallowdale House, Flynn wondered. That was the address that Alison said they'd been enquiring about. And if that was the case, what the hell were they doing here, what did they want and who were they calling on at Mallowdale House?

Flynn dug deep within his mind and regurgitated the names of the two minders: Roy Napier and Sim Riddick, two very evil men who were smiling civilly at Alison. She eyed them cautiously, then glanced in Flynn's direction. The faces of the two men turned the same way and this time they saw Flynn in the alcove, although they gave no sign that they had recognized him.

Quickly he tugged up his collar, gave Alison a quick wave and stepped out into the harsh snowstorm that engulfed the village.

In his right hand was the message about the possible presence of a poacher on Mallowdale House land.

NINE

'Karl! Karl!' Henry bellowed against the heavy snow smashing into his face as he scrambled back up the path. Panic didn't need to rise in him – it was there instantly. He had walked maybe thirty metres along the path from the point at which he and Donaldson had stopped, then, for no reason really, just the hint of the suggestion of an out-of-place noise, he'd looked back to check on the Yank – and he wasn't there. Henry could so easily have walked half a mile with his head down before looking over his shoulder, and if he'd done that and Donaldson hadn't been there . . . That horrendous thought was just one of the many that tumbled though his mind. 'Karl,' he screamed again, reaching the point where they had rested briefly. Henry faced directly into the weather, shouting his friend's name through hands cupped around his mouth.

The path was narrow and precarious. Stepping off it could have serious consequences under any circumstances as the hillside fell sharply away. It was particularly dangerous underfoot because of the steep angle and the loose shale.

It was obvious to Henry what Donaldson had done: taken a step off the path, or simply lost his balance and pitched over the edge.

Henry blasphemed. He had once had food poisoning himself. He recalled it vividly, the whole experience. The creasing gut pain, the shits, the nausea. It had drained him completely of any will power, sucked all the energy out of him. All he had wanted to do was go to bed and curl up like a foetus and pull the sheets over his head and die. At least until the next desperate urge to race to the toilet came. It had also made him woozy and light-headed, and he guessed that could be what had happened to Donaldson.

Henry stood at the edge of what was virtually a precipice, his head shaking as he dithered about what to do. The wind howled around his head and he cocked his ear to one side, trying to listen. He shouted the American's name again.

He was sure he heard some sort of response. The wind swirled away and then there was nothing but the buffeting of the snow, drowning out everything.

Henry shuffled sideways, tentatively placing one foot off the track into the shale. It slid down straight away, but he knew he had to go for it. Angling his whole body to counteract the steepness of the slope he moved down, inches at a time, grinding his feet into the ground with each step.

Within seconds he was enveloped by the snow and had lost sight of the track.

Then he fell and slithered down the hill, emitting a roar, grappling with his fingers, trying to stop his descent. And then he stopped suddenly as he crashed into something hard – which screamed.

'Fuck, Henry,' Donaldson said, as Henry regained his feet and crouched by the curled-up body of his friend.

'What the hell happened? Why did you leave the track?'

'Thought it would be a wheeze,' he gasped. 'A quick way down.'

'You hurt?'

'Yeah – busted my ankle.'

Henry's heart could not have sunk any lower at the words. He crouched over Donaldson with his back to the weather, digging his heels into the shale. Donaldson had managed to sit up.

'Which one?'

'Left.'

'Can you move it?' Henry looked at the left foot as Donaldson tried to rotate it. He grunted as it moved slightly.

'Yep, it moves – but I can feel it swelling in the boot.'

'Hopefully not broken, then?'

'Dunno – feels bad.' He raised his eyes and looked at Henry. 'Pisser, eh?'

Henry nodded. 'Pisser.'

From the directions given, Flynn knew that Mallowdale House was out of the village, beyond the police house, meaning he would have to drive out past Cathy's place again. But he could not bring himself to drive past without speaking to Tom once more. He wasn't remotely happy with what Tom had said to him and he was increasingly concerned about Cathy. He knew she was a big girl, an experienced cop and all that, could look after herself . . . but until he heard from her he wasn't going to be satisfied. His still very active cop instinct told him he needed to dot the i's and cross the t's.

He stopped outside the police station, drumming his fingers on the steering wheel. Decision made, he got out and went up to the front door and pounded it with the side of his fist. Roger the dog responded as before, barking angrily. Flynn kept up the pounding, standing back and checking the windows for any signs of Tom avoiding him. Nothing happened. The dog, from somewhere inside the house, continued to bark.

Flynn then saw there were tyre tracks and footprints in the snow at the garage door, almost filled in again by the snowfall. He walked across to the garage, turned the handle and found it to be unlocked. He pushed open the up-and-over door, which rose easily on its runners and revealed an empty space. Tom's car had gone and the tracks had obviously been made by the vehicle reversing out down the drive. Maybe he had gone to work.

Flynn stepped into the garage and saw there was actually an inner door at the back that led through to the house, into the kitchen. He went to it and heard the snuffling of the dog at the gap along the bottom of the door. Flynn's hand went to the handle, turning it slowly, opening it just a crack and peeking through, seeing the dog's eye.

'Roger,' he cooed softly. 'Roger . . . it's me, Flynnie.' The dog reacted by going frighteningly still. He opened the door another inch. 'Hiya, Roger . . . good lad.' The dog shuffled back a few inches, its eyes watching Flynn intently. Its hackles were up and for an old dog, it looked nasty to Flynn. 'Roger, good lad . . . it's me . . . remember me?'

Roger's ears twitched uncertainly, the beast not knowing what to do – attack or roll over and expose its tummy.

Flynn pushed the door open a little further then extended his hand, not too enticingly he hoped. He saw that it would just about fit into Roger's old jaws very nicely, like a T-bone steak. 'Good lad, come on.' He clicked his tongue. 'That's a boy . . .' Roger blinked, his tail wagged uncertainly, his ears flickering. Flynn opened the door a little further, keeping one hand on the knob, ready to slam it shut if necessary. 'Come on, it's Flynnie . . .'

Then, as if the dog was shedding a raincoat, his whole demeanour changed and he walked forward, head lowered, tail a-wag, ears back, submissive. Flynn was top dog. He patted him on the head, scratched his ears, then took the risk of fully opening the door and stepping into the kitchen. He squatted low, eyes level, and gave Roger a few hearty slaps, watching for any change of mind, but it looked as though Roger was going to do the decent thing – and not rip Flynn's throat out.

'Where's your mum?' Flynn asked. Roger's ears perked up and the big bushy tail wagged enthusiastically. 'Let's find her, shall we?' Flynn stood up and called out Tom's name – just in case. There was no reply. 'Come on,' he said to Roger and walked out of the kitchen, down the hall and into the office.

A quick search did not reveal very much but it did give him some information. A photograph on the wall showed Cathy standing next to a vehicle against the backdrop of the police house. New cop taking up a new beat, Flynn guessed, and the vehicle in question was a short-wheelbase Mitsubishi Shogun, probably the one she used for work and pleasure, part paid for by the county, part paid for by her.

He took out his mobile phone, thinking he would try Cathy's number again, but there was no signal. He picked up the phone on the desk and called it instead, but there was no reply other than the automated response that told him no one was available. He called another number.

'Jerry, old mate . . .' Flynn heard a groan at the other end of the line. 'Sorry to bother you again so soon.'

'You are going to get me sacked,' Jerry Tope said.

'Just a teensy favour.'

'Tch!'

'Knew you'd understand. Just check Cathy James's duty states again, will you?' There was a deep sigh and the tapping of computer keys.

'Rest day, like I said.'

'And Tom James?'

More tapping. 'Nine-five. That it?' Tope asked hopefully.

'Can you get into the computerized incident logs for Kendleton up in Northern Division? Course you can.' Another very pissed-off sigh. 'For yesterday. Can you see if a poacher was reported on land at Mallowdale House?'

Flynn waited. 'Nothing,' Tope said.

'So she didn't call it in, then?' Flynn mused out loud, frowning.

'What?' Jerry asked.

'Nothing – thanks matey.' Flynn was about to hang up when he thought he heard Tope saying something more. 'What was that?'

'I just want to confirm something.'

'What would that be?'

'Are you talking about Mallowdale House in Kendleton?'

'Yes.'

'I assume you know who lives there?'

'Unfriendly people, I gather. Lord of the manor, I suppose. Shoots commoners just as soon as look at them.'

'Not quite. An OC target,' Tope said. 'A very big OC target.'

'Organized crime as in . . .?'

'You didn't hear this from me.'

'Just tell me.'

'Jack Vincent.'

Flynn's brain cogs whirred. 'No bells,' he admitted.

'Rich, connected, usually operates down below the radar, business fronts mainly in haulage and construction.'

'Drugs?'

'Big style. Came into our sights say three years ago.'

'Which is why I don't know him.'

'And that's all I'm saying – especially on an open line.'

'I happen to be sitting in Cathy James's office, using her phone, buddy.'

'Why the hell are you asking me what shift she's working, then?'

'Because she isn't here. I broke in.' Flynn hung up quickly, smiling at the wind-up. Then he leaned forward and looked at the message logs, as he thought this through. He knew it wouldn't be unusual for a deployment at a rural station not to be logged immediately with the control room, although eventually it would be; nor was it unusual for a rural beat officer to turn out on a rest day. That was the downside that came with working a rural beat, you were at the behest of the community 24/7 and rest days were a luxury. Having said that, Flynn would have expected Cathy to inform control room that she was attending the report of a poacher, if only from a health and safety perspective. He frowned, flicked idly through a few days' worth of messages, some handwritten, others word processed, and realized with shock that he'd made a very big assumption about something. He took out the now very crumpled message he'd stolen earlier that day from the top of the pad, straightened it out and re-read it.

Somehow they managed to make it back up the steep hillside to the track, Henry taking Donaldson's weight and half lifting, half dragging him. By the time they were back on the narrow track, Henry was seriously exhausted. He settled the big man down and re-checked the mobile phones, shaking his head angrily, again resisting the compulsion to fling the useless items into the snow when they showed no signal.

'I reckon we've got about two miles to go, max, before we hit the village. By my estimation we should be pretty close to an unused quarry which we'll skirt around and from there we should be able to find a decent road down to the main road, then we'll be near the village.'

'Is this good news?'

'It's all good news. How's the foot, ankle, whatever?'

'I don't think it's broken, but it's a bad sprain.'

'So it might as well be broken?'

Donaldson shrugged helplessly. 'Guess so.'

'We'll do it bit by bit, yard by yard, eh?' He patted Donaldson's shoulder, dreading how hard this was going to be. Henry was big and strong enough, but Donaldson was bigger and heavier and the prospect of keeping him upright for the next two miles across treacherous terrain and against the weather did not fill Henry with glee. The drag back up the hill, only a matter of fifty metres, had been tough enough. 'All I ask is that you don't go on any unauthorized excursions again,' Henry said.

'Are we going to find your mummy?' Flynn asked the dog in his most patronizing tone. 'Yes we are, yes we are.' Roger barked happily. 'Are you going to come with me? For a walk?' Roger's ears shot up at the 'W' word and Flynn could have sworn he smiled and went, 'Yeah, yeah.'

Flynn had a quick scout around the kitchen and found a selection of leads hanging behind the back door, chunky thick leather ones, ones that looked like chains from a work gang, and an extendable one. Flynn picked a leather one, clipped it to Roger's collar and looped the handle a couple of times around his hand to keep a firm hold of him, otherwise the dog would probably do just what it wanted to do. Before leaving, Flynn cast his eyes around the room and saw a lady's headscarf tossed across a kitchen stool. Assuming it was Cathy's, he grabbed it and stuffed it in his pocket.

'Come on then, Roger.' Even before he had completed the sentence the dog lunged for the door, almost yanking Flynn's shoulder out of its socket. He heaved back. 'Whoa there.'

It had some effect, but Flynn was still basically dragged out of the door, into the garage and out to the front of the house where the dog made a beeline for a big tree at the bottom of the drive and cocked his leg up. After the relief, Flynn took better command and led the dog to his hire car, opened the passenger door and indicated for Roger to climb in. After a suspicious glance, the dog climbed stiffly in and Flynn noticed for the first time that its back legs were on their way out, as is often the case with German shepherds, or so he had heard.

Flynn went to the driver's side, got in. Roger was almost as large as a human passenger and Flynn felt like he was sitting next to Scooby-Doo, the cartoon dog.

'Ready?'

Roger eyed him, his tongue hanging out, slavering all over the gear lever.

Donaldson did his utmost to help Henry, but it was clear that the pain of the ankle injury and the continuing griping in the stomach from the food poisoning had combined to knock him for six. Henry had Donaldson's arm across his shoulder, acting as a crutch for his friend, but the going underfoot was slippery and the track hardly wide enough for two to walk abreast. But Henry held on and they made slow progress. The weather did not let up and daylight was fading fast.

Henry had no reason to suspect his estimation of their position was anything other than correct, but they still had to get down off the hill and into the village before nightfall. To be caught even a hundred yards away from the main road would be just as deadly as being trapped on the hill.

Steve Flynn drove up the narrow road. It was filling with snow, which was starting to drift and bank up in various places. He cursed the weather and had another quick flashback to the sunshine he'd abandoned two thousand miles south of here.

With the weather being so bad, he realized he didn't have time for more than a cursory drive around the roads that formed the perimeter of some of the land surrounding Mallowdale House. It didn't help that he was a stranger to the area, didn't know where he was going, didn't know what he was looking for and was probably wasting his time anyway.

The road dipped, the car fishtailed through some deep snow, then began to rise. On his left was a high security fence and he spotted a sign written in red letters which he guessed warned against trespassing. On a post behind one of the signs, behind the fence, he also saw a CCTV camera. He didn't stop to read the signs, but drove on another hundred metres and found a wide double gate, maybe ten feet high, but dipping slightly in the centre where the two halves met. He pulled up at it, peered through the windscreen and considered it for a moment. It seemed to be the entrance to Mallowdale House.

'You stay here,' he told Roger, who nodded.

He got out and walked up to the gate, which was made of solid wood, reinforced with steel belts, and was electronically operated. On a pole behind one of the gate posts was another CCTV camera, focused on him. There was another sign on the gate itself which read, its tone unfriendly, 'MALLOWDALE HOUSE. NO TRESPASSING. GROUNDS PATROLLED BY SECURITY GUARDS AND DOGS. BEWARE. KEEP AWAY. CCTV CAMERAS ALSO IN USE.' Like the sign further down the road, it was written in red. He tried to peer through the tiny gap in the middle of the gate. With one eye he could just about see a curved driveway, with a couple of sets of tyre tracks in the snow, and beyond, behind the snow-laden trees, almost out of sight, a large house, but he couldn't make out its detail in the fading light. He could also make out some cars parked outside, but again, no detail.

'Can I help you?' Flynn jumped as a metallic voice came from an intercom speaker set in the gate post. Automatically he glanced at the CCTV camera again. He gave a little wave, walked over to the intercom and pressed the talk button.

'I'd like to see Mr Vincent,' Flynn said, off the cuff.

'What's your business?'

Still winging it, Flynn ad-libbed, 'Police business. I believe he's had poachers on his land.'

'Show your warrant card to the camera,' the voice instructed him.

Flynn made a weedy show of patting his pockets. 'I think I've forgotten it.'

'In that case, come back when you've got it – and make an appointment beforehand.' The intercom clicked dead.

Flynn toyed with the idea of pressing the talk button again, but decided against it. He got back in the car and looked at his travelling companion. 'Have you got your warrant card?' he asked the dog. Roger looked dumbly at him, dipped his head forward to be stroked and dribbled on to Flynn's lap. 'Thought not.'

He engaged first gear and carefully started the car, the wheels spinning in the snow. He drove on up the hill. The high fencing with warning signs continued for another quarter of a mile parallel with the road before doing a right-hand turn. Flynn drove on up the hillside, which got steeper and steeper, passing the entrance to Mallowdale Quarry. He wondered if this had any connection with the house, recalling what Jerry Tope had said about Jack Vincent's legitimate businesses, haulage and construction. The light car became even more difficult to control and the snow seemed to be getting even heavier the higher up he got.

Flynn realized he was driving blind in more senses than one and he might simply be reacting to something that didn't even exist. Chances were that Cathy was completely safe and unharmed. She'd probably stormed out of the house with no intention of looking for a poacher and was safe and sound somewhere, licking her wounds, phone turned off to stop incoming calls from Tom. Flynn still felt uneasy about the situation and was worried that Cathy wasn't returning his calls, but he could see there was very little he could do about it and a big part of his instinct was telling him not to get involved. Domestic disputes equalled messy nightmares.

He decided to give it another mile or so then – literally, probably – spin around, slide back down to the village and see how the weather panned out.

The road twisted. The car slid and the steering wheel spun out of his grip, and he almost ended up nose first in a snow bank.

'Enough's enough, yeah?' he asked Roger, who had only just managed to stay seated. Flynn reversed carefully, keeping the revs

low and using the clutch tenderly to edge back off the road into a
forest track. His intention was to return to Kendleton and, if there
was no chance of leaving the village because of the weather, throw
his charming self on the mercy of Alison the curvy landlady for the
night. He tried not to think about the possibility of laying his weary
head on her bosom . . . the car slithered backwards on to the track,
making him concentrate on driving again. He braked, went back
into first gear and let out the clutch slowly. The tyres spun, not
gripping. He eased off and tried again.

It was then he happened to glance in the rear view mirror.
Something dark amongst the pine trees had caught his eye. Puzzled,
not even sure if he had seen anything, he yanked on the handbrake
and looked over his shoulder through the back window, which was
covered with big spats of snow. It cleared with a sweep of the
wiper blade and confirmed the glimpse. There was a dark vehicle
parked some thirty metres up the track, virtually out of sight of
the road.

Flynn's guts felt as though they'd been scraped out as he fumbled
with his seat belt, scrambled out of the car and ran up the track.

They staggered towards the remains of a farmhouse, nothing more
than a shell of stone and rubble, no roof, most of the walls missing.
It looked as though it had been bombed, but it was a good sight for
Henry to behold. Breathing heavily, he was close to falling over.
Cold pervaded his whole being and his energy reserves had dwindled
almost to zero as he fought to keep Donaldson upright, as he had
been doing for the last two tortuous miles.

He was relieved to see the building because it was a feature on
his map, overlooking the edge of the disused quarry which was also
on the map. This meant they were not far from a track that would
lead them down to the minor road, thence to the village of Kendleton
where they could rest and recuperate and possibly get medical
attention. The end was in sight.

He guided Donaldson to the farmhouse and eased him down
under the lee of one of the walls that remained standing, blocking
off some of the wind and snow.

Henry's relief was incredible, but tempered by the thought he
might have made a mistake in stopping. Should they have carried
on? The thought of heaving his friend back up to his feet was
demoralizing. Henry stretched his back, muscles he didn't know he

had ached agonizingly. He looked at Donaldson massaging his injured ankle. His tanned face was pale and sickly.

'Couple of minutes, then we get going again.'

'Sure thing,' Donaldson mumbled, not even raising his eyes to look at Henry.

Henry resisted the urge to sink down next to him, knowing he would not want to get back up again and also wanting to give his friend the impression that he was OK, even if he wasn't. A psychological thing, his desire to keep Donaldson's spirits up.

Instead he wandered around the building that had once been a large farmhouse, curious as to why it had never been renovated. To Henry it looked like it would have made a stunning house. He wandered around the walls then got the probable answer to the question. Within ten feet of the gable end was a high, wire-mesh fence. Henry walked towards it, slipped his fingers through the mesh and gave it a rattle, reading the *Danger – Keep Out* sign in red. Underneath these words was written *Disused Quarry*. And that was why the farmhouse had never been done up, he guessed. Too near the rim of the quarry, although as he peered through the fence he couldn't actually see this. But he assumed it wasn't too far away. Once, the farmhouse would have been situated in a stunning location on the hillside, but as the quarry had been excavated and crept closer, it wasn't so nice.

'Whatever,' Henry said, ending his speculation. He turned, had his back to the fence when suddenly the hairs on the back of his neck rose and a very strange sensation rippled down his spine as he became aware of a presence behind him. For a brief moment every organ in his body seemed to seize as the certainty overwhelmed him that somewhere behind him, not too far away, something was stalking him.

He went rigid. Out of the corner of his eye he was utterly convinced he had seen a movement, a shape on the other side of the fence. His mouth opened slightly and he swallowed. Something deep inside him, some long-buried intuition, told him he was being hunted, that he was the prey.

Catching his breath, his neck muscles taut like wire, his nostrils flaring, his mouth now a tight 'O', he spun quickly. Was there something? An indistinguishable shape on the other side of the fence? Yes. Then it was gone and there was just the faintest scent in the air. Henry stared dumbly at the fence, at the exact point where he was certain he'd seen something. But there was nothing and he became conscious of how wound up his body had become.

Relief wafted over him and he laughed with embarrassment.

'A deer,' he thought. Couldn't have been anything else. Might not even have been a deer – just nothing, a combination of tiredness and over-imagination and light-headedness. Maybe the equivalent of the thirsty desert traveller seeing an oasis, then realizing it was a mirage, pure hallucination.

He shook his head, exhaled, relaxed himself and returned to his friend. This time Donaldson lifted his face weakly when Henry stood in front of him.

'Not far to go, pal,' Henry said, proffering his hand. Donaldson reached out pathetically and Henry tried to ease him up. The big man rose slowly, painfully and almost got to his feet, then seemed to stagger and lose balance as he put weight inadvertently on his injured ankle. Henry's hands shot out to steady him, but Donaldson moaned and slid back down on to his backside, dragging Henry with him.

'Jeez, sorry pal. It just went.'

'It's OK,' Henry reassured him. 'Lct's do it slow and sure.' Henry positioned himself on his haunches, slightly to one side of Donaldson, and took hold of his left arm with both hands, but when he looked up he was staring into the golden eyes of a beast.

TEN

F lynn jogged through the snow, slowed and eventually walked the remaining few yards to the vehicle, a black, short-wheelbase Mitsubishi Shogun: Cathy's car. The one Flynn had seen in the photograph in the office, the one she was proudly standing against with the police house in the background. About two inches of snow had settled on the roof and bonnet.

It was parked on the track in the trees and as Flynn glanced around and back he confirmed it was just out of sight of the road, being parked on a slight right-hand kink in the track. It would be virtually impossible for anyone driving past to have spotted it, and even if it had been seen, so what? Nothing that suspicious.

Other than the fact it belonged to the local bobby, who hadn't been seen or heard of for a day . . . but again, who would know that?

Flynn's horrible gut feeling started to become even more painful.

He peered in through the side windows, wiping the snow off with the blade of his right hand, shading his eyes to see inside. The vehicle was empty. He tried the driver's door, found it unlocked. He pulled it open and leaned inside, looking over into the back seat, seeing nothing of interest. However, on the front passenger seat was a sturdy leather handbag of the type issued to female officers. Flynn dragged it across to him, opened it and peered at the contents. A pink duty diary, a couple of bits and pieces of make-up, a CS spray canister, an extendable baton, a pair of rigid handcuffs and a mobile phone.

'Not happy,' he said, 'not happy.' He was tempted to handle the items but held back for the time being, because he thought this could well be part of a crime scene and he didn't want to contaminate any possible evidence with his fingerprints. Again he considered he was maybe being over-dramatic. But, he thought, recalling good police practice, it was better than having egg chucked in your face. You can laugh off making an arse of yourself, but you can never shrug off overlooking something of importance.

He just didn't like it – at all.

Then he noticed the key was still slotted into the ignition. He extracted it carefully, closed the door and locked the car with the remote. He quickly ran his hand under the thick blanket of snow on the bonnet and confirmed to himself that the engine really was cold. Then he walked back to his hire car and looked in at Roger, still sitting patiently. Well trained, these county dogs, he thought.

Flynn opened the door, muttering to the dog, 'You're not going to like this, pal.' He attached the extending lead and hooked it on to Roger's collar. The dog clambered stiffly out and dashed to the nearest tree to cock his leg up. Flynn waited for the flow to end, then said, 'C'mon Roger, where's your mum? Come on, find your mum.' He pulled out the scarf he'd taken from the kitchen and let the dog sniff it.

Roger's ears perked up and he lunged excitedly up the track with a woof, almost dislocating Flynn's shoulder from its socket, and headed towards the Shogun. Flynn tried to rein him back to get more control. To some degree he was successful, but Roger certainly had a mind of his own and obviously knew his job, so Flynn let the lead reel out a little.

At the car, the dog sniffed around, encouraged by Flynn's words. He rose up on his back legs and placed his massive front paws on the driver's door window, making Flynn appreciate just what a huge dog he was, more like a fully grown man in a dog suit. He shoved his wet nose to the glass and slavered on it, then pushed himself away from the vehicle and dragged Flynn up the track, zigzagging as he went, nose-down in the snow, foraging, pausing occasionally to sniff the air, or a particularly interesting tree trunk.

Flynn sensed the dog was on to something. At least up to the point where he stopped, sniffed and pawed the ground. Flynn approached with trepidation, drawing the lead back on to the inertia reel, thinking that something – someone – had been found in a shallow grave. His imagination ran riot.

The dog circled tightly, dropped his back end and started to shit.

Flynn didn't know whether to be relieved or annoyed, but the expression of pure pleasure on Roger's face actually made him chuckle. Then, with one last squeeze, Roger had completed his task and was ready to resume the search. He went up the track, pulling Flynn behind him. Flynn remarked philosophically, 'When you gotta go, you gotta go.'

For an old dog with arthritic joints, Roger moved quickly and with purpose. It was all Flynn could do to keep up and prevent the lead from wrapping around trees and snagging bushes. Flynn knew that police dog handlers usually allowed their dogs to roam freely on wide searches, but he didn't want to face the prospect of never seeing Roger again and having to explain that away.

The ground was broken and uneven underneath the snow and it was hard to keep upright, but Flynn was fit and agile and controlling Roger reminded him, in a way, of playing a marlin. Not as much fun, obviously. The path rose steeply and Flynn saw they were making their way up alongside a high fence on their right. Suddenly they reached a plateau which opened up at a dilapidated farm building.

Then it was as though Roger had an injection of speed. He surged ahead, uttering a growl, and hurtled towards the building. The lead played out like a fishing line from a spool. The dog skittered and half-disappeared behind a wall that had once been one of the gable-ends of the old farmhouse.

Flynn rushed up behind him as Roger stopped abruptly and dropped into a rigid attacking stance, hackles rising, ears flattened back, a very dangerous snarl, revealing thick, long, sharp canines. His teeth were stained brown with age, but even so they looked like they could still tear off a man's biceps when combined with the powerful muscles in the jaw.

Flynn skidded around the corner, the inertia reel clattering like a broken tape measure as it gathered back the lead. He almost collided with Roger, whose training had taken over as he stood looking ferociously at the two bedraggled, exhausted and weather-beaten men he had discovered sheltering in the protection provided by the crumbling wall.

Roger glanced at Flynn, waiting for the attack signal. Flynn let the lead rattle all the way back in until it was as short as it could be, then he thumbed on the locking mechanism. Only then did he look properly at the men.

The one who'd been on his haunches, almost eye-to-eye with Roger, rose unsteadily, knees cracking. The other one, sitting against the wall, stayed where he was.

'Bloody hell,' Flynn gasped. 'Henry-freaking-Christie. What are you doing here?'

'I could ask you the same question,' Henry croaked.

'Walking my dog, obviously,' Flynn said.

'I never thought I'd be glad to see you,' Henry admitted. 'Need some help here.'

As they helped Donaldson to his feet, Flynn inadvertently knocked the locking catch on the lead and Roger, now uninterested in his find, moseyed off towards the fence. Flynn kept hold of the lead, but did not watch what he was doing.

Roger raised his sensitive nose and sniffed the air. A change came over him: his head fell and his hackles rose again as they had done on finding the two men, but this time he stepped backwards, his throat rumbling uncertainly. There was a terrible growl from the other side of the fence. Roger leapt a foot high, all four paws leaving the ground, turned tail and ran back to Flynn, coming around him and wrapping the lead around his legs, taking cover.

Henry and Flynn looked from the dog to the fence and back again.

'What the hell was that?' Flynn said, stepping out of the lasso formed by the lead and hunching one of Donaldson's arms around his shoulders.

'Don't know – an owl?' Henry suggested.

'Big owl,' Flynn said.

They manhandled the sick and lame Donaldson between them the mile or so back down the hill, passing the Shogun on the way, and eased him on to the back seat of Flynn's hired Peugeot where he slumped gratefully across the upholstery with a groan. Flynn switched on the engine and turned up the fan heater a few notches.

'It's not far to the village from here,' Flynn said, blowing into his cupped hands. Darkness was almost upon them, the snow unrelenting. 'This could cut the place off,' he said, gesturing at the weather. 'We probably need to get going, otherwise the road from here could be impassable, too.'

'Yeah, good idea,' Henry agreed. 'Shall we?' He indicated the car.

'But not just yet,' Flynn said.

'He needs to get somewhere warm,' Henry said.

'And I reckon I've got another ten minutes of looking,' Flynn said.

Henry regarded him. His face felt frozen and unfeeling, his fingers inside his gloves like ice-pops, and all he wanted to do was defrost. 'Just what the hell are you doing here?' he asked. 'What are you looking for? I'm here because an ill-judged jaunt went wrong, but you're two thousand miles off your patch, aren't you?' If he was honest, he did not care what Flynn was up to or why, he was simply grateful their paths had collided, thankful for his assistance with Donaldson, and now he just wanted a hot bath, hot food and to get his friend sorted. He had no interest in Flynn's circumstances.

'I couldn't resist a plea from a husky maiden,' Flynn said, not giving Henry the additional reasons he'd left Gran Canaria, such as the possibility of an assault complaint, or the lack of work. 'So I've turned up here and, to cut a long story short, I think I'm looking for a body.' He pointed to the Shogun up the track. 'That's her car. Her keys and possessions were in it, but she's nowhere to be found. I'm thinking bad things.'

'And who is the dusky maiden?' Henry said, playing along with reluctance.

'Cathy James, the rural beat officer out here.'

Henry would have frowned, but the cold had made his forehead as smooth and fixed as if he'd had a Botox injection. 'A police officer?'

'You might remember her as Cathy Turnbull – if you know her at all.'

Henry's internal light bulb flickered. 'She married Tom James, a detective from Lancaster.'

'The very one.'

'He's a good lad,' Henry said. Flynn emitted a doubtful noise. Henry relented a little and tried to show some interest. 'So what's going on?'

'Nutshell? I got a few frantic calls from Cathy – we go way back,' he explained. 'I turned up here and found she hasn't been seen since a domestic ding-dong. Good lad Tom acts like he doesn't give a shit and now I've found her car.' He opened his arms helplessly.

'Where does the dog come into it?'

Flynn gave Henry a pissed-off look. 'Does it matter? Fact is, I can't contact her, I've found her car in the middle of nowhere and I'm worried – as you would be,' he concluded cynically.

'But no sign of any body?' Henry asked.

'No . . . but I also know she might've been checking up on a report of a poacher on this land, so that's an add-on worry. I mean, she could've come a cropper challenging a poacher, dunno. It's happened before, hasn't it? And as for the dog, it's hers, so I borrowed him to look for her.'

Flynn was not one of Henry's favourite people, and their history was one of conflict. However, as a cop, he felt some responsibility to act on Flynn's story, half-baked as it was. He looked up at the sky, then at the Peugeot with Donaldson in the back seat. If he insisted on getting Donaldson to the village, there would be no light left at all, and as there was only a few minutes' worth left anyway, he decided that he would humour Flynn. At least then he couldn't be criticized. 'Let's have a look at the car, then.'

'What about your mate?'

'A few more minutes won't do him any harm. It'll be pitch black then anyway and there won't be any time to look for anything.'

Flynn gave a short, grateful nod. He tugged Roger's lead and the three of them walked back up to Cathy's Shogun. Flynn took the opportunity to give Henry a few more details of what had been going on. Henry listened as he trudged. Flynn pointed the remote at the car and unlocked it as they got to it, the inner light coming on. Henry opened the driver's door, leaned carefully in, checking the interior. He picked up the leather handbag Flynn had told him about and peered at the contents, glancing sideways at Flynn.

'Admittedly, looks sus,' Henry conceded. 'If she was getting out to deal with a poacher, why would she leave this stuff behind?'

'Maybe she didn't get the chance,' Flynn said.

Henry jerked his head in acknowledgement, and thought, *Or maybe she didn't feel the need to have the stuff with her, or maybe this is just the set-up of a hysterical person trying to draw attention to herself.* He kept those musings to himself.

'Did she actually say what the problem was with her and Tom?' Henry asked.

'Not really,' Flynn said in a strained way. 'But she did say something weird.'

Henry waited.

'She said her husband was bent.'

'As in gay, or cop?'

'Cop.'

'Mm, I find that hard to believe, knowing what I do of Tom James.'

'You didn't seem to find it hard to believe when you were investigating me,' Flynn blurted, displaying deep-rooted resentment.

Henry blinked. 'A million quid did go missing,' he pointed out.

'And I didn't take it, as I've since proved.'

'Let's not go there.' Henry raised his eyebrows.

Flynn pursed his lips and said, 'Whatever.'

Henry reached back inside the Shogun and lugged out a big Maglite torch from the passenger footwell. 'Let's give it a once round the vehicle, say a ten-metre circle, the vehicle being the centre. I reckon we take a quick look and if we find nothing, we come back in the morning.'

Sullenly, Flynn nodded, unable to believe his own little outburst, still surprised at how much his past dealings with Henry still rankled with him. Scratch the surface, he thought bitterly, you uncover a cancer.

'You want to try the dog again?'

'On the whole, I think he might have lost the knack,' Flynn admitted sadly, patting Roger's head.

Henry switched on the torch. The strong beam cut through the gloom, the snow looking eerie as it fell through the light. He walked to the front of the car and tried to fix his mind on the situation. It didn't help that all he wanted was to get off the damned hillside, not go scratting around in the undergrowth. Every bit of him was cold. His feet were sopping wet now, his gloves had been penetrated by the damp and although his outer clothing had done its job well, he was chilled to the marrow and fed up with it.

Truth was, he didn't want to do this. His instinct was to remove Cathy's property from the car, lock the vehicle up and leave it in situ overnight; get back to civilization, then start from scratch in the morning. What he was doing now was just a sop to appease Flynn, someone he didn't like very much and who was developing a nasty habit of coming back into his life to haunt him.

'I'll have a look over there,' he said, no enthusiasm in his voice.

'Don't try too hard,' Flynn said, responding to Henry's tone.

Henry set off from the front radiator grille of the Shogun. He intended to walk ten yards dead ahead, five yards to the left, left again, then back to the car, kicking up snow and dirt as he went. His feeling was that if Cathy had come to grief, and this wasn't an elaborate ploy to get attention, the grief would have happened in fairly close proximity to the car. Not that her body couldn't have been dragged further into the trees after the deed had been done.

As he walked forward, he wondered why he hadn't switched on the car headlights. Brain freeze, he thought. Knackered. No time for this shit. Want to go home.

The snow got deeper the further he walked from the car. He glanced over his shoulder and saw the shadowy figure of Flynn covering the area on the nearside of the car, accompanied by what looked in the dark like a wolf.

It didn't matter that he wasn't looking where he was going because he would probably have caught his foot and stumbled on the snow-covered root anyway. He kicked the obstruction angrily, but it wasn't quite solid enough to be part of a tree, because it moved. Curious, he poked at it again with his toe and unearthed a frozen arm. He dropped to one knee, brushed away the snow until he revealed the white, frozen face of a dead woman.

'Over here,' he said, then louder, 'Steve, over here.'

ELEVEN

Flynn stared incredulously at Henry. They were standing either side of the body in the snow and Flynn could not quite believe the words that had just spilled from Henry's cold-hearted mouth.

'Let me put this in simple terms,' Flynn's voice rose angrily. 'I owe you at least one good punch in the mouth for the way you stitched me up way back when, and I'm damn sure I can get away with it out here. So, if you do what I think you want to do, I won't hang back.' He paused. 'No way on earth is this body going to stay out here.'

Henry allowed Flynn his little rant and could not resist saying, 'And when I hear shit like that coming out of your mouth, I realize Lancashire Constabulary is a much better organization without people like you in it.'

Flynn bridled like a prodded Rottweiler.

Henry went on quickly, sensing Flynn's inner burning. 'All I'm saying is that if we start messing around here and moving the body, we're likely to lose evidence. You don't get a second chance . . .'

'At a crime scene,' Flynn completed the sentence sourly for him, quoting the Murder Investigation Manual. 'I know all that, but by implication you are actually suggesting that somehow her body should be left here until you can get the circus out to it. That could be . . . fuck knows when!'

'I'm simply considering all the angles, pros and cons.' Henry had to raise his voice against an ever strengthening wind. He jabbed his finger downwards at the body between them, already re-covered in snow after Henry had brushed some of it away only moments before. 'She's been murdered and I don't want to lose any evidence that might help catch a killer. Especially as she's a colleague.'

'And that would mean leaving her here?' Flynn demanded.

'In an ideal world, yes. If the weather was fine and we could actually communicate with someone and I could get the circus out and I could protect it and leave it guarded – that's exactly what I'd do.'

'But none of those things apply.'

'I know – but what I need to do is find out the true situation, OK? Our mobiles don't seem to work out here, but are we actually cut off by road yet? Until I get to a landline and put a call through to headquarters I won't know for certain. Can I get a helicopter up? Can I get a team here? Until I get those questions answered I won't make a decision.' Henry's jaw jutted challengingly.

Flynn relented slightly. 'Tell you what, you go to the village, use my motor, and see if you can contact your precious HQ and find out what the score is. I'll lay odds nothing's moving, not in this neck of the woods anyway. I'll stay and cover the scene – if you'll allow me to sit in the Shogun.'

And then there was the other aspect: Henry was also suspicious of Flynn, as he would be of anyone so closely connected to a murder victim. Did he do it?

As if Flynn could read Henry's mind, he said, 'No – I didn't.'

They weighed each other up for a few moments, then Henry nodded and said, 'Start the car to keep warm, but don't touch anything.'

'I was a cop for twenty years,' Flynn said. 'I know what to do.' Henry handed him the torch. 'And if you can't get anyone out, this body is being moved, whatever the hell you say or want.'

Unfazed by Flynn, Henry said, 'I'll be making the decisions.'

Flynn watched Henry stumble back past the Shogun to the hire car, shaking his head at the detective's back, somehow stopping himself from jerking a middle finger up at his back. Then he looked down at the body at his feet, squatted down and shone the torch beam on to her distorted face, or at least what was left of it. The top right-hand quadrant had been effectively blown off, undoubtedly from a shotgun blast at close range. The right eye had also been removed, but even though the force of the blast had caused the remaining three-quarters to be hideously misshapen, the lips baring the teeth, the cheek distended, Flynn could still clearly recognize Cathy James.

'Oh babe,' he whispered, trying to hold back his anguish, 'who the hell did this to you?' But even as he asked a dead body, Flynn was pretty positive that the husband had some very difficult questions to answer.

Henry dropped heavily into Flynn's hire car and dragged the seat belt cross his chest.

'What's happening?' Donaldson's weak voice came from the rear. He was lying in a foetal position across the back seat, knees brought up tightly to his chest.

'Tell you later. I'm going to get you down to the pub, then I need to get back up here.'

'You found a body or something?'

'Something like that.'

'Oh,' he said with little interest, showing how poorly he was.

Thick snow covered the windscreen, heavy and wet. The wipers had to work hard to clear the glass before Henry put the car into first and slowly eased out the clutch.

'How're you feeling?' he asked. The car crept forward, off the forest track, on to the road. He turned left into the gradient and instantly the front wheels failed to grip. The car slewed in slow motion across the snow. Henry wrestled with the wheel, turned into the skid and corrected it. He realized that although there was only a couple of miles or so to go, it was going to have to be a slow journey.

'Jeepers,' Donaldson said, grabbing the back of Henry's seat to stop himself pitching off his own seat into the footwell.

'Sorry,' Henry said.

'And in answer to your question, not good. Ankle's throbbing like it's on a hotplate and the insides are still churning. Should I elaborate?'

'No.' Henry leaned forward as he drove, his chin almost on the rim of the steering wheel, nose nearly touching the screen as though this position made it easier to see ahead and control the car.

'Who was that guy anyway? Why – how – do you know him?'

'Ex-cop,' Henry said. 'I gave him a helping hand in the ex department.'

'Ahh.' Donaldson's stomach cramped tightly. 'Need a restroom,' he said, and added, 'pretty urgently.'

'I'm going as fast as I can,' Henry said, trying to concentrate on the road and not put the car into a ditch. Going at this snail's pace required all his skill and focus, even though several other things were tumbling simultaneously through his mind, mainly the dead body of a cop and the presence of Steve Flynn, with whom he had crossed swords five years earlier and who had reappeared the previous year in connection with a case Henry had been investigating – a case that had links with the reason Flynn had left the police.

In respect of the body – the important thing – Henry knew the scene had to be protected, hence his quandary about how to proceed for the best. Despite being en route to check it out, he was as sure as Flynn that because of the atrocious weather, there would be no chance of turning anyone out to assist him. His call to HQ would serve no purpose other than to alert the powers that be that a colleague had been murdered and a team had to be on standby, ready to deploy as soon as the weather allowed. He really wanted to leave the body in situ, and the evidence-gathering part of him was convinced this was the sensible thing to do, for the reason he'd lectured Flynn: no second chance at a crime scene.

But Henry knew this was unlikely to be an option, either practically – who would guard the scene on the worst night of the year? – or from a humanitarian point of view. And because of the weather, evidence would be destroyed anyway. Based on that, Henry knew that, somehow, he had to recover the body and try to maintain the integrity of the scene at the same time.

As he corralled the car down the hill, Henry was suddenly confronted by the appearance of a black Range Rover coming up in the opposite direction, headlights blazing on full beam. Henry squinted and flashed his own lights, but the big car continued to hog two-thirds of the road and forced the smaller car on to the grass verge. Henry just managed to keep control.

He cursed, flicked the wheel this way and that, and the two cars passed within centimetres of each other. He added a few more colourful phrases, but the incident passed without anyone dying, so Henry stuffed it out of his mind and continued on, very bloody annoyed by everything: the adventure – two mates on a well-deserved walking break – had gone boobs-up and now he had to put on his Senior Investigating Officer cap when all he wanted to do was chill out and recover. He knew that this day was far from over.

Passing the snow-covered sign declaring he was entering the village of Kendleton – safe drivers welcome – he kept his eyes on scan, taking in a few things of interest that might be of assistance to him in the coming hours, such as a tractor parked on the main road, before slithering to a stop outside the Tawny Owl. The old pub was a welcoming sight, promising warmth and comfort.

'Let's get you into your room,' he said over his shoulder to Donaldson, who was emitting weak, pathetic noises as he clung on desperately to prevent a bowel movement. 'Toilet first, though,' Henry corrected himself.

He helped him out, in through the front door, and propelled him gently along in the direction of the loo before turning to the bar.

There were only a handful of customers, unsurprisingly considering the weather. Henry approached the bar, his finger-ends tingling as he took off his gloves, and the warmth of the roaring fire immediately caressed him. He peeled off his outer jacket, fighting the urge to order a double scotch and sink into the battered, empty armchair by the fireplace. The last thing he wanted to do was turn out again, but relaxation and recovery were distant concepts at the moment, and were soon to get further away.

The lady behind the bar turned away from the two men she'd been serving at the far end and came towards Henry. Even in his tired state he could not fail to appreciate her looks and figure and, as if by years of conditioning, he tilted his head slightly and gave her his boyish grin. On a man his age, it probably came across as more of a leer.

'What can I get you?'

'My friend and I have two rooms booked for tonight,' he said. Instantly the expression on her face changed to one of horror.

'Ahh,' she said, drawing out the word.

'Under the name of Christie,' he added helpfully.

'Mm, yes . . . unfortunately I've had to let the rooms to someone else,' she said apologetically, dropping a bombshell.

'Must be some mistake.' Henry smiled, but his heart was beating just that little bit faster. 'I booked the rooms through the Internet and I have a confirmation e-mail.' He tapped his back pocket and kept his voice reasonable.

'I know, I'm sorry.' Henry saw her gulp. 'I assumed that because of the weather you wouldn't be coming.' She shrugged awkwardly, not really knowing what to do with her body language.

'I would have informed you if that had been the case.' His voice had become as cold as the weather.

'I'm sorry, but the rooms have been let to someone else now.'

'We'll have two more rooms, then.'

'I have only the two rooms, unfortunately.'

Moments before Henry had been half-visualizing this woman naked, a sad trait he'd had, since being a penis-led teenager, of mentally undressing women as soon as he met them, and one that had stayed with him all his life. Now he was imagining tightening his hands around her throat.

'I won't even try to explain what my friend and I have been through today to get here. Just to say we need those rooms urgently. He's very poorly and injured and as we speak he is affixed to a toilet bowl. I am exhausted. We need rest – and I have paid a deposit.' He tried to hold it together, but he was cracking at the edges. The rising inflection in his voice gave the game away. His right hand had started a little jig of agitation.

'I'm sorry, Mr Christie, I truly am.' Henry saw something in her eyes that puzzled him: fear. 'But I had no choice in the matter.'

'So where does that leave us?'

'I'll refund the deposit, obviously.'

'Is there another hotel in the vicinity?'

She shook her head and Henry tried to stop his own from jerking in exasperation. He tried to work through the immediate future: sick/lame friend, dead cop, crime scene, body, snow, ice, cut off from civilization, nowhere to fucking sleep! 'Right,' he declared, 'as it happens I haven't got time to argue the toss just at the moment. But at the very least, can my friend change into his dry clothing, maybe have a shower – i.e., use yours? And can he get sat down here in the warmth while I sort something out?'

'What's up with him?'

'Food poisoning and a sprained ankle – both pretty extreme.'

'He can change in the back and he can use my bathroom.'

'It's a start and it would be a big help for him.'

'What about you? You look as though you could do with the same.'

'A room would have helped.' He gave her a pointed look. 'But I have things to do first. What's the weather situation?' he asked, checking his phone for a signal at the same time, seeing no bars whatsoever.

'Bad and getting worse.'

'Is Kendleton cut off yet?'

She nodded. 'The road in and out is blocked with snowdrifts.'

'Great. Can I use your phone please? My mobile signal is non-existent.'

She handed him the cordless phone. 'Be my guest.' She looked contrite.

'An ironic statement if ever I heard one.' He snatched the phone and wandered across to the roaring fire, glancing crossly at the few customers, assuming they were locals, although the young woman sitting alone in one corner seemed slightly out of place. As he dialled, Donaldson limped into the bar, pale, ill looking. Henry gestured for him to take a seat and he slumped into a big old chair. As the phone dialled the number Henry had put in, he eyed the two men at the end of the bar, who were in deep conversation. Were they locals, or were they the bastards who had snaffled his rooms?

The connection was made and Henry was put through to the Force Incident Manager in the control room, who had an up-to-date overview of road and weather conditions in the county. The news was not good. The helicopter was grounded, all roads in the north of the county were becoming impassable as the snow fell. Councils, unprepared for the sudden change, were fighting to keep the main routes open and minor roads in the sticks were filling up with snowdrifts. Deflated, Henry briefed him of the situation he had encountered and gave him certain instructions to follow, putting a list of people on standby, but even as he went through this preparation, it seemed a futile exercise. No one could physically even get here before the morning, and even that was doubtful.

As he guessed, he was on his own.

TWELVE

Jack Vincent watched the Range Rover pull away from the front of his large house, head slowly down the gravel drive towards the automatic gates, which opened on its approach. It passed through them and turned towards the village. Vincent closed the heavy door with a clunk and turned to the two men behind him in the hallway.

Neither of these two men spoke. Breaking the silence was Vincent's prerogative. He was the boss, almost.

He hustled back to the lounge where he poured himself a large shot of whisky and sat down on a wide leather armchair, his eyes blazing. He sipped the pale liquid, holding the glass tight to his lips, and stared dead ahead.

The two men had followed him, hardly daring to speak.

Eventually he turned his gaze to them. 'Well?' he said quietly.

Neither man had an answer, but both knew what Jack Vincent was thinking. Then another man, who had been keeping out of sight, came into the room and all eyes turned to him.

The sudden appearance had caught Vincent off guard, but not for long. He had fully expected Jonny Cain to come knocking, but not so soon. He'd anticipated the visit would come later, when it was realized that H. Diller and Haltenorth had not reported back. There was no way Cain could have had any inkling as to the crushing fate that had befallen the two enforcers, so Vincent guessed that the follow-up had been pre-planned, to keep him off balance.

Diller and Haltenorth had been the advance warning, Cain the real thing. Obviously Cain had expected that the two heavies would achieve nothing, Vincent not being a man to be threatened or intimidated, and they would not have returned with good news, so the idea to come in their immediate wake was designed to demonstrate how seriously – and personally – Cain viewed matters.

When the intercom on the gate had buzzed, Vincent had been at the dining table in the kitchen with Henderson, the fitter, a man called Chris Shannon who managed Vincent's quarry, and another man. They had been drinking strong coffee and discussing the situation.

Henderson rose and answered the intercom, next to which was a CCTV monitor on the kitchen wall. Henderson had also answered the intercom a short while earlier to a man who had purported to be on 'police business' but had been unable to flash any ID at the camera on the gate. On that occasion, Henderson had turned to his companions and asked if either knew the visitor. Vincent and Shannon said no, but the other man crossed to the screen, looked at the image and said, 'I know him, but he isn't a cop – tell him to get lost.'

Henderson had complied, a little more politely, and the man went.

But the appearance of Jonny Cain didn't give Henderson that right.

'Boss.' Henderson flicked a finger at the monitor.

Vincent rose slowly and looked at the monitor linked to the camera at the gate. It was good quality equipment and clearly showed the stern-faced Jonny Cain, arms folded, staring expressionlessly at the lens.

'Shit,' Vincent said. 'Let him in.'

'But boss . . .'

'Just do it.'

Henderson pressed the gate release button and they watched Cain get back into the Range Rover, then the vehicle entered the grounds.

Vincent greeted him at the front door.

Cain and another man got out of the car and came up the steps. The Range Rover did a full circle and headed back down the drive, tyres crunching the gravel.

'Jonny, to what do I owe this pleasure?' Vincent said.

'I've told them to be back for me in half an hour,' Cain said. 'Now let's cut the bullshit and get inside out of this shite weather.' He ignored Vincent's outstretched hand and walked past him into the house.

'Hey, whatever,' Vincent said, trying to keep a note of levity in his voice. 'Nice to see you too, Jonny,' he said under his breath, turning in behind his unexpected guest and almost colliding with him. Cain had stopped abruptly, having heard Vincent's snide remark.

'This isn't a social visit, Jack.'

Cain declined the offer of strong drink, opted for coffee instead. Vincent had shown him into the lounge, trying to display a measure of confusion and pleasure at Cain's presence.

'Nice.'

'Colombian,' Vincent said with a grin. 'Obviously.'

The drink was in a large mug and Vincent winced when Cain, still holding it, settled into the soft, expansive leather of the armchair that was his own, placed the mug on the chair arm and dug it into the surface of the leather. It was part of a four-piece suite that had cost Vincent almost ten grand and that particular chair was his favourite.

It was just Cain displaying the top-dog psychology of the moment. He was the man and wanted Vincent to be completely aware of that. And Jonny Cain did not usually turn out to deal with things in person. That was why he had underlings, so if he had taken the trouble to show his face, it meant big trouble.

Vincent reined in his response to the mug wind-up.

'You'll already have had a visit from my men,' Cain started without any prologue.

Vincent frowned, glanced at Henderson who hovered by the door. 'No,' he said, puzzled. 'No, I haven't.'

'Really?' Cain said, unfazed. 'It's a good job I've come to see you then, isn't it.' He smiled.

'Why are you here, Jonny? Not social, you say?'

'No, it isn't.' He took a sip of the coffee. 'Purely fucking business.'

'And that business would be?' Vincent asked, acting dumb.

'Debt collection.'

Vincent pouted. 'Debt collection?'

'Jack, I'm not playing around with words or playing fucking games here. You owe me and I've come to collect.'

'You know as well as I do that I – we – were ripped off by a mule. A guy who thought he could get away with it. He's been dealt with now, Jonny. He won't be ripping anyone off again, but as to the loss . . .' Vincent opened his arms as if to say, *That's life, get used to it.* What he actually said was, 'The money's gone, the drugs've gone – irrecoverable . . . shit happens.'

Cain listened patiently. His accomplice, a man called Danny Bispham, stood at the back of the room, six feet away from Henderson, watching him like a hawk.

Cain balanced the coffee cup on the arm of the chair, stood up and walked around the room, looking at the displays in glass cases – stuffed birds of prey, mostly protected species, each one standing over a kill, a small bird or rabbit. He paused in front of one, a superbly mounted hen harrier. 'This is nice,' he said.

'I like predators,' Vincent said.

Cain sighed and turned. 'You know the sums.'

'The money doesn't exist any more, it's gone. I was ripped off and the guy who did it has had his head ripped off for his trouble. Quid pro quo, I think they say. The circle of life. If you want the money back, claim on your insurance,' Vincent guffawed.

Cain's narrow, harshly lined face remained expressionless. He checked his slim, gold wristwatch, which probably cost more than Vincent's suite. 'My other two men are securing rooms down at the local pub for the night. You have five hours to get the money. I'll settle for eighteen grand today and the rest in produce. The rest later.'

'I owe you nothing, Jonny.'

'Yes you do. How you handle your business is your business and dealing with a bent mule doesn't make the money you owe me vanish. If you don't show up with the money, we will be back, Jack, and then I'll mount your head in one of these glass cases.' His eyebrows angled upwards. 'Five hours – max.'

The Range Rover arrived on time to pick up Jonny Cain and Vincent watched it drive away. Back in the lounge, he looked at his colleagues, Henderson and Shannon. 'Well?' Vincent had asked, his eyes flickering between the two men, neither of whom ventured an opinion.

A door opened and another man entered the room. He had been listening to the exchange and Vincent now looked at him.

'You heard it all?' Vincent said.

'Every word,' the man confirmed.

'And? From a police perspective, what's your opinion?'

Without hesitation, Tom James said, 'Well, now that he's out in the open, I think it would be wise to do the decent thing, exactly what we've been planning to do for the last six months. Kill him and then take over his business.'

THIRTEEN

Having seated Donaldson by the crackling fire, Henry returned to the bar. 'See,' he said triumphantly to Alison, 'he's not well at all. He needs a room.'

'I'm really, really, really sorry,' she said. 'I . . . I didn't have a choice.'

Henry gave her his best grimace. 'Whatever . . . look, I'm going to drive up to the police station, I have some business up there. I'd be really grateful if you could just keep an eye on him.' Henry fumbled in his jacket. 'I'm a detective superintendent, by the way, and he's an FBI agent – honestly.' He showed his ID.

'You're a police officer?'

Henry nodded. 'And I've a few things to do before I can chill out – or warm up, so please look after him. He's a big galumph, but he's pretty harmless.'

'I will.'

Henry regarded her, liking what he saw. 'I'm still miffed about the rooms and I need to sort something out.'

'I'm sorry . . .' She seemed on the verge of saying something more, but held back, and Henry did not have the time to hang about.

'I'll be back when I've sorted this – *thing* – out.' He went to Donaldson and squatted down by him. 'The landlady's going to fix you up, hopefully. I need to go and see if anyone's in at the police house.' Donaldson stared uncomprehendingly at Henry, not far from being totally out of it. 'Don't worry, I'll be back soon.'

He got up, patting his friend on the shoulder, slid himself back into his weatherbeaten coat and set off outside. As he emerged through the revolving door, the same Range Rover that had almost barged him off the road drew up in the car park, disgorging four occupants. Henry flicked his hood over his head and walked to Flynn's hire car, one eye on the four tough-looking guys who barged past him into the pub, in much the same way that the car had been driven, without a thought for anyone else.

With his hand on the cold car door, Henry watched the men entering the pub, waiting for each other to use the door. The last man stood in line patiently and glanced briefly in Henry's direction.

About thirty metres separated the two men. Snow was falling heavily, darkness was upon them, the street lights were on, the doorway to the pub was illuminated and Henry saw only three-quarters of the man's face for a maximum of three seconds before he looked away. Long enough for Henry to make an ID.

'Holy shit,' he said, got into the hire car and drove off towards the police house.

The nature of coincidence was something that had always intrigued Henry. Things sometimes happened and people who knew each other could easily meet in unexpected circumstances of which they would never have dreamed. Such as the time he'd been on holiday in the Canaries and bumped into a man wanted by the cops in Lancashire. Or the time he'd been at a Rolling Stones concert and amongst eighty thousand other people, he'd met the only other person he knew, another cop who he never even thought could be a Stones fan. That sort of coincidence he believed in.

What he didn't believe was that it was a coincidence that Jonny Cain, a ruthless drug dealer and – unproven maybe – murderer, alleged hirer of contract killers to take out pesky rivals, had walked into a pub in the middle of nowhere with three of his hairy-arsed goons, whilst at the same time, lying there amongst the trees, was the dead body of the local rural beat officer, brutally slaughtered.

Jonny Cain just passing through – *and* a dead cop?

'Call me a cynic, but I don't think so,' Henry breathed. 'Highly friggin' unlikely.' He had an uneasy feeling about why his pre-booked rooms had been re-let, and to whom. He recalled the glint of fear in the landlady's eyes. 'That is no coincidence, no freak of fate. If it is, I'll show my hairy buttocks in the local butcher's window . . .' A musing that gave him an idea.

He drove carefully along the main road up to the police house, the car slithering in the snow. Henry knew the location of the police house – he'd passed it on the way to the village anyway – as he did every police station, large or tiny, in the county. Thirty-plus years in the job ensured that crumb of knowledge.

He wasn't completely sure what he hoped to achieve by coming here. To find Tom James at home and break the awful news to him? And then what? Flynn had said that Tom wasn't home and Henry was relieved to find that was still the case. The house was in darkness, unoccupied. He didn't even bother to knock. He thought about Flynn again, what the man had said, or not said, about Cathy and Tom. He knew that he and the ex-cop would be having a long discussion when Henry had sorted out the issue of Cathy's body and what to do with it.

He spun the car around, heading back to the village, parking outside the pub. He committed the registration number of the Range Rover to memory and was pleased to see that the tractor he had noticed earlier was still parked down the road.

Re-entering he saw that Donaldson and both rucksacks were missing, nor was there any sign of the landlady. A bonny teenage girl was now on duty behind the bar. Neither was there any sign of Jonny Cain or the goon squad. Henry's mouth twisted acrimoniously. 'In my room,' he mumbled, 'no doubt.'

The two men who'd been at the bar earlier were still there, having a chat and a laugh into each other's ears whilst the barmaid pulled new pints for them. The lone girl was still sitting by herself near the fire, nursing what looked like the same drink. A couple of other snow-covered punters had also appeared and were parked in an alcove with their drinks. Henry sidled up to the men at the bar and asked, 'Either of you two gents know who owns that tractor outside?'

Conversation interrupted, their heads turned slowly to him. He was close enough for their breath to catch him off balance, even in a pub.

One said, 'Who wants to know?'

Henry flashed his warrant card. 'Me. Detective Superintendent Christie, Lancashire Constabulary.'

'And why would you be wanting to know?' the same man demanded. He was big, thickset, in his sixties, with no hair and bushy, ginger sideburns, a matching ruddy complexion and eyes as sharp as a hawk. He was dressed in a thick check shirt with rolled-up sleeves, loose corduroy trousers, wellington boots, with a heavy coat thrown over a stool next to him. *If you're not a farmer . . .* Henry thought.

'I need a favour,' Henry said, 'and I presume it's yours.'

'Yup.' He drew his right hand, the one holding his pint, up to his mouth. Henry laid a hand on his wide forearm, preventing the emptying of the glass down the man's gullet. 'What the—?'

'How much have you had to drink?'

'This is my second pint – why? You going to breathalyse me?'

Henry studied him, guessing that two probably meant four in his language. 'Like I said, I need a favour and it involves the tractor. Police business,' he added.

The man pouted. 'OK,' he shrugged, then necked about half of the pint. Henry watched the beer disappear, trying not to look too concerned.

'Would you also know if there's a doctor in the village?' he asked the man, who wiped his mouth dry.

'That would be me,' the other man at the bar declared. He spun off his stool, staggered slightly and proffered his hand to Henry. 'Doctor Lott, and for some reason, my younger patients have started calling me Pixie.' He pronounced the last word as 'Pickshie' and Henry wondered how long he had been propping up the bar. 'At your service.' He stifled a burp and looked up at Henry through a sea of thick facial hair.

'I could do with your help, too,' Henry said, deciding that a pair of inebriated assistants would be preferable to none.

Both men looked expectantly at him.

'What you wan' us to do?' the doctor asked.

'One minute,' Henry said, raising a delaying finger. 'I need a quick word with the landlady.' He asked the barmaid where she'd got to and was told into the living accommodation.

'Aye, she took your big, good-looking mate with her,' Dr Lott said. 'Lucky bleeder.'

With a despairing glance at his two new assistants, neither of whom stood particularly steadily, Henry said to the barmaid, 'I need to have a quick chat with her, please.'

'Are you Mr Christie?' Henry nodded. 'She said you could go through if you came back.'

Henry gave her a nice smile and followed her to a very robust, thick wooden door marked *Private – staff only*. The barmaid entered a four-digit number on a security keypad and the door clicked open.

'Door at the end,' he was directed by her. He went through and entered the living area, which he estimated made up a big chunk of the rear ground floor of the pub. He shouted hello as he walked down a long, poorly lit corridor, then through another door that opened into a large, comfortable, but slightly dated and careworn lounge. He repeated his greeting, heard a mumble of voices behind another door, which then opened. The landlady appeared carrying a large fluffy bath towel.

'You're back soon.'

'No one in. What've you done with my friend?'

The landlady smiled indulgently. 'I'm running a hot bath for him. He needs it.'

'That's very kind of you. He's had a bad day.'

'I'll dry his clothes, and he can change into the clothes in his rucksack,' she said, then, 'I'm a very kind person.'

'No doubt. So kind you re-let our rooms.'

The smile faded. 'You won't let me forget that, will you?'

'Not in a hurry.'

'Your friend said you found a body in the forest?'

'Yeah. I need to try and sort some things out, a problem not made easy by the weather and the place being cut off.' He paused. 'Quick question. Did my previously booked rooms, y'know, the ones I booked on the Internet and which I paid a deposit for, go to the four guys who came in just after I left?'

'Yes.'

'Then I sort of understand why you did it.'

'You know them?'

'Oh yeah,' he said dubiously. 'You did right under the circumstances. I'm presuming they made you an offer you couldn't refuse?'

'They were scary.'

'Mm . . . look, I need to get back out and do a bit of police work. I'm not sure how long I'll be, but would there be any chance of me getting a shower later, and changing, and then some food?'

'Of course. And you and your friend can bed down here, if you like. I'll sort out some bedding and stuff. One of you can use the settee.' She looked penitent. 'Sorry about the rooms.'

Henry shrugged. 'What's done's done . . . I notice there's a butcher's shop down the road. You wouldn't happen to know the name and address of the owner, would you? I could do with a chat.'

'Better than that, he's in the bar. The man with the check shirt and red sideboards? Don Singleton.'

'The tractor owner?'

'One and the same.'

'Three out of three,' Henry almost whooped.

'Pardon?'

'Nothing. I also wonder if I could just use your phone again. I need to check in at home . . . and also, do you have a digital camera I could borrow?'

'Yeah, I do. Use that phone if you want.' She pointed to the phone on the sideboard, next to a bowl of fruit and a framed photograph.

Henry picked up the phone and glanced at the photo. It was a snap of the landlady, a girl he recognized as the one now serving behind the bar, although much younger, and a man. Obviously a family shot, all smiling happily at the lens. As he dialled the number, Henry said, 'Nice photo.' He glanced at the woman, whose name he did not yet know – although he assumed she was the one named on the pub licence plate over the front door, Alison Marsh – and saw her mouth contract sadly. He was a little puzzled by the expression, but looked away from her as his connection was made.

Steve Flynn hunched forward in the front seat of the Shogun and twisted the heating control up another notch. He was sitting in the dark now, watching the snow fall steadily, the wipers clearing the screen every ten seconds. Initially he had sat there with the headlights on main beam, the light piercing through the snowflakes into the trees ahead, up to the point where Cathy James's body lay. But that view had soon depressed him, knowing that a very dear friend – and briefly lover – was lying murdered about thirty feet away. Although Henry had warned him not to touch anything, he couldn't resist checking the mobile phone, which showed a list of his unanswered calls to it.

Roger, the German shepherd, had jumped into the back seat, stretched out and fallen asleep, making grunting noises and chasing rabbits. Thanks to the strenuous exercise of going up the hill in search of Cathy, the old dog was whacked. Not that he'd been much use in rooting her out. That pleasure had fallen to Henry Christie.

He began to think about Henry and the history they shared.

Flynn had thought of himself fundamentally as a good cop, but had developed a hard-man reputation when dealing with criminals and had built on that by being seen as someone who also cut corners in the criminal justice system if he could. He loved catching crims, particularly career-minded ones who were professional and organized. He'd managed to get on the drugs branch, devoting his energies to nailing big-time dealers. He and his long-time partner, Jack Hoyle, were seen as tough cops who had brought down many criminal empires.

What Flynn didn't know – initially – was that Jack was both massively in debt and was also nailing his wife Faye behind his back.

All these things came to light following one of those shit-hits-the-fan raids when almost everything had gone wrong.

Naively Flynn, a detective sergeant, thought it would be a career-making bust. With Jack, he had been building a case against a major drugs dealer, Felix Deakin, and had identified a counting house in Blackpool where Deakin's takings were being collected. Flynn had decided to raid the house just as Deakin was paying it a visit. He turned up, the cops hit the place – and then it went wrong. A cop got shot and Deakin alleged that a million pounds in drugs money had disappeared into the pockets of bent cops – specifically Flynn's and Hoyle's.

Although Deakin was successfully prosecuted and jailed, and it was never proved that the million pounds actually existed, a very dark cloud of suspicion hung over Flynn and Hoyle. Both men were withdrawn from front-line policing and given tedious desk jobs at opposite ends of the county. Henry Christie was pulled in to investigate Flynn and although he could not prove anything against him,

Flynn's life as a cop became untenable. So much shit, and much of it stuck. That, together with a private life that was unravelling faster than a reel of cotton, drove Flynn to quit the job and scuttle to Gran Canaria to try and rebuild his life.

Only when two of Deakin's heavies came along and asked him in fairly unpleasant terms where the million pounds was did Flynn put the sums together and realize that Jack Hoyle had stolen the dirty money right under everyone's noses. Then things got very nasty indeed. Not just for Flynn, but for Deakin, too.

'Felix Deakin,' Flynn breathed out loud. 'Jonny Cain . . . now that's some connection.' ·

But Deakin was now dead, killed by a hit man's perfectly aimed bullet; killed because he was supposed to have volunteered to give evidence against Cain, who had been up on a murder charge. Not being a cop any more meant Flynn didn't know the complete background to all that, but what he did know was that Cain was acquitted of the original murder charge and as far as he knew, it was never proved that he'd hired someone to whack Deakin. And Cain had resumed his old ways.

And now Flynn had seen two of Cain's lieutenants in Kendleton, which meant Cain wouldn't be far behind. Chuck Jack Vincent into this little casserole. And a dead cop. 'What the hell's going on in this village?' he asked himself.

And Henry Christie too . . . Flynn's slightly disconnected thoughts focused on Henry again. Not his favourite character, but not many did like Henry. He had a tendency to rub even the most mild-mannered folk up the wrong way. Flynn closed his eyes. But instantly he was bathed in bright white light, as though a flying saucer had landed behind him. Startled, he jumped around in his seat as four beams of light burned into his retinas like four mini suns.

The tractor was massive. What's happened to the tractors of my youth, Henry had thought when he climbed on to the running board of the huge machine. The ones that pottered amiably around country lanes with wobbly wheels and a stereotypical farmer hunched over the iron-rimmed steering wheel, often with a collie dog trotting at the back wheel, tongue lolling.

Now they were monsters. Complicated, powerful vehicles designed to carry out all manner of tasks.

'Welcome aboard,' Don Singleton, farmer and butcher, announced proudly, taking his seat in the centre of what Henry could only describe as a cockpit. He was amazed by its size and the relative comfort it offered, from the big leather driver's chair to the two jump seats either side of it, set back slightly, for passengers. Henry sat in one of these seats and Dr Lott in the other, rubbing his hands together keenly.

'This is a John Deere 5M,' Singleton continued. 'Lovely, lovely beast.'

He turned a key, pressed a button and the engine came to life – diesel, but as smooth as a car engine. All the lights came on, even the four positioned across the roof of the cab. He released the clutch and the beast on wheels moved. Henry was very much aware that the cab now reeked of exhaled alcohol. The only good thing was that there was no chance of a cop appearing, breath kit in hand.

From Henry's description, Singleton knew exactly where he was going and the heavy tractor mashed its way easily through the deep snow, past the police house, then past the entrance to Mallowdale House. Following Henry's last directions, Singleton came off the road and swung the tractor on to the forest track, stopping just behind the Shogun, out of which Flynn emerged blinking and shading his eyes, probably thinking that a plane had crash-landed behind him.

Henry swung down from the cab.

'Got some help,' he shouted to Flynn over the din of the powerful engine. Flynn opened his mouth to speak, but Henry cut him short. 'Don't ask. This is the local GP,' Henry introduced Dr Lott, who had clambered down, 'and the gent at the wheel is a farmer and butcher. The way I see it,' Henry went on, 'is that we'll have to do the best we can under the circumstances. Obviously we can't leave her here,' he said, eyeing Flynn, 'yet this is the scene of a serious crime that needs protecting.'

'What are you going to do?'

Henry pulled out the digital camera that Alison had let him borrow. 'I'll try and record it as best I can and I'll get the doctor here to pronounce life extinct and offer any opinions he may have.'

'I can tell you she's dead,' Flynn grunted. 'Don't need a quack.'

'Like I said, we'll make the best of a tough job. We need a doctor's certificate.' Henry tapped Dr Lott on the shoulder and led him past the Shogun.

'I'm not that good with death,' the doctor admitted. 'Old fogies are the most I usually deal with.'

'I understand,' Henry said. He had also snaffled a soft-bristled sweeping brush from the landlady's utility room and he used it carefully to brush the newly dropped snow off Cathy's body. Flynn and the doctor both held torches for Henry as he carried out this task.

'Oh my lord,' the doctor sobbed. Henry detected that he had suddenly become sober.

'You all right?'

'I'll be fine,' he assured Henry. 'It's just, I knew her. Not well, but I knew her,' He lowered himself down and shone his torch on to Cathy's disfigured face. 'Oh my gosh, oh my gosh,' he repeated. Henry knew that normal, run-of-the-mill doctors had very little contact with violent death and it could affect them as badly as any member of the public. Even more so when they'd had a drink or two.

'Oh hell!' Henry heard from behind as Singleton got his first view of the body. He guessed there was a difference in seeing butchered animals as opposed to human beings.

Dr Lott did a swift visual examination of the body, not touching it.

'Just confirm the time and date you pronounced life extinct,' Henry told him, 'though any observations you might have could be useful.'

'Yeah, um,' the doctor nodded, clearly shaken. 'I can confirm death at . . .' He consulted his watch, read out the time and added the date. 'Massive head trauma,' he added, 'consistent with a shotgun wound, I'd say.'

'Thanks for that,' Henry said. 'If you can back off, I'll do some photography.'

He moved everyone out of the way and started to take numerous shots of the body, the surrounding scene and the approach. The camera was twelve megapixels, of good quality, and the flash bright, but he was unimpressed by his results as he checked the screen. Not that they weren't adequate, but he was no crime scene photographer.

And the snow still fell, the wind continued to blow.

'What's the plan for moving her and where is she going to be kept? Is there an undertaker's in the village? Are they on the way?' Flynn fired the questions like a Gatling gun.

'In answer to the last part, there is no undertaker, but I've sorted out the next best thing and my plan for moving her is *that*.' He pointed at the huge bucket affixed to the hydraulic lifting gear on the front of the John Deere.

Flynn's eyes followed Henry's finger. 'You must be joking.'

Next to Cathy's body, Henry laid out one of the tarpaulin sheets that had been folded up in the tractor bucket. The four men lifted her carefully, Henry gently taking her head and neck, and placed her on the sheet. She was light and easy to move.

'She's as stiff as a board,' Singleton commented. 'Rigor mortis?'

'Frozen solid,' Lott answered.

Henry took more photographs of her, then the sheet was folded over her. Between them they carried her down to the tractor and put her in the bucket. It was just a little too short for her and her legs stuck out.

All four men took a moment to consider their handiwork.

'Talk about respect for the dead,' Flynn commented.

Henry made a '*Harrumph!*' noise, then walked back up to the scene. With Singleton's assistance he unravelled a second sheet of tarpaulin which was about twenty feet square. They laid it over the spot where the body had been, and secured it using stones and chunks of rock.

Henry weighed up the job and shook his head in frustration. It was a far cry from what he would have preferred to do: erecting a crime scene tent, special lighting, the scientific teams, police search personnel, securing the scene . . . bringing in the circus, as Flynn had so disparagingly referred to the constituent parts of a murder squad. The professional approach, not this half-baked cockamamie crap. He prayed silently that what he'd done would not turn into an alligator ripping his arse to shreds sometime in the future. And the mantra, also sneered at by Flynn, 'You don't get a second chance at a crime scene,' kept looping through his mind – because it was a good mantra.

'It's the best you're going to do,' Flynn said, picking up on his thoughts.

'It's rubbish,' Henry said, 'and goes completely against my professional instincts.'

'You and your professionalism, eh?'

'Yeah, bummer. Fancy wanting to get the job done right.' The atmosphere between the two grew colder by a few degrees. 'But you wouldn't know about that, would you, Steve?'

A strong gust of snow-laden wind suddenly pushed both men off balance. They staggered against each other, almost into an embrace, in order to stay upright. They broke off the clinch with much facial distaste and bodily quivers of disgust.

'Are we going, or what?' Don Singleton shouted as he and Dr Lott climbed into the tractor cab.

'OK if I use the Shogun?'

'Yeah, sure, but don't forget it could be part of the crime scene. Having said that, I suppose we can always eliminate your prints.'

'Except that, as you know, my prints aren't in the system, because, guess what? I don't have any convictions. You'd have to take them specially.'

'Yeah – bullet well dodged.' Henry could have got in the Shogun with Flynn, but could not bring himself to do so. He hauled himself back into the tractor cab. Singleton reversed out of the forest, then headed back to the village. Flynn followed in the Shogun.

As Henry had noticed earlier when he'd driven into the village using Flynn's car, there was only a handful of shops, one being a butcher's. This was the one that had given him the idea. The fact that it belonged to Singleton was a bonus and made the facilitation of the matter that much easier.

Singleton slowed the John Deere down outside his shop, then expertly turned right into a narrow ginnel running down the gable-end of the shop, just wide enough for the tractor. From the way he handled the machine, even though he was well under alcoholic influence, Henry assumed he must have driven down the alley many times. Either that or the alcohol just made him blasé.

Behind the shop he wheeled into a small customer car park and stopped.

'Back entrance,' he said. 'Those double doors open into the cold storage room.'

Henry jumped down from the cab. Singleton and Lott followed. The butcher/farmer let himself in through the back door and a few moments later the double steel doors opened on what was simply a huge walk-in freezer, big enough to live in. Singleton pushed the doors wide, the strip lighting flickering on behind him. Slabs of meat swung from rows of ceiling hooks, lamb, beef, pork, venison and a long line of big fat turkeys. An icy mist seemed to surround everything spookily.

'Wow,' Henry said.

'Health and safety nightmare, this,' Singleton said. 'A dead human.'

'Needs must.'

Flynn pulled into the car park in the Shogun and trotted over to them. 'The new public mortuary, eh?'

Henry gave him a sour look. 'Help us,' he said.

The four men went to the tractor bucket and lifted Cathy's tarpaulin-swathed body out of it, carried it into the freezer and at Singleton's direction, laid her on a steel slab in one corner that had previously been cleaned and disinfected ready for the following day's business. They took a step back as Henry unfolded the sheet and revealed her.

He blew out his cheeks. Under the bright lights of the room, it was possible to see her injuries in much more detail. The head wound was horrific, much of her face having been blasted away at close range.

'She would have been face to face with her killer,' Henry said.

'I agree,' Lott said.

'Talking to him or her?' Henry asked himself, glancing down at the rest of her, noting she was dressed in jeans, a warm zip-up anorak over a tracksuit top, walking boots on her feet.

'She looked prepared for the weather,' Flynn observed. Henry glanced at him, seeing his face strained.

'You OK?'

Flynn nodded.

'What's your plan, Superintendent?' the doctor asked, no longer slurring his words in his new-found sobriety.

'I need to take some more photographs,' he said, his mind working things out. 'Then I'd like this place to be secured?' It was a question aimed at Singleton, who nodded, said it wouldn't be a problem. 'Then I need to report all this in, start a murder book and see if we can find Tom James.' He turned to Flynn. 'From what you said, he told you she stormed out after a domestic, so he could possibly have been the last person to see her alive . . .'

'Or the first person to see her dead,' Flynn said. 'You know the stats.'

'Yeah, most people are murdered by their nearest and dearest, or other close family members . . . but there is that message about the poacher.' Henry turned to the local men. 'Is there much to poach around here at this time of year?'

'The deer come down from the hills in bad weather,' Singleton said. 'So yes, plenty.'

'OK. I'll get some photos, then we can lock up. Can I ask you gents to keep shtum about this for the time being? I know it's a big ask, but the fewer people who know, the better at the moment.' They both nodded and assured him of their silence. 'And then, I'm afraid I need to get showered and changed before I start looking into this. Also need some food down me, which hopefully will come via the landlady at the Owl.'

'Alison?' Flynn said.

'Never got as far as her name.'

Despite knowing that Karl Donaldson had recently stretched out in the same bath, Henry only took his time entering the hot soapy water so that he could enjoy every inch of his body's response to the bliss. He eased himself carefully into the deep water, his bottom burning at first dip, slowly submerging the whole of his six-two frame and allowing the heat to permeate his freezing bones. He exhaled slowly and the tip of his nose started to burn strangely.

He was in the bathroom situated in the private living accommodation at the rear of the Tawny Owl and the room looked as though it had been recently refurbished, with a large question-mark shaped bath/shower, matching loo, bidet and wash basin. The walls were tiled in white from top to bottom. It was quite a feminine room, Henry observed in passing, no evidence of a man.

The landlady, Alison Marsh – Henry had thought it appropriate to ask her name as he was going to be using her facilities – had been kind enough to show him straight through to the bathroom, in which she'd unpacked his rucksack and laid out a change of clothes from therein. And run the bath. Fact was, she couldn't do enough for him and Donaldson since the unauthorized re-letting of their rooms. She was trying her best to make amends.

Henry pinched his nose and sank under the water like a submarine, then surfaced like a whale, his head covered in nice-smelling bubbles.

He uttered a short laugh at the memory of the phone call he'd made to Kate before heading up to the crime scene on the tractor.

Neither she nor Karen, Donaldson's expectant wife, had any inkling whatsoever of the peril in which their two men had found themselves. Since depositing them in the Trough of Bowland, they had dropped Henry's car in Kirkby Lonsdale, then they'd driven like the clappers in the Jeep to the Trafford Centre in Manchester to have an indulgent shopping trip and they simply had no idea about the weather. Which was a good thing, Henry thought. There had been no worrying on their part and Kate had taken the news of Karl's twisted ankle and food poisoning as though it was nothing. Neither did the fact that the men were now snowed in seem to bother her too much. She and Karen had booked into a hotel close to the Trafford Centre and were going for a meal, then catching a film at the multiplex cinema. There was no concern, either, when Henry told her about finding a dead body.

'Henry,' she said knowingly, 'I wouldn't have expected anything less.'

He shook his head, grinned, scooped the bubbles off his head, then shot bolt upright when someone knocked on the door. 'Hello.'

'It's me,' the landlady called. 'Sorry to bother you, but I've brought that bath towel I promised – and I've got those photos printed off. Can I just stick my hand through and drop them in?'

'Hold on.' Henry gathered suds and built a pile of them to cover his nether regions. 'OK,' he said.

The door opened. Alison leaned in and dropped a towel, then a few sheets of A4 paper.

Henry, having to peer slightly over his left shoulder, caught her eye. She smiled shyly.

'I hope the photos weren't too upsetting for you. You really didn't have to print them off. I would've done it.' Henry had of course checked that Alison wasn't Cathy's closest friend and had warned her severely of the content.

'Like I said, I've seen worse.'

Henry didn't go there. 'Well, thanks.'

She paused. Henry grinned self-consciously.

'The food's almost ready. I got the chef to prepare a roast beef dinner. I hope that's OK. Whenever you're ready, Superintendent.'

Henry chortled. He hated officers junior to himself addressing him by his rank, let alone a strange woman whilst he was naked in her bath. 'That was a bit formal, all things considered. Henry will do nicely.'

'Henry, then.'

She withdrew, closing the door softly. Henry leaned out of the bath, stretching to reach the towel, dragging it towards him with the photographs on top that Alison had kindly downloaded from her digital camera on to her PC and printed off. There were four photos on each sheet. He dried his hands, picked up the sheets, and settled back to examine what had been produced.

They weren't brilliant, but they did the job well enough. He hoped there would be a chance of enhancing them later, just to sharpen them up. The ones of Cathy's body in situ showed the scene well enough, but the ones he'd taken in the walk-in freezer were very clear, if not terribly well composed. He shuffled through them several times.

As well as his favourite mantra about only getting one chance at a crime scene, another one from the Murder Investigation Manual also went through his head: find out how they lived, discover why they died. For most murders he investigated, this held true. Often the circumstances of a murder reflected the way the victim had lived in the first place. So, he asked himself, how did this apply to Cathy James?

Was she merely doing her job, investigating the report of a poacher, and was she killed just because of that? Or was there something more to her death? Modern, organized poachers were violent men, Henry knew, but the killing of a cop was way extreme. Not that he would discount this theory, but he was already thinking that Cathy James's death was more than a bad luck encounter.

He placed the photos back down on the bathroom floor, sank deep under the suds again, revelling in the sensation, wishing he'd stayed at home instead of turning out for a stupid walk. Donaldson would still have got food poisoning, but he, Henry, could be sipping Jack Daniel's and watching a film without a care in the world.

He dressed in the change of clothing from the rucksack – light trousers, a polo shirt, trainers. The idea had been that they would have time to dry their outdoor clothing and change back into it the day after for the second half of the walk to Kirkby Lonsdale. Rubbing his close-cropped hair dry as he entered the landlady's dining room, he found Donaldson sitting at the table next to Steve Flynn. Roger the dog was laid out asleep on the floor. Henry winced at the sight of Flynn.

'You smell wonderful tonight,' Flynn said. 'All feminine.'

Henry ignored him. 'How are you feeling?' he asked Donaldson, who had also changed after his bath and looked much better. His right foot was strapped up and propped on a dining chair.

'Bit better. Guts still churning,' he said, giving Henry a sit-rep. 'But I'm hellish hungry and need some nourishment. The foot is very sore and swollen, but I don't think it's broken. Alison got the doctor to check it.'

'Could he focus on it?' Henry asked, settling at the table. 'I see you two have met.'

'Yep. You're old friends,' Donaldson said with irony.

'Old somethings,' Henry said.

Flynn eyed him malignly. 'Whatever, he'll always believe I took that million, won't you, Henry?'

'Until you can show different, I'll find it hard to move on.'

'You know it was my partner, Jack Hoyle.'

'So you say.'

'And I found him living the high life in the States.' He exchanged a look with Donaldson. 'Skippering a fishing boat out of Key West,' he explained.

'But yet, somehow he wasn't to be found when the cops arrived to question him, detain him, whatever,' Henry pointed out. 'A real will o' the wisp.'

'Not my fault if the forces of law and order move with the speed of a tortoise.'

'Whoa, guys! Knock it on the head, as they say,' Donaldson interjected. 'Leave it for another time.'

Henry shook his head despairingly.

A door opened and Alison came through balancing three plates on her arms, each with a succulent serving of beef steaming thereon. She placed one in front of each man, instantly picking up the tension. 'I'll be back shortly with the veg,' she said and withdrew, but not before she caught Henry's eye with a questioning frown, an exchange both Donaldson and Flynn noticed. They waited until she'd gone before speaking.

'Nice woman,' Flynn said.

'Pity about the rooms,' Henry said. 'Don't really fancy bedding down here for the night.'

'Judging from that look, it's only something me and Steve here will have to worry about.' Donaldson arched his eyebrows.

Henry shot him a withering look. 'I won't be taking a leaf out of *your* book,' he said, seeing Donaldson redden at the under-the-belt jibe at his recent indiscretion. Henry instantly regretted the dig, but at least it ended that line of conversation.

Alison reappeared with a couple of stainless steel serving dishes, crammed with steaming vegetables, and a gravy boat. 'Help yourself, guys.'

They fell like ravenous wolves on the food.

Henry felt its immediate effect, warming him from the inside and meeting up with the outside warmth from the bath. Energy returned to him and though he was still shattered from the day's exertions he felt more capable of dealing with the night ahead, which he knew might be very fraught and long.

They ate heartily and in silence, the main course being supplemented by a dessert of sticky toffee pudding and custard that had Henry purring with delight.

Once the food was over, Alison brought in coffee and Henry got down to business.

'OK, Steve, let's hear your story – all of it.'

Flynn squinted thoughtfully, arranging his brain, and began to relate everything from start to finish. From receiving Cathy's frantic phone calls, the unpleasant encounter with Tom James, finding Henry and Donaldson and then Cathy's body. At least that was his plan, but just as he opened his mouth to speak, Alison burst in.

'I need some help,' she said, clearly distressed. 'There's trouble in the bar.'

FOURTEEN

'Him there,' Alison whispered. She had led Henry and Flynn through to the bar. She pointed out a big, unruly-looking man sitting in the far corner of the room at a brass-topped table, diagonally opposite where Henry was now standing by the side of the bar.

Henry looked at the guy, dressed in a heavy, mud-stained donkey jacket, jeans, steel-toecapped work boots with the caps exposed. He was a big, broad man, looked like he could be a handful, with thick, calloused hands and a brooding, menacing expression enhanced by heavy eyebrows. Henry put him mid-forties and in manual labour.

He had one big hand wrapped around a half-drunk pint of beer, next to which were a couple of empty whisky tumblers. He was hunched over the table, staring, deeply thoughtful – troubled, Henry surmised – into what remained of the beer.

'What's he done?' Henry asked.

'Nothing so far, but he's obviously been drinking before he came in, and he was really nasty to Ginny, who was too scared to refuse him a drink.'

'Then what?'

'He went and sat at that table.'

Henry considered this, tried to assimilate what she'd just told him. A pissed-up guy comes into the pub, orders more drinks, is offhand with the staff, then goes and sits down with his drinks and, basically, does nothing.

'I think I'm missing something here,' Henry said. 'I take it you want him ejecting, is that it?'

'No . . . no . . . yes . . . but . . .'

'But what?'

'He's got a gun.'

One of the things Henry had loved most about being a uniformed cop – back in the day – was dealing with pub brawls and incidents in licensed premises. Bread and butter stuff for uniforms, and Henry had been witness to, or involved in, many disturbances that wouldn't have been out of place in Dodge City. He had also been called out to a few reports of people in pubs carrying weapons, firearms or knives. The customer who had tried to conceal something that someone else had spotted, such as this man.

These incidents were fraught with much more danger and unpredictability than good old-fashioned fisticuffs, with many awkward questions zooming through a cop's head as the suspect was approached. Not least of which was, 'Am I going to be the one the weapon gets used on?'

Henry said, 'You sure?'

'Yes, well, Ginny said she saw what looked like a double pipe thing inside his jacket.'

'A sawn-off shotgun?' Flynn said. He, too, had attended numerous pub fights when he'd been a uniformed constable on the beat, and had revelled in the excitement as well as the opportunity to land punches of his own in the melee.

'We think so,' Alison said.

Ginny was still at the bar, serving a new customer. The place was getting a little busier, a few more locals braving the weather to get stiff drinks inside them in the warm atmosphere. There was a pleasant buzz about the place, people coming together to face the adverse weather and all that. There was, however, a space around the sullen man, rather like a no-fly zone.

'Is he local?' Henry asked.

'Yeah, Larry Callard. Local tough guy, or so he reckons. He's one of Jack Vincent's drivers. Was in here yesterday, pissed up.'

The mention of Vincent gave Henry a jolt and he flicked a glance at Flynn, who had listened to all this eagerly. Henry sensed he wanted to get involved. 'Not your call, Steve, no need to pitch in.'

'Not much chance of that,' Flynn responded. 'I'm here, mate.'

'What do you think, then?'

Flynn pouted. 'Play it cool, get a drink at the bar, gravitate to him, sit down, strike up a pleasant conversation. See where it leads.'

'I thought you'd be for the more direct approach,' Henry said cynically, but was secretly pleased that Flynn had volunteered to help.

'Not when there's a chance of getting my guts blasted.'

'Ahh,' Alison said knowingly. 'You used to be a cop, too? That's how you know each other. I wondered.'

'Now you know,' Flynn said.

'Amazing.' She shook her head.

'OK, then, that's what we'll do,' Henry said. 'I don't think the guy's clocked us, so we'll go to the front of the bar, you give us a coke each and we'll take it from there, Alison.'

She went behind the bar whilst Henry and Flynn leaned on it, pouring them two colas from the soft drinks dispenser. They turned, elbows on the bar, and watched Callard.

'Be careful,' Alison said. Both men nodded.

'If he's right handed and he's got a big pocket inside his jacket to hide the thing, then it'll be on his left side. Not rocket science,' Henry said. Flynn nodded. 'So keep an eye on the right hand and let's see how close we can get to him.'

They pushed themselves off the bar and weaved, pretending to chat, through the few customers towards Callard, who didn't look up once. The brass-topped table next to him, and the two chairs with it, were unoccupied.

'Mind if we sit here, pal?' Henry asked.

Callard's watery eyes angled up slightly, his face a deep-lined, vicious scowl. He said nothing, turned his eyes back to his drinks, his shoulders turned away from the two men. Henry saw a deep, recent cut on his head, still weeping blood and a bit of slime. Looked like he'd been hit hard or caught his head on a lorry door or something.

'Obviously not,' Henry muttered. The two of them manoeuvred around and seated themselves on the low stools. Henry was about four feet away from Callard, who was on his right-hand side. Flynn slid his chair around so he was sitting opposite Henry across the table. When they were settled, Henry said, 'A hell of a night,' directing his voice at Callard.

The man's head stayed low, he did not acknowledge Henry.

'I said—'

'I heard you,' Callard growled, jerking his head round and staring venomously at Henry. 'Just piss off, OK?'

Henry nodded slightly and tried to give the impression he was offended by the reaction. 'OK,' he said, between unmoving lips. He glanced at Flynn.

'So much for a nice conversation,' the ex-cop commented. 'I thought this was a welcoming village . . . no strangers here, just friends we haven't met.'

'Obviously doesn't apply to all members of the indigenous population.' Henry scanned the customers at the bar. Don Singleton and Dr Lott were still just about propping up the bar. Both gave him a knowing nod from their unsteady perches. The young woman who'd been in the bar when Henry first arrived was still in the same spot. Henry caught her eyeing him and Flynn and his brow creased. She was definitely out of place. Maybe she'd been stood up. But it was only a transitory thought because Henry's problem was how to deal safely with a suspected armed man without getting anyone else – or worse, himself – injured. He sighed down his nose and spoke close to Flynn's ear. 'You get on his other side and grab his arm if necessary and I'll speak into his . . .' Henry was going to say 'shell-like', but the truth was that Callard's ears were an amalgamation of cauliflower florets and walnuts. 'Lug hole . . . see if we can charm him.'

Flynn nodded, took a few steps and quickly seated himself on a stool on the opposite side of Callard as Henry shuffled his own stool up to Callard's left-hand side. He held out the palm of his left hand in the gap between Callard's face and his drinks on the table. In the hand was Henry's warrant card and county badge.

'Detective Superintendent Christie,' he said into Callard's ugly ear. Callard's face jolted around, his whole being tensed up instantly. 'And that's my colleague.' Callard took a quick look at Flynn, then back at Henry, remaining hunched over his drinks. 'Now then, Larry – it is Larry, isn't it? I don't want any aggro here, understand?' Callard's eyes widened at Henry's use of his name. Henry decided to keep it more formal than chatty, so there would be no misunderstandings. 'I have reason to believe you are carrying a shotgun under your coat, Larry, and what I want you to do is simple. Put your arms around your back and link hands, then let me and my colleague escort you out, each of us holding one of your arms, yeah? Then I'll search you outside.' Henry's voice was soft, firm, yet audible.

Callard's tongue stuck out between his lips. 'Dunno what you're talking about.' He looked into Henry's eyes with defiance. But from the expression in the eyes, Henry saw that the allegation was true. Callard did have a weapon on him, Henry would have placed a month's wages on it.

'If you've got it for a legal reason, then it's not a problem – but we both know that guns and booze don't mix, so let's do this nice and slowly and compliantly.' Henry arched his eyebrows. 'Don't even think about kicking off.'

Callard's thick neck rose and fell as he swallowed, his eyes taking in Henry, then cautiously moving to Flynn. All three of them were big men. Flynn six-four, lean, muscular, with broad shoulders and strong legs from years of hauling in big fish for wimpy clients. Callard was smaller, stockier, but had the power that came from driving big wagons and helping to move heavy loads. Henry at six-two was the eldest of the three, but although he did not have the developed muscle of the other two, he was as fit as could be for a man in his early fifties. If they came to blows, it would be an interesting contest, Henry visualizing that tackling Callard would be like fighting an ogre.

Callard wiped his mouth with the back of his hand. He sat slowly upright, still gripping his pint glass, weighing up the situation.

Henry's heart rammed against his ribcage as adrenalin spurted into his system. He could taste it.

Gut feeling told him that this encounter was not going to turn out well. Sometimes you could just tell. There was something desperate about Callard, like a wild animal trapped.

Callard looked across the room.

The door to the steps leading up to the first floor accommodation opened and a man appeared, glancing around the room. Henry recognized him as one of the three who had arrived earlier with Jonny Cain. The henchman looked back up the stairs and made a thumbs-up gesture and a moment later, the man himself appeared, leather jacketed, looking cool. And it was this appearance that ignited Callard. Just for the briefest moment Henry and Flynn had lost their concentrated focus on Callard because of Jonny Cain, and Callard, despite the amount of alcohol in his system, acted with incredible speed.

His right hand, the one in which he was holding his pint, flicked upwards and sideways at Flynn, covering him with almost half a pint of bitter, then in the same movement he opened his fingers and let the glass go. It flew into Flynn's face, bouncing off the side of his head, just above the right eyebrow. Callard had thrown it hard and although it did not shatter as it connected with Flynn's face, the rim of the glass split Flynn's skin like a knife, causing him to flinch backwards.

The glass crashed to pieces on the wooden floor of the bar.

Callard rose with a roar like Samson breaking off his shackles. The hand that had thrown the glass went inside his unfastened donkey jacket, reaching for the weapon he had concealed in the inner pocket. His fingers grabbed the butt and his forefinger slid into the trigger guard.

At the same time, he backhanded Henry with his left hand, a fierce, hard blow which, had it connected cleanly, would have easily pulped Henry's nose. As it was, Henry was already reacting to Callard's sudden surge. He saw the hand coming in a blur, ducked instinctively, but in so doing moved away from Callard and unbalanced himself temporarily.

With Flynn flinching in one direction and Henry the other, this opened up a route for Callard and gave him time and space, the extra microseconds he needed, to draw the weapon from beneath the jacket.

Henry was dimly aware of screams and shouts of warning coming from the other customers, but it was just white noise to him as, horrified, he saw the shotgun emerge. It was only inches from him.

He could see every minute detail of it. The ends of the barrels that had been roughly sawn off, then filed down, the double-cocked hammers, the taped sawn-off butt, Callard's calloused hands and the fat tip of his forefinger on the double triggers.

It was as though Henry had stuck his head in a tumble drier. A roaring, pounding noise in his cranium. Then nothing, just his reactions, him operating.

He swung back round, his right arm moving in an upward arc, knocking the shotgun upwards in the moment before Callard managed to yank back the triggers. He didn't need to force them back as they had obviously been set to operate at the whisper of a touch. The weapon of a desperate criminal.

Callard blasted the ceiling, taking out a mini disco ball that hung as a kind of ornament. It exploded spectacularly like an expensive firework, the sound of the weapon deafening and terrifying.

Henry's arm carried on in its upward trajectory, then he twisted his whole body, contorted as his forearm slid down the short barrel and he was able to grab both barrels with his hand and tear it from Callard's grip. He threw the hot-barrelled gun across the room like it was a cobra.

Flynn had recovered. He pushed his body into Callard and his left hand went around his neck. He started to power the man down to his knees, scattering table, chairs and glasses as both men thumped to the floor. Callard hadn't stopped fighting. He shouted and swore and attempted to free himself from Flynn's ever-tightening grip.

Flynn held on. Callard managed to gut-punch him in the lower belly and the air shot out of Flynn.

Henry moved in to assist, grabbing the back of Callard's donkey jacket, and forced him down until he was on all fours. Then, in a combined effort, he and Flynn completely flattened him. Flynn's right knee dropped on to Callard's spine right between the shoulder blades, pinning him to the bar room floor. Henry positioned himself on Callard's legs, preventing any movement from them, and he dragged the man's thick arms around his back, holding them together . . . at which point he would usually have applied handcuffs.

Callard continued to fight and squirm to try and break free, far from being subdued. Henry and Flynn caught their breath and looked at each other.

'You're the cop,' Flynn said. 'What's the next move?'

'Would this be of any help to you?' Don Singleton was approaching them, reaching into his pocket and producing a tangle of plastic cable ties that he used for fastening around pipes, engine components, hedging, the type that ratcheted up tight.

'Yeah, ta.' Henry took one and looped it around Callard's big wrists, pulling the free end tight as he dare without cutting into the skin, drawing the man's hands together.

Flynn eased some of the pressure on Callard's spine by taking some of the weight off his kneecap. He drew his palm across his face, wiping away the blood from the cut inflicted by the pint glass. It was a good inch long and would need medical attention. Flynn glanced at the blood, a sardonic twist on his lips, then wiped his hands on his jeans.

'You OK?' Henry asked.

'Never better.'

Henry looked around the bar. Every face was aimed in his direction, expecting him to take the lead. One noticeable exception was that of Jonny Cain, who had done a smart U-turn back up the stairs.

'What're we – well, you actually – going to do with him?' Flynn asked, smirking.

Henry barked a short laugh. 'Good question.' Hell of a good question, he thought. What the hell have I done to deserve this to happen to my day? A pleasant stroll across the moors that turned into an epic. A policewoman murdered. Trapped in a small village that should have been a peaceful place. Bumping into Steve Flynn . . . ugh! Now sitting astride the legs of a man who'd gone loopy in a bar – and, surely the glue that connected some of those strands together, Jonny Cain was in town.

'Can't let him go,' Henry said. 'Best option might be to get him out of here and take him up to the police station and tie him to a radiator, or something. You said the garage door was open?'

'Yes, but . . .'

'No buts. He's under arrest for a very serious offence and I know it's not ideal, but what's the choice? Can't just brush him down and let him go, because he might come back, or disappear, or whatever . . . I'll start a handwritten custody record and keep him up there – somehow.'

'Do you want to chuck him in the bucket?' Singleton asked. He'd been listening in.

'No, thanks for the offer, but we'll take him up in the Shogun.'

Flynn nodded, eased a little more pressure off Callard's back. Henry rolled forwards and spoke into Callard's mashed ear. 'Listen, Larry, we can do this easy or hard. Sounds corny, I know, but it's how it is. You're under arrest for attempted murder, plus loads of other things, so you're going nowhere. If you want to make it hard, that's your problem. I'll gladly run your head into a brick wall, understand?'

'Fuck you.'

'I'll take that as a yes. Now, me and my friend here' – Henry cringed slightly at the use of the word 'friend' – 'are going to help you to your feet. If you want to fight, that's up to you.'

Henry and Flynn took an arm each and raised him slowly to his knees. It was no mean feat. The will to fight had evidently left Callard but he wasn't exactly cooperating and they had to work hard, lifting an unresponsive dead weight, sullen drunk, unpleasant and still with the possibility of kicking off again if the chance arose. They heaved him to his feet and began to steer him towards the door.

As they passed the sawn-off shotgun, Henry scooped it up, gave Alison a nod, and also Donaldson, who had made his way through to the bar, annoyed at having missed a fracas. Henry told them, 'We'll take him up to the police house and decide what to do from there.' The trio went out through the exit door next to the revolving one and virtually dragged Callard towards Cathy James's Shogun, which Flynn had parked outside the pub.

Dispiritingly, the snow was still falling just as thickly and a gusting wind whipped it in flurries around them. They forced Callard into the back seat, then caught their collective breath.

'How's this going to pan out?' Flynn asked. He wiped away more blood from the side of his face. It was streaming from the cut.

'How should I know?' Henry answered truthfully. 'You need to get that seen to, though.'

'I'll be fine. I'll try not to bleed on you.'

'No – it needs sorting. There's a doctor in there.'

Flynn shrugged. It was just a cut. He'd had worse injuries from fishing hooks and the fish themselves. But then Alison came out of the pub, hitching an outer coat on, a small zip-up bag in her hand.

'I'll come with you,' she announced. She held up the bag. 'First aid kit, and Dr Lott's given me some butterfly strips, so I'll fix you up,' she said to Flynn. 'The doctor's too drunk to do anything. He'd probably stitch your eyelids up . . . I did used to be a nurse, in case you were wondering.'

'Yeah, thanks,' Flynn said gratefully. 'It really needs sorting.'

Henry shook his head at Flynn's sudden desire to seek medical attention.

'I'll follow in my car,' she said and pointed to a Hyundai four-wheel drive. 'I'll bring that dog back up, too . . .'

'What the fuckin' hell you bastards doing?' Callard demanded from his face-down position in the back seat.

Henry looked sadly at the Shogun, realizing that if the car did have any connection with Cathy's murder, any evidence inside it was now completely screwed.

The police house was still in darkness, no sign of habitation. Flynn parked the Shogun in the snow-covered drive, wondering where the hell Tom James had disappeared to.

Henry was sitting alongside Callard in the back seat, having righted him for the journey. The shotgun had been placed in the front passenger footwell, out of reach. On the way Henry had made sure Callard understood exactly that he was under arrest and cautioned him, giving him the 'full hit', though the words did not seem to mean much to him at that stage. He hung his head miserably and avoided all communication. Henry had gone on to ask questions in a conversational way, but Callard stonewalled him, refused to speak and stared at his knees, his jaw rotating, his facial features angry and grim.

By the time they drew up to the house, Henry didn't know anything more than what he had personally witnessed and been involved in: Callard pulling a shotgun from underneath his jacket and blasting it in the general direction of Jonny Cain, who had just appeared in the bar. That, again, was no coincidence, not one that Henry would ever believe. That Callard was just a madman with a festering grudge against society in general who'd decided to wreak havoc and death in the community in which he lived, a sort of Hungerford massacre . . . Was it simply fortunate that Henry and Flynn had been on hand to prevent it happening?

Henry doubted it. He was certain that if Ginny had not spotted him concealing a weapon, a bloodbath would have ensued, but only the eight pints in Jonny Cain would have been spilled.

Cain again, Henry thought. The catalyst, something it didn't take a nuclear physicist to work out.

They heaved Callard out of the back seat and propelled him roughly up the drive. Whatever Callard's motive had been, whoever his intended target had been, Henry still didn't feel terribly warm and fuzzy towards him and he got a bit of pleasure from shoving him between the shoulder blades. Inside, he was still worked up about the incident and knew it would be quite hard to keep his hands off the prisoner, remain detached and professional. Hence the flat of the hand between the shoulder blades.

Flynn opened the up-and-over garage door, flicked on the light to illuminate the empty garage. Henry continued to shove the cable-tied Callard ahead of him.

Behind them, Alison had arrived. She followed them into the house, having brought Roger the dog back with her. Flynn led them through the connecting door into the kitchen, then into the hallway, switching on lights as he went. Roger wormed his way through, went into the living room and crashed out.

'You think this'll be all right?' he asked Henry over his shoulder.

'Using the house, you mean?' Flynn nodded. 'Well, it's police owned and I can't believe for one moment Tom would object, even in the present circumstances.'

'Got some news for you,' Flynn said. 'Cathy and Tom bought the house from the county when they got spliced. It's theirs, not the force's.'

'Bugger,' Henry said. 'Didn't think of that. Why didn't you—?'

'Just remembered.'

'Ah well, needs must, eh? Let's suck it and see. The county must provide some of the costs for the office bit.'

As he said this, Flynn opened the office door. Henry pushed Callard through and forced him down on to the plastic chair on the public side of the desk. He sat awkwardly and complained, 'These things are digging into my skin. You have to take them off. I know my rights.'

'You pull out a gun, you ain't got no rights,' Flynn blurted angrily, the ball of his hand pressed on to the cut, trying to stem the bleeding.

Henry gave him a 'shut it' look and perched himself on the corner of the desk. Unfortunately the bastard did have rights and Henry would make sure he got them as best he could under the circumstances. However, taking off the makeshift handcuffs did not enter the equation.

'I'll sort out your rights as and when. At the moment you need to know you're under arrest for many serious offences and you're going nowhere, and you're too drunk to have your rights given to you anyway.'

'I am fuck!'

There was a radiator on the outside wall of the office, with short copper pipes coming out of the wall. Henry smiled. Just as he predicted, that was where the prisoner was going to be fastened. He pulled out the half-dozen or so cable ties that Don Singleton had given him as he'd left the pub with Callard.

'My advice to you is get your head down,' Henry told Callard, who was now attached to the radiator pipe via a series of looped cable ties, one around the pipe, another looped into that one and a final one around Callard's right wrist. It was not ideal, but the ties were strong and could not be unfastened by hand, although if he kicked off again, he was probably capable of ripping the radiator off the wall. However, Callard was now sitting dumbly on the carpet, scowling at Henry, seemingly resigned to his fate.

'Henry – can I have a word?' Flynn said into his ear. He beckoned Henry into the office doorway, out of whispering earshot of Callard who watched them all the time, but then started to work himself into a prone position. Henry had provided him with a pillow and he grumbled as he adjusted himself and stretched out on the floor. 'You need to question him, urgently,' Flynn said.

Henry shook his head. 'Nope. If he was locked up properly, we'd not be able to interview him even then, because he's so pissed. As far as I can see, the moment of violence has passed, no one else is in danger, so I couldn't even justify an urgent interview if he was in a police cell. You know all this.'

'Because I was a cop?'

'Exactly.'

'But I was bent – apparently.'

'Let's not get into that.'

'OK then, what about the shotgun? He's got a shotgun, Cathy was murdered with a shotgun, by the looks. Uh?'

'And we have the shotgun, we have Cathy's body and we have someone to interview – when he sobers up and he's in a real interview room with a real solicitor and all that garbage. For now, nothing.'

'You're just going to keep him here?'

'It's not ideal. I didn't order the fucking weather.'

'You need to speak to Jonny Cain,' Flynn insisted.

Henry gave Flynn a withering look. 'I know – but I've got a prisoner and I can't leave him, unfortunately.'

'I'll look after him.'

Henry considered Flynn, his mind going back to his previous dealings with the man in whom Henry saw much of himself reflected. The desire to lock up high-class criminals, the way Flynn had approached his job when he'd been a cop. The big difference had been Flynn's excessive use of violence and intimidation. Deep down, Henry knew Flynn was honest, but there was too much of a cloud over him, especially when a million pounds in cash of drug dealer's money went missing on a botched-up raid. Henry hadn't personally made Flynn's life in the cops unbearable. The organization, together with Flynn's paranoia, had done that.

'We can get Jonny Cain here, if we—'

'We?' Henry butted in.

'OK, you. Whatever. What's he doing here? Why did this idiot try and shoot him, an idiot who incidentally drives for Jack Vincent? Y'know, what's going on here? Two top crims in one location – why is that?' Flynn said. 'We might be trapped here by the weather, but so are they and it gives us – you – a chance to grab 'em by the balls. I was after Cain for years and I'd still like to get him nailed.' Flynn was almost shaking as he spoke. 'It's not often you know where he is, for cryin' out loud! You know something big's happening here, don't you?'

'I'll think about it.' Henry's lips pursed tightly, bringing the conversation to an end. 'Anyway, how do you know Jack Vincent?' he queried.

'I used to be a drug squad detective,' Flynn blustered. Truth was, he'd only just learned of Vincent's existence following his phone call to Jerry Tope in the intelligence unit, but Henry didn't need to know that. Flynn was happy to have him believe that he still had a finger on the pulse of the drug scene.

'Hm,' Henry said doubtfully. 'I need to make some phone calls, bring the control room up to date and start the paperwork.' The two men's eyes clashed for a moment, then Henry went back into the office, started looking for some forms to fill in.

'And what's more – what happens when he wants a piss?' Flynn asked.

Henry gave him a blank stare and Flynn shook his head with frustration.

Henry found an unused custody record in a drawer, sat down at the desk and started to complete the form. His mind wanted to shut down, really. He'd had food and a bath, but he was exhausted. He knew though that he couldn't allow himself the pleasure of switching off. He also knew that the night was yet young.

Flynn sat on the edge of the bath, presenting his profile for Alison, who cleared away the blood from his cut, then dabbed the wound clean, applied antiseptic cream, which made him recoil slightly, and started to seal the cut with butterfly strips.

As she worked on him, their faces were only inches apart. Flynn could smell her perfume and it reminded him of a tragically lost love from his recent past. Exactly the same heady aroma worn by the woman he had loved, albeit briefly. He could not remember what it was called, though. He went slightly misty-eyed at the memory.

'Are you OK?' Alison asked, drawing back slightly, concern in her eyes.

He half smiled. 'Yeah, fine . . . your perfume . . . I kinda know it.'

'Just Chanel Number 5.'

'Ah, yes.'

'Sweet memories?'

'Bittersweet.'

Alison smiled as she laid a butterfly strip across the cut, pulling the skin together in what seemed to Flynn a very intimate, caring act. 'What happened?' she asked quietly.

'I screwed it up, drove her away,' he said ruefully. 'It was a while ago now.'

'Was marriage in the air?'

'I had been married once, screwed that up, too. Then this woman came along who I'd known for years and suddenly, click! In love.' Alison applied another strip. 'But as I say, I messed it up.' He pouted. 'What about you? You said you were a nurse.'

'In the army. I was a soldier first, then trained as a nurse.'

'Oh – I was a Marine as a kid.'

'I'm impressed.'

'And . . . go on,' he encouraged her.

'I met my husband in the army. It was a short marriage. He was killed in Afghanistan when his unit were trapped in a village and the population came out and beat them to death.' She peeled another strip and placed it over the wound.

'How long ago was that?'

'Six years, give or take.'

'I'm sorry.'

'Shit happens.'

Flynn's brow furrowed. 'Is Ginny your daughter? I noticed a photo . . .'

'She's Robert's daughter from his first marriage, Robert being my husband. We're kind of inseparable and when I left the forces and came up here, she tagged along. She's a good lass. There.' The final strip was applied and smoothed down, fully closing the wound. 'You still need to go to A&E. It's a while since I patched anyone up.'

Flynn touched it gingerly. 'Seems like a good job.'

Their faces were only inches apart.

Henry had completed the custody record. Separately he jotted down on a scrap of paper some notes which would form the basis of his arrest statement. When he'd done that, he phoned through to control room and spoke to the Force Incident Manager, brought him up to date. An incident log had been started from his previous call and Henry was keen to keep things updated, mainly to cover his own back.

During the course of the conversation with the FIM he was told that Rik Dean was trying to get a message through and could Henry call him back as soon as possible.

Henry gave Rik a call to his mobile, but it went straight through to voice mail. Henry left a short message, then sat back as a wave of exhaustion swept through him like the tidal bore on a river. He looked at Callard, attached by the plastic hoops to the central heating system. He had fallen asleep for a while, but had woken himself with a loud snore and was staring uncomprehendingly at Henry.

Don't spew and don't piss your pants, Henry thought, recalling the days when he'd been a custody officer, one of the toughest jobs in the police, and one of the most unpleasant. Henry had cleaned up a lot of shit in his time.

'It's not over,' Callard growled thickly.

'What's not over?'

'Tonight . . . more to come.'

'Meaning?'

But Callard just closed his eyes and was instantly asleep again.

Fending off the urge to kick him repeatedly, Henry stood up slowly, his limbs and muscles screaming with annoyance. All they wanted to do was curl up and go beddy-byes, as did his brain. The phone rang. He grabbed it.

'Superintendent Christie.'

'Henry – what the hell's going on?' Rik Dean demanded to know. 'I've been trying to contact you for hours.'

'I'm trapped in the middle of nowhere with a dead cop, a nutter with a shotgun and a sus ex-cop, so I hope what you have to tell me is important, Rikky boy.'

'Uh – dunno then.'

'Spit.'

'You know I went to speak to Calcutt after the trial?'

Henry screwed up his face, trying to recall. It seemed such a long time ago, but he remembered Calcutt, the professional killer, had asked to speak to Henry after the trial had ended. Henry, eager to get away, had delegated the job to Rik, then promptly forgotten about it. Calcutt, he reflected, suspected of being hired by none other than Jonny Cain to whack a rival. The only thing the trial had proved, and all that was needed, was that Calcutt had killed Deakin. The 'why' had never been established because Calcutt had admitted nothing. Henry tensed. 'Yes.'

'Well, big dos, little dos, I only actually got to see him on remand at Manchester prison today. He spoke – actually spoke! Said he knew he was screwed, was going down for life and wanted to unburden himself.'

'Bollocks,' Henry said in disbelief.

'Exactly,' Rik said. 'And he told me nothing, except for one thing.' Rik paused dramatically. 'He said the world he operates in is very cloistered, y'know, Assassins Anon, and there are only a handful of people who do what he does and they sort of know each other-ish.'

'The point, Rik.'

'Told me that the person who hired him, the identity of whom we'll never know, had hired someone else to do some more dirty work.'

Henry waited for the revelation. It never came. 'And?'

'That's it. Reading between the lines, he's telling us that Jonny Cain has hired a hit man to whack some other guy.'

Henry soaked this up. 'Nothing else? Just teased us like that?'

'Yes. Calcutt said that if he told us anything else, he would end up dead in prison.'

Henry thanked Rik and hung up slowly, churning this new information. He sighed deeply, knowing that, interesting as it was, it probably had no bearing on what had happened or what was happening in the village on this snowy evening. But it was interesting, needed to be borne in mind.

Callard was asleep, groaning, snoring obscenely. Henry went out of the office to find Flynn.

The cough snapped the moment between Flynn and Alison. They jumped back from each other to see Henry standing at the bathroom door, a scornful expression on his face.

'When you've finished,' he said, his voice brittle.

Alison ran her thumb across the butterfly strips on Flynn's wound, then gathered the medical kit together, not looking at Henry.

Flynn grinned triumphantly.

'Callard's asleep,' Henry said. 'I will go and speak to Jonny Cain. Do you think you can look after him?'

'Not my problem,' Flynn teased him.

'I know, but if you don't do it, I'll be stuck here watching him all night and I'll miss the chance to collar one of the country's biggest drug dealers.' Alison spun to look at Henry, shock on her face at this revelation. 'And you were so desperate to nail him way back when, so I don't want to miss the chance, yeah? Even if he only gets roped into this as a witness, at least we'll have some hold over him.'

'I'll do it.'

Alison stood up. 'I'll run you back down to the Owl,' she said to Henry, who hid a smirk when he saw Flynn's crestfallen face.

FIFTEEN

Even for a senior detective, actually coming face to face with a top-notch criminal was a rare treat. Such people were usually only spoken to – and usually by lower-ranking detectives – when all the background work had been done and it was time to move in. Only then did the cop and criminal, hunter and prey, come into contact.

After Felix Deakin had taken the bullet that parted his hair, and Jonny Cain had walked free from a murder trial when all the other potential witnesses gave thought to their own futures – then suddenly developed severe memory loss – it was pretty obvious that Cain had ordered the hit on his rival. Even when Calcutt, the hit man, had been arrested, the link to Cain was never proved despite the lengthy investigation. Cain, of course, was interviewed but Henry did not meet him, did not carry out the interviews. That had been left to Rik Dean and other detectives on the team. It proved to be a useless exercise, but one that had to be carried out. It was simply going through the motions, knowing that unless he held up his hand and said fair cop and confessed, he would be walking.

The cocky man had even presented himself at a police station for interview, with his solicitor, knowing that he would be laughing all the way to liberty. He had been relaxed, smug, confident, constantly saying, 'I just don't know what you're talking about,' and even gave Rik Dean a kiss-wave goodbye when he strolled out of the cop shop.

Nailing Cain would have been great, but Henry was nothing if not pragmatic. As such, he decided to back off in the knowledge that in the future, Cain would do something that would seal his own fate. Plus, Cain was a Serious and Organized Crime Agency target and it was up to them now. Henry was an SIO and had his own workload to deal with.

Two years down the line, Henry guessed, SOCA would probably have amassed enough to pull him in again. Until that time came, as Cain was known to be super cautious in his dealings, activities and communications, it was unlikely that any cop would come into personal contact with him.

Which is why Henry, despite having to leave a prisoner guarded by a volunteer, was actually relishing the prospect of speaking to him. Any chance to get into his face was not to be missed, and Henry had a bloody good excuse to have words.

It was the sort of confrontation Henry lived for. He loved baiting crims, didn't do enough of it these days.

Alison drove him back to the Tawny Owl.

'You mentioned that Callard is one of Jack Vincent's drivers?' Henry said on the way.

'Yes.'

'What do you know about Jack Vincent?'

'Not a lot. Runs a haulage business from the quarries he owns. Lives in Mallowdale House and owns a huge amount of land around it. And doesn't like people trespassing – why?'

'Nothing,' Henry said. For he too knew of Jack Vincent. It was his job to know. Not personally, but knew Vincent was, or had been, a SOCA target too. Henry dredged his mind of what he knew about Vincent, but details were sparse and he had to admit he'd forgotten that Vincent lived out here in the sticks. He would have to find out more . . . *two* OC targets in one village, he mused.

'I think you misinterpreted what you saw,' Alison blurted, subject changed.

'None of my business,' Henry said genuinely. 'You don't have to explain anything to me.' She glanced sideways at him and he caught her look. 'What?' he said, perplexed.

'You're a fool,' she quipped with a laugh. 'I don't like *him* at all.'

Henry gulped, knocked slightly off track. 'What do you mean?'

'Idiot.'

They had reached the car park at the front of the pub and she pulled in alongside Cain's Range Rover, Henry noticing some damage to the offside door mirror. Singleton's tractor was still parked in the road and a few other vehicles had arrived, showing that movement in and around the village itself was possible – just not out of it. He climbed out and met Alison at the front radiator grille of her car. Still in his shirtsleeves, he shivered.

'What you do is your own business.'

She grasped the front of his shirt and pulled him towards her, so they were eyeball to eyeball. Now it was Henry's turn to smell her perfume. Her lower jaw jutted slightly as her eyes played over his face.

'If we get chance,' she breathed, 'you and me . . . can I make it any more clear?'

Henry blinked, got a rush of blood, then she yanked him the extra six inches towards her, pulled him down and forced her full lips on to his.

For a moment he was completely stunned. As he tasted her, felt her warmth against him, he responded before he knew what was happening. Fortunately common sense kicked in. He pushed himself gently away from her.

'You no like?' she asked, a wicked smile on her face.

'Me like a lot . . . but I thought . . .'

'Not my type. Brash, arrogant.'

'Oh.' Henry's lips pursed and the 'oh' became an 'Ooh!'

'However, there are more pressing things to deal with.'

'Yeah, yeah.' Henry's shivering returned.

They walked side by side, silently into the pub. Henry sneaked a covert look at her and tried to get a grip of what had just happened. If nothing else, he thought meanly, it was a poke in the eye with a shitty stick for Flynn, and that gave him an immature glow of warmth.

He stood aside, allowing Alison to enter ahead of him, their eyes meeting fleetingly, then followed her into the welcoming heat. The main bar in which the shotgun fracas had taken place was back to normal, with the exception of the shotgun pellet-peppered ceiling. The remains of the disco ball hung limply from a thread, and all the shattered fragments had been swept up by Ginny. With hindsight, Henry wondered if he should have asked for the area to be cordoned off somehow, but in the excitement of the tussle with Callard, protecting the scene hadn't been his first priority. It was too late now. New customers were even sitting where the fight had taken place.

The bar had filled up with a few more locals. On Henry's entrance, the chatter died down for a few beats, but resumed when Alison let herself through to the living area and Henry went to his two assistants, the butcher/farmer and the GP. The bar was now propping them up.

'Thanks for the handcuffs,' Henry said to Singleton.

'No probs. I always carry cable ties with me. Never know when they'll come in useful in my trade – as has just been proven.'

'Absolutely. Do you have any more?'

Singleton pulled a tangle of them out of his back pocket and gave them to Henry. 'Just in case,' Henry said, slipping them into his pocket.

'What've you done with chummy?' Dr Lott asked.

'He's a bit tied up, shall we say?'

'You know – and it's just me talking aloud,' the doctor said. 'Putting two 'n' two together, but Larry Callard is known to do a bit of poaching, and he had that shotgun . . .' His bottom lip stuck out, he blinked repeatedly and shook his head.

'It's something I'll bear in mind.'

Alison had returned to the bar and taken up her usual position behind it. She pointed discreetly towards the dining room and mouthed, 'In there.'

To the left of the pub entrance, just inside the door, was a small dining room with a low-beamed ceiling. It held half a dozen tables, there was a roaring fire and hunting prints on the wall. Henry had to duck to enter. It was like stepping back in time, into a room that had managed, either by accident or design, to miss any modernization at all.

This was where Jonny Cain and his three cronies, all of whom Henry knew from their files, were sitting around one of the tables that had been pulled in front of the fire, eating a hearty meal, with bottles of red wine and beer on the table. There were no other diners and as Henry entered the room he was reminded of a scene from the Hellfire Club, particularly when he saw Ginny, who was collecting some dishes, lean over the table and one of the men – the pony-tailed Danny Bispham – jab the blade of his hand up her short skirt, much to the raucous amusement of the other men.

Red-faced and embarrassed, she scuttled past Henry, her eyes averted in shame. The men watched her retreat, then their faces turned to him, all with threatening expressions. Who else would want to dine alongside four such uncouth men, he thought.

Bispham stood up and Henry's assumption about why they were dining alone was confirmed. Bispham took two strides – he was a seriously violent-looking man with a rodent-like face – and growled, 'This is a private function, no one's allowed in here, so fuck off out.' He actually laid the palm of his hand on Henry's chest to stop any further progress.

'Unfortunately for you, I'm a police officer and I have the power of entry into licensed premises, in particular where private functions are taking place.' The last bit was slightly over-egging the pudding, but Henry was more than confident of the powers vested in constables to enter pubs, clubs and all other types of drinking establishments. 'But I do know this isn't a private function. Take your hand away, Danny,' he added, pleased when Bispham responded with puzzled shock at the use of his name. People like him did not like to be known. He produced his warrant card and county crest and flashed it close into the guy's face, then held it aloft so the others could also see it clearly. He wanted no misunderstandings. 'Detective Superintendent Henry Christie,' he introduced himself, 'Lancashire Constabulary Force Major Investigation Team. And I want to speak to Jonny Cain.'

'No Jonny Cain here,' Bispham said defiantly.

'In that case, I'll speak to that man there.' Henry pointed to Cain, whose attention had returned to his food, but was also keeping an eye on the interaction as he chewed on a thick steak. Cain sat back, wiped his mouth with a napkin. His jerked his head at Bispham, who retreated a half-step, scowling at Henry.

'I like hurting cops,' he hissed.

'I like arresting shit-bags,' Henry came back, unfazed, but real-izing that in this situation, with no cavalry on the horizon, he would be in a very invidious position if things kicked off.

'Stop the bollocks,' Cain said irritably, 'and check him.'

'Pleasure . . . I want to see if you're carrying.'

Henry, dressed in his light trousers and a short-sleeved shirt, would have been hard pressed to secrete anything on him, but Bispham wanted to pat him down for concealed weapons. Henry said, 'Don't even think of touching me again, Danny.'

'Right now I'm thinking about beating the crap out of you.'

'Just step aside,' Henry said, holding his ground.

'Henry? You got a problem here?' an American voice came from the doorway. Karl Donaldson had put in an appearance, was standing a few paces behind him, with Alison and Ginny a little further behind.

'Jeez,' Bispham laughed contemptuously, 'you brought your tame gorilla with you? What is this shite?' He looked Donaldson up and down, sneering, then made a bad error by stepping up to him and calling him the most obscene word in the English language, a short, guttural insult.

Donaldson moved so quickly that Bispham did not see anything coming, was just suddenly aware of a flash, then massive pain in his face, before he found himself on his backside on the carpet. He sat there for a moment, trying to figure out how he'd got there. Delicately he brought his fingertips up to his face, expecting to feel his nose – but it had been completely flattened by Donaldson's huge iron fist. There was a rush through his brain and he fell backwards, unconscious, blood pouring out of his face.

Henry had not quite been expecting it either, but went with the flow.

Cain's remaining two men, Napier and Riddick, pushed their chairs back, dropped their cutlery.

'Guys, guys,' Henry said placatingly, 'you'd join him even before you got to your feet. Now shall we start again?' he asked Cain.

Cain gave a flat-handed calm-down gesture. 'Get him cleaned up,' he told Napier. The man screwed up his napkin and threw it angrily on to the plate, stood up and crossed to his colleague, who was groaning and trying to sit up.

Henry walked to Cain's table, spun a chair around and straddled it. Cain continued to eat his food. The steak looked excellent.

'I know who you are,' he said to Henry.

'Really.'

'Make it my business to know every cop who gets on my case. Everything. History, family, dislikes . . . weaknesses.'

Henry bridled at the implicit threat. 'In that case you'll probably know my greatest weakness.'

'Which is?'

'And strength – the desire to put villains like you behind bars, people who think they're above the law, who intimidate and kill . . .'

Cain raised a finger. 'Have to stop you there, Superintendent . . . I don't kill people.' He smiled.

'A matter of conjecture.' Henry stopped as Danny Bispham was raised unsteadily to his feet and assisted out of the dining room, past Donaldson who had a cheeky grin on his face.

'And I don't talk to cops.'

'Not even the one who just saved your life?'

A forkful of fried onion paused on the way to Cain's mouth. 'What do you mean by that?'

'The fact that some guy with a shotgun tried to shoot you, and I stopped him. Silly me.'

'I don't think so.' The onions went in.

'He went for you as soon as you appeared.'

'Nah, don't think so.'

Henry wasn't fazed. He hadn't expected Cain to be anything other than obstructive and a liar. People like him did not like cops getting into their lives under any circumstances. But Henry had a message to get across. He leaned over the back of the chair. 'I don't know why you're in this village and I've no doubt that you won't share it with me, but let me tell you something. Whatever it is, it better not spill out and affect anyone else. You've already been shot at and, yes, I saved your life, but don't count on it happening again, because next time I might not be there.'

Cain smiled broadly and said, 'I have no idea what you're talking about.'

Henry and Donaldson were back in the living area.

'Figured you'd need a helping hand. A guardian angel.'

'Or a pet gorilla. That was a hell of a punch.'

'He shouldn't have cussed me like that, not with ladies in earshot. He got what was coming and he knows it.'

'I just hope we haven't poked a stick in a hornet's nest,' Henry said.

'We will've done.' Donaldson eased himself slowly into an armchair.

'How are you feeling?' Henry asked him.

'Bad. Ankle's swollen up to twice its normal size and I know I'll need to rush to the toilet again very soon.'

'Thanks anyway.' Henry regarded his friend who, despite his incapacitating illness and injury had turned out, unbidden, to back him up, just in case things got hairy. Donaldson had fought the stomach cramps, covered up his limp and appeared behind Henry as though nothing was ailing him. Then he'd landed a killer punch that had poleaxed Bispham, a man who, without doubt, was tough and mean.

Now that the moment had passed, Donaldson was debilitated again and a kid with a feather could have knocked him for six.

'And on that note,' the American said, grabbing the chair arms and propelling himself to his feet. Half running, half limping, he hobbled out of the room, his last words being 'Need to go.'

Alison returned from the bar, standing aside to allow him past.

'Now you two are good mates, not like you and Steve.'

'Up to a point.'

'To infinity, I'd guess.'

Henry took a quick but detailed look at her. She was probably fifteen years younger than him, a thought that jolted him somewhat, made him realize how old he was getting. He had passed fifty, was too quickly approaching the middle of that decade, and sixty – *sixty* – was just over the horizon. By the way time was passing so quickly, he'd be there sooner rather than later. Most of his landmark birthdays hadn't bothered him, but the prospect of six-zero scared the crap out of him.

Alison came towards him. 'I'm sorry about before, being a bit forward.'

'Don't be. I'm very flattered that someone as gorgeous as you would even give a grizzled old bugger like me a second glance.' Oh God, he thought, so smooth.

She scrunched her lips thoughtfully together. 'I might be sorry, but that doesn't mean I've changed my mind.'

They smiled at each other, knowing that anything between them had gone as far as it was going. It was an unsaid conclusion.

'There is still an overnight problem to solve,' she said.

'Well, I'll be spending the witching hour looking after Callard,' Henry said. 'He's my responsibility and I don't want Flynn to do it.'

'You'll be up at the police house?'

'That said, I'd be really obliged if you could still look after Karl.'

'I'll put him up in Ginny's room. She can sleep with me tonight – I've got a huge king-size bed.' She looked longingly at Henry. 'I'm sure Ginny will be fine with that. What about Steve, though?'

'What about Steve? He didn't book a room here, did he?'

'He'll need somewhere to get his head down.'

'Perhaps he could use your settee?' He wasn't too concerned about Flynn's sleeping arrangements.

'I'll offer it to him.'

The phone rang and Alison answered, listened for a moment, looked sharply at Henry and then handed it to him.

'Yep?'

'Henry, Flynn. You'd better get back up here right now. Tom James has turned up.'

SIXTEEN

With a touch of longing, Flynn watched Alison and Henry climb into her car and drive back to the Tawny Owl. He closed the door slowly and touched the repaired cut on his head, so tenderly fixed by Alison's gentle fingers.

It had been some time since Flynn had been with a woman. He had lost interest, become bored and wary of the 'man-woman' love thing, preferred to concentrate on his job as skipper of the best sportfishing boat in the Canaries. He had a lot of ground to make up with Adam Castle, the owner, and had paid him back by effort and dedication to the cause, that being bringing in the biggest fish most consistently. The last customer had been somewhat unfortunate. Never assault a customer. Never – even if they deserve it.

Flynn had done some playing about in the foggy aftermath of the relationship with the woman he had so unexpectedly fallen in love with. One night stands, meaningless fornication with a succession of willing ladies, easily seduced by the hot weather, a muscle-bound, suntanned skipper and jugs of Sangria. But Flynn had soon tired of it. It was a lifestyle he'd once enjoyed, but the glint of the future he'd seen with 'that woman', as he now referred to his tragic lover, now made him want much more from a – the hated word – relationship. He'd retired into his shell and concentrated on work instead.

But Alison's touch, her closeness, her breath, had stirred something inside him. And the signal it gave was that he now wanted to move on in his life, and possibly Alison might be just the lady to drag him out of his emotional doldrums.

That's if he read her right. He knew he was a bit of a Neanderthal when it came to sussing out what the female of the species meant or wanted. So perhaps he'd got it wrong. Maybe she was just being nice.

And, he thought realistically, what chance would there be of any relationship with her? It would, by simple fact of geography, be a hit and miss job. She didn't strike him as someone who would want a long-distance relationship, and to be truthful, nor did he.

'Think I'm getting ahead of myself here,' he muttered as he

walked back into the office and checked on Callard. Still affixed to the radiator, asleep and making one hell of a medically dodgy noise. Flynn backed off into the hallway and picked up the sawn-off shotgun that had been left propped up there. He hooked his thumb under the trigger guard and carried it through to the kitchen, laying it gently on a worktop.

As he inspected it his mind shuffled back over the day he'd just had. He blew out his cheeks as his intuition told him that something very horrible was happening in this village. Not a great insight, bearing in mind what had happened so far on his watch, but incredible just the same. He dearly wanted to speak to Tom James again, because he knew, gut feeling, that he had a lot to answer for.

He was aware of the lights, the sound of a revving engine, the slamming of a car door.

Flynn stirred listlessly, shaking his head, not even remembering falling asleep on the settee in the front lounge. It must have come over him without warning. He rubbed his eyes, wondering how long he'd been under. He sat forward, trying to recall what had woken him, then jumped up and almost went headlong over the prone figure of Roger, spreadeagled at his feet, oblivious to any noise, in a deep slumber, not even reacting to Flynn's feet.

Then he heard the front door crash open.

'Cathy, Cathy, where the hell have you been?' Tom James shouted angrily as he came into the hallway.

Flynn's mind clicked into gear. Cathy's Shogun was parked outside. The sound that Flynn had heard must have been Tom returning from wherever he'd been. He twisted into the hall and came face to face with the detective.

Flynn's appearance caught him unawares. 'You! What the hell are you doing here? Where's Cathy?' Then he saw Callard laid out by the radiator in the office. 'What the fuck's been going on here?' he demanded. 'Who's that? What the hell's—?

'Hey, man, calm down,' Flynn said peaceably. 'That bloke's a prisoner.'

Tom glowered. 'Whose prisoner?'

'Hey, long story, pal . . .'

'Don't you freakin' "pal" me . . . where's Cathy? Is she here?' Flynn couldn't find the words for a reply. 'Well, come on, numbnuts, what's going on, where the hell is she?' He barged past Flynn into the kitchen, calling her name and coming to a jarring halt when his eyes clamped on the sawn-off shotgun.

Flynn was behind him, at his shoulder.

'What is that doing here?' Tom asked coldly and turned slowly to Flynn. 'What's going on? Why is this gun in my house? Where is Cathy? What's that bastard doing in my house? And why are you here?'

Roger, having eventually been roused from his deep sleep, snaked around Flynn's legs, came between him and Tom, then rose delightedly on his creaky hind legs, placing his massive front paws on Tom's chest, giving a little 'woof' of greeting.

Tom's right forearm drove the dog roughly sideways, twisting his arthritic hips, so Roger went down awkwardly with a squeal of pain.

'Fuck off, dog.'

'Hey – no need for that,' Flynn said.

Roger cowered, ears back, tail turned inwards between his back legs. If there could have been an expression of disbelief on his face, it would have been there.

Tom jammed a finger into Flynn's chest. 'My house, pal – now where is she?' He had a rage that was becoming uncontrollable and Flynn was wondering why. Why would he be so incensed to find his wife's car back home? Even if they'd parted on bad terms, surely Tom wouldn't be so annoyed to have her return? OK, a drunken prisoner in the house might well infuriate him, especially as the stench emanating from that direction was telling them he had pissed himself. But under the circumstances, with the weather having cut the village off, Tom would surely have understood that if Cathy had been obliged to make an arrest, then she would have been just as obliged to keep the prisoner here.

Obviously Flynn knew what had happened to Cathy. But, he speculated as he listened to the policeman's rant, did Tom also know? And was the sight of her Shogun and the shotgun a warning that her body had also been found? Was he now putting on an act?

'You need to calm down,' Flynn said evenly.

'Why, exactly? Why do I need to calm down? I come home and find my house violated and you here.' He pointed at Flynn, his face ugly with hatred. 'Someone my bitch of a wife called and blabbed to, who then turns up like a puppy dog, because you shagged her, didn't you?'

Flynn coloured uncomfortably. 'That's not why I'm here – and you know it.'

'So why are you here? And where is she? And what's going on with that prisoner? Who arrested him? It can't have been—' He stopped himself mid-sentence. 'Start talking.'

Flynn sighed. 'You need to calm down. Look, come and sit in the lounge and we'll get all this sorted. I need to make a phone call.'

'To Cathy? Where the hell is she?'

'Just sit down, eh?' Flynn was frantically using his hands in calming gestures. 'Let me phone Henry Christie – it's down to him to explain everything.'

Flynn had to be quick to see it because Tom covered it up well – a look of horror at the mention of Henry's name. But see it he did, and it made him think this outburst from Tom was a complete charade. 'Why Henry Christie?' Tom demanded.

'He's down at the pub.'

'Why him?'

'Just let me call him.'

'What the fuck is Henry Christie doing here?'

'He's probably asking himself the same question . . . come on, Tom – try to chill for a few minutes and I'll get him up here to explain things.'

'Why can't you explain things?'

'Because Henry's a cop and I'm an innocent bystander.'

He arrived in Flynn's hired Peugeot, which he noticed now was missing a driver's door mirror. He parked behind Tom's Golf and his heart sank a little at the task that lay ahead. He always thought that delivering a death message chipped away at something inside every cop, even though every cop knew it came with the territory. Henry had delivered many in his time – too many. Some of the toughest ones were linked to murders or suspicious and sudden deaths. By the nature of his role he often had to break the most awful news to families of people who had been brutally killed, their lives brought to unnatural and violent ends. Additionally, unless there was a suspect in mind, Henry also had to realize that the person he was delivering the news to could also have been the offender. It was a fine balancing line between empathy and cold calculation, compassion and evidence gathering, all these things running in parallel.

He thought briefly about what he knew of Tom James, detective and husband of the deceased. He knew Tom distantly in the way that SIOs knew the detectives who worked in the geographical areas for which they were responsible. Henry's area included the north of the county, which therefore included the city of Lancaster, where Tom worked as a DC. Henry had come across him on a couple of straightforward domestic murders that he'd overseen in his SIO role. Tom had been professional and his performance had been excellent. He guessed that one day, Tom might become a DS, maybe a DI in the fullness of time. He seemed steady, diligent and reliable, could talk to people, the latter skill being the most important criteria in a decent detective.

So, nothing much, nothing outstanding. Except for the additional information fed to him by Steve Flynn, a man of dubious character himself. He'd told Henry what Cathy had said in a desperate phone call: the marriage was going south and Tom was corrupt. And it could all be bullshit. Henry didn't know Cathy James well, could not comment on her character, but Flynn thought highly of her, for what that was worth.

Henry decided simply to bear these things in mind and, as ever, wing it. OK, he was dealing with the murder of a cop, but he didn't know her, nor did he know Tom well, so that was good – nothing personal to queer the pitch. No preconceived notions that would sway him. He would simply deal with this as he would any other case. Thing was, of course, as he had already discussed with Flynn, murder victims usually knew their attackers and often the killer turned out to be a close friend or relative.

He hoped that would not be the case here. He opened the car door, stepped out into the deep snow, trudging and leaving footprints all the way up to the front door. 'Open mind,' he told himself firmly.

'Christ boss, what the hell's happening?' Tom James asked desperately, having rushed to the front door to greet Henry, worry and fear pasted over his face.

'Need to sit down and talk,' Henry said.

'What's going on? Tell me, please.'

'Living room,' Henry said firmly.

'OK,' Tom said, tight-lipped. He walked stiffly into the front room.

Flynn was standing in the hallway. He gave Henry a shrug and

Henry returned it with a shake of the head, followed Tom into the lounge and closed the door softly.

Tom sat primly on an armchair, wringing his hands.

'This is going to be bad news, isn't it?' Tom said.

'Tom, I want you to bear with me. I need to ask you some questions, to establish some facts. You know the score.'

'Just tell me what's going on,' he pleaded.

'Tom,' Henry said firmly, trying to judge the best way ahead, part of the balancing act. If Tom knew nothing, if he and Cathy had simply had a barney and she'd stormed out and he didn't know where she'd gone and it was as simple as that, Henry should just tell him that her body had been found and all the rest. However, if Tom was responsible for blowing his wife's brains out, Henry had to get some details first. Henry knew he really had no choice. Whatever he believed, Tom James had to be up there in the top two prime suspects, alongside the mystery poacher, if indeed that person did exist. It was like defusing a bomb. Lots of wires, one of them lethal. 'When did you last see Cathy?'

'Oh God,' he wailed, 'she's dead, isn't she?'

'Why would you say that?'

'You being here. All this.' He waved his arms around wildly. 'Her car, Flynn – I don't fuckin' know!'

'I'm here by accident.'

'Then if there's nothing going on, you don't need to be involved, do you? Can you see where I'm coming from?'

Henry pursed his lips. 'Yeah, except I am here and I am involved, and you're right to be concerned.' Henry stopped a moment. 'What has Steve Flynn told you?'

'Nothing.'

Henry nodded. 'Right – just answer me, when did you last see Cathy?'

'Uh, yesterday, OK. We had a row, she split . . .'

'And? Is there anything else I should know? What time did she go? What did she say when she left?'

'Called me a tosser . . . and she said she was going to check out the report of a poacher, then she was leaving me. That was about half three, I guess.'

'OK . . . Steve went looking for her because he was worried about her. He found her car in some woods near Mallowdale House . . .' Tom leaned forward tensely. Henry made a judgement call and went into bluff mode to gauge the reaction. 'But there was no sign of Cathy, so I am somewhat worried about her. With the weather, the deep snow, it was obviously impossible to do any sort of search. It may be that she did challenge a poacher in the woods who could've been armed . . . maybe.'

Henry watched Tom's eyes and his facial muscles carefully. There was a crease of the forehead, a narrowing of the eyes and a sigh. He looked warily at Henry, as if he was choosing with precision what he was going to say.

At the same time, Henry's anus was twitching nervously. If Tom had no involvement with Cathy's death, Henry knew he could possibly have thrown himself into the mire with the lie about not finding her. But if Tom was involved, then keeping the discovery of the body from him could be worthwhile for the time being. Like poker, but with more at stake.

Henry watched the reaction. Tom had been so utterly and completely wound up that Henry could not quite work out what the sigh meant. Relief, yes, but from what? No body found, meaning Cathy was still out there somewhere, alive, or no body found, thank God, now I've got some manoeuvring space.

Henry hoped to hell he wasn't reading this all wrong. He was playing a game with someone's life here and if he misjudged it . . . he didn't even want to think about the implications.

'So you haven't found her body?'

'No,' Henry said. There, done it. Now be prepared to live with whatever the consequences might be. Was that a smile that twitched on Tom's face? Henry went on, 'Steve Flynn found the car, but not Cathy. Her stuff was still in it, so it looks as though she could possibly have met someone she knew.'

'Someone like Steve Flynn?'

'It's a possibility, but whatever, I'm very concerned about her whereabouts. D'you think she's capable of doing something silly?'

'Nah, not her. So why's that drunk in my house?'

'He pulled a shotgun in the pub. Steve and I wrestled it from him and there was nowhere else to bring him,' Henry answered. 'Where have you been since Flynn came to see you earlier?'

Tom shrugged. 'Out and about.'

'You told him you were going to work.'

'Well, that'd never be possible. Getting over to Lancaster in this, no way.'

'Did you tell them you wouldn't be in?'

'Course I did.'

'So where have you been?'

'As I said, out and about – look, what are we going to do about searching for Cathy?'

'Nothing until tomorrow. The night and weather are against us and we'll need extra resources, too.' Henry paused. 'So you haven't seen her or heard from her or tried to contact her since yesterday. Is that right, Tom?'

'Yes.' Tom's head sagged. 'I hope she's OK.'

'Mm,' Henry said, still trying to read him. 'I'm sure she will be . . . What were you arguing about?' he asked softly.

Tom's eyes rose, met Henry's. 'She was taunting me about having slept with Flynn once, years ago. I knew she'd been on the phone to him, then next thing, here he is in the flesh. Mr Ex-lover.'

'The marriage was in trouble, then?'

'I didn't think so. It came as a shock to me.'

And now I just know you're lying, Henry thought.

Flynn moved into the office when Henry and Tom went into the living room, excluding him. He sat at the desk on the revolving chair and looked at the sleeping prisoner, who had wet himself spectacularly. Flynn screwed up his nose at the reek.

Listlessly, he started to flick through the message pad from which he'd snaffled the message about the poacher.

Frowning, he took out the now very crumpled form from his back pocket and laid it out, flattening it with the palm of his hand. The message had been taken by Cathy at 15.30hrs on the day before. That was about an hour before she had called him whilst he was sitting in the beach bar in Puerto Rico, eating paella. Then he remembered something, the assumption he had made when he had first read the message, and what he had discovered when he'd had the chance to recheck it. The message under the one about the poacher, and most of the others underneath that, had been taken by Cathy. She had signed the pro-forma pads as the person receiving the message. But the handwriting on the poacher's message was not hers. It could only have been Tom's. Flynn had thought it was Cathy's writing, but clearly it wasn't. Tom had written this message, not Cathy.

Not sure whether this meant anything at all, he picked up the cordless phone and was glad to see it was a very up-to-date one that recorded the numbers, time and dates of all incoming and outgoing calls. He began to tab through the menu.

'This is going to be a hell of a night. No way am I going to sleep.'

'I don't think any of us are,' Henry said.

'What are you thinking, Henry? That I've done away with Cathy?'

Henry's only response as a detective was, 'Have you?' He would have been sacked if he'd said anything else.

'Don't be a dick. I loved her.'

'Loved? Or love? Present tense, past tense.'

'Don't pervert my words. You know what I mean.'

'What's going on in the village?' Henry asked, a quick change of subject.

'In what way?'

'What's Jonny Cain doing here?'

'The Jonny Cain?'

'The one and only.'

'Didn't know he was.'

'When he showed his face in the pub, that's when our drunken friend Callard tried to blow his head off.'

'Jeez.'

'What's the connection between Callard and Cain?'

'Have you thought of asking them?'

'I spoke to Cain – not very forthcoming. Callard's too drunk to speak to.'

Tom shrugged.

'I'm told Callard's a driver. What do you know about him?'

'Not much. Just a drunk who's lucky to have a job. Works for the company that own the quarries in the hills.'

'That'd be Jack Vincent's operation?'

'Yeah, yeah, him,' Tom said.

'So what's Jack Vincent up to? I assume you know who he is?'

'I do, but he's not on my radar. I'm just a small-town CID officer, catching burglars and car thieves. Big-time drug dealers aren't my remit. And I don't know what he's up to.'

'Jack Vincent, Jonny Cain in town . . . do you think something might be happening?'

Tom sighed. 'How would I know, Henry? And to be honest I don't give a toss. My wife is missing. That's what I'm bothered about.'

'Coming back to the subject of Cathy . . .'

'You really think I've done something to her, don't you?'

Well, Henry thought, I've got a dead policewoman on a meat slab in a butcher's shop and her husband sitting here in front of me and I'm not impressed by him. Being a detective doesn't make him innocent, but just because he's her hubby doesn't make him guilty either . . . Ahh, love the double negatives . . .

'You know what it's like being a detective, Tom.'

'You don't believe a word anyone is telling you, at least to start with . . . Look, we had a bust-up. Things weren't working out. We wanted different things. Then she brought up fuck-face in there—' He gestured angrily towards the door. 'You know, the guy who was good enough to provide us with a free honeymoon. I'll bet he re-shagged her then. Yeah, it was going tits-up and she stormed out. And if you have nothing more for me,' he checked his watch, 'I'm off to the pub for last orders because I feel pretty shitty. You just continue to use my house for whatever purpose you see fit. You seem to be doing that anyway.'

He made a move to stand up, just as a *rat-tat* came on the lounge door and Flynn poked his head around. 'Quick word, Henry?' Flynn glanced at Tom, who scowled.

'Yeah – look Tom, just hang on here for a few moments, will you?' Henry rose, as did Tom. 'No,' Henry said firmly to him. 'Stay here and I'll be back shortly.'

Tom hesitated and Henry thought he was going to kick off on the subject of being ordered about in his own home. Henry prepared himself, but Tom backed down and sank slowly on to the settee, his face telling the story of his unhappiness with the situation. Henry gave him a curt nod, left the room and followed Flynn into the office.

'I thought you'd want to see this,' Flynn whispered. He had the crumpled, but flattened message on the desk next to the message pad binder. Henry looked, but his mind wasn't completely on what Flynn was showing him. The two men were standing side by side at the desk, two big men, but Flynn had the upper hand in terms of height, breadth, fitness, age and sun tan.

Almost without moving his lips, Henry said, 'He tells me you and Cathy were lovers.' His eyes moved sideways, like an Action

Man figure, checking Flynn's reaction. 'Something you failed to mention . . . Oh, what a tangled web,' he added cynically.

Flynn's nostrils dilated and he coloured, his tan glowing extra red. 'If you call a one night stand twenty-odd years ago at training school being lovers, and nothing since, just a distant friendship.' His face tilted a few degrees, eyes searching the detective's face.

'Seems she didn't think the same.'

Flynn swallowed, clearly shocked. 'BS. He's throwing you a line – and you know it.'

'Bullshit you didn't care to share with me.'

'As I recall, we were rudely interrupted by chummy here.' Flynn pointed to Callard. 'Just as I was about to reveal everything. And it's not as if you needed to know.'

'Oh, I think I did. Puts a whole different complexion on things, don't you think?'

'She called me for help, as a friend – yesterday, when I was in Gran Canaria. I came, found her dead – who the hell do you believe? Me or him?'

Henry could not find it within him to respond instantly – a pause, a beat that told its own story, which made Flynn tut and roll his eyes with frustration. His history with Flynn and all the controversy surrounding his departure from the police had clearly soured him towards the man. He knew it, fought it, but could not hide the surfacing prejudice. 'Put it this way,' he conceded, 'I haven't told him she's dead yet.'

Flynn exhaled with relief. 'You've been playing him.'

'Oh yeah . . . So, what am I supposed to be looking at here?'

Pulling himself together, Flynn explained. 'This is the message about the poacher, dated yesterday, anonymous caller, timed fifteen thirty hours.'

'Why is it so crumpled?'

'You don't need to know.'

'I probably do, but go on.'

'It's in Tom's writing.'

'And your point is?'

'I've checked through the phone's memory and there is no record of anyone having called here at that time. Someone called earlier about straying animals, which is logged, but the only other calls received here are the unanswered ones I made. There's no record of a call where the number is withheld and this phone does record them. No one called here at three thirty, anonymous or otherwise, unless it's been deleted.'

'Could have been a personal caller at the door,' Henry ventured.

'Or made up.'

As they were talking, the phone rang and Henry picked it up. 'Yes, this is he . . . Oh, hello . . . go on . . .' Henry listened carefully, then said thank you and hung up.

'As I was saying . . . I think this is a lie, made up by Tom for some reason. He sent her out to get killed, or something,' Flynn concluded hazily. 'It doesn't add up, anyway.'

Henry nodded, trying to take in what Flynn was trying to say, and the content of the phone call just received.

'That was Alison on the phone,' he said quietly. 'She's been talking to Ginny, her stepdaughter . . . Apparently Ginny saw Cathy drive past the pub yesterday, just after five o'clock. In the Shogun . . . only she wasn't alone, Tom was with her. Thing is, she also saw Tom walk back about an hour later, alone . . . he told me she went out alone to the poacher.'

The two men digested the words, then slowly turned to a noise at the office door.

Tom James stood there, a tired, desperate-looking individual. But in his hands he held the sawn-off shotgun, the one that had been taken from Callard and which Flynn had left unattended in the kitchen. He raised the weapon to gut height and aimed it loosely at a point somewhere between the two men. His finger hovered over the double trigger.

'Guys, you're too smart for your own good and I really don't have time for this.'

SEVENTEEN

He rocked the weapon. 'Move back to the wall. Go on, or I'll blast you both.'

They hesitated, the initial shock on their faces now morphed into disbelief.

Henry, his mouth suddenly dry with fear, said, 'Tom—'

'Don't speak,' Tom barked.

'You don't have to do this,' Henry said.

'I said, shut your face.'

'I don't know what's going on,' Henry said, 'but I'm ordering you to put the weapon down.' By his own admission, Henry's voice was shaky and nervous, but he tried to sound authoritative, hoping for once in his life he could pull rank.

Tom laughed harshly. 'Just get back to the wall,' he said calmly and gestured with the gun, making them realize that if it was discharged in this small area, both would be seriously injured if they were standing close to each other. Effectively they would form one big target.

Henry nodded. 'Do as he says.' He touched Flynn and pushed him gently backwards and slightly away. His thought was that if there was some distance between them there would be more chance of survival and maybe the possibility of overpowering Tom. The latter option, though, was not Henry's favourite. Flynn picked up on Henry's chain of thought, taking a pace backwards and outwards away from Henry.

'Stop,' Tom said. 'Keep together, backwards, side by side, nice 'n' slow, then face the wall. If you go one foot apart from each other, I'll kill you. Simple.'

They backed off carefully.

'You know the gun's not loaded, don't you?' Flynn said.

Tom gave him a pitying look, then said, 'You screwed my wife.'

'She wasn't your wife. Not then, not even close.'

'But she rubbed it in my face. Hey – you stopped moving. Keep going, right back to the wall.'

'What's going on, Tom? Is that what this is all about? Whatever it is, I can help you.'

'Which cop drama did you get that line from?'

'It's true. Whatever's happening, I can help.'

'Henry – I very much doubt it.' Their backs were up to the wall now. Next to the radiator to which Callard was affixed. 'Turn round, noses to the wall.'

Both men rotated slowly, the shotgun trained on them. Tom had moved with them, keeping the same distance away from them, just out of arms' length, enough of a gap for him to react if either should be foolish enough to make a heroic lunge. As they turned inward, their eyes met.

Henry's lips were an inch from the wallpaper and when he next spoke, his voice was muffled. 'Are you going to shoot us in cold blood?'

'The only way.'

'Just like you did Cathy?' Flynn blurted.

Tom was directly behind them now. In a furious response he jammed the double muzzle of the shotgun into the back of Flynn's neck, screwing the roughly sawn ends into his flesh. He pushed hard and banged Flynn's mouth against the wall, knocking the inside of his lips against his teeth. Flynn screwed his eyes tight shut, tasting the blood, and imagining his throat being blown out. Tom leaned into him, mouth close to Flynn's ear, breath hot on it. 'Yeah – just like that.'

'What did she find out about you?' Flynn asked.

'Too much, too much.'

'You'll never pull this off,' Henry said, squinting sideways.

Tom backed away a few inches, the gun coming out of Flynn's neck. 'Oh, I will. Thing is, you guys turned up too soon, before I could get everything tickety-boo, so I need to wing it now. And as you know, Henry, the beauty of being first detective on the scene is that you can do anything you want. Mr Callard here, such a bad man, gets out of his makeshift cuffs, finds the weapon and blasts the brave detectives who arrested him, but then kills himself in drunken self-loathing. Take a bit of doing, but it won't be a problem. As regards Cathy,' he shrugged, 'Mr Callard here is a known poacher, so I'll pin that on him, too. Always planned to anyway. Him being dead will make that easy, too. Just another reason for him to take his own life, which was going down the shitter anyway.'

Henry tried to peer round at him. 'Not a chance in hell, Tom – any detective worth his salt will see through that in a flash. It'll all get too complicated. Your lies will screw you – as they already have done.'

'Nah – cops're thick.'

'We'll see.'

Tom raised the weapon up to the side of Henry's face. Henry ground his teeth together and closed his eyes, but Tom swung the gun away in a short, flat arc and pointed it at Flynn.

'For screwing my wife . . .'

Flynn gasped in terror as Tom's fingertip curled on to the trigger.

But then from his position on the floor, Callard kicked out and smashed the steel toecap on his right foot hard into Tom's shin, causing him to scream out in agony, twist around and discharge a single barrel upwards, tearing a huge hole in the ceiling above the men.

Flynn spun, as did Henry, as a cloud of white plasterboard poured over them.

Tom staggered backwards, but wasn't going to be put off his chosen course of action because of a kick on the leg. He tried to bring the shotgun down, but Flynn launched himself low and hard. Flynn was extremely fit and fast and he moved quicker than Tom could have anticipated, but he still clicked his finger back on the second trigger, firing the second barrel at a slight upward angle.

Henry jolted back with a scream, clutching his upper chest and left shoulder.

Flynn ignored this and powered into Tom, who hacked down at Flynn's unprotected head, catching him a glancing blow off the side of his head and cutting his ear. It knocked Flynn off track, and he smashed into the desk awkwardly.

Tom shrieked something incomprehensible, hurled the gun across the room, ran out of the office, slamming the door behind him, down the hallway to the kitchen.

Flynn came up into a one-kneed starting position and looked worriedly over at Henry.

Pale and wounded, Henry had crashed against the wall and slithered down, sitting there dumbly, his right hand holding his left shoulder. Blood oozed through his fingers.

'Shit,' Flynn uttered and scrambled over on all fours to Henry, whose terrified eyes played over Flynn's face.

'Just get him,' he said to Flynn. 'Don't let him get away, whatever happens.'

'You sure?'

'What're you going to do – operate on me? Go!'

Flynn gave a short nod, glanced at Callard who, still drunk and glassy-eyed, was sitting up, a look of horror on his face. Flynn got up and ran to the door.

The pain in Henry's shoulder was incredible. It was like a dozen blunt needles had been hammered deep into his flesh. He took a long steadying breath and began to unbutton his shirt.

Flynn opened the office door cautiously, stepped into the hallway, paused, listened. He kept to the wall, using the staircase as part cover, and edged towards the kitchen, moved across the last gap and flattened himself against the wall next to the door frame. He reached for the handle, turned it slowly and opened the door a crack, trying to remember the layout of the room.

Pretty standard. A work surface immediately to the left of the door, on which he'd foolishly left the shotgun. Then ninety degrees to the sink and draining board, a gap where the back door was, another ninety degrees to another work surface, with cupboards along the walls, the door to the garage, cooker, and a huge fridge-freezer.

So – open the door and diagonally opposite, basically, was the back door.

Flynn felt something around his legs and his heart leapt. Roger, the German shepherd, had nudged him with his forehead. The old dog looked up kind of sadly.

'I think you're going to be an orphan,' Flynn said and patted him.

But then the dog did what Flynn was hesitating to do – simply barged through the door into the kitchen.

Tom fired from the back door, two bullets smashing through the door panel by Flynn's head. Flynn leapt backwards, slamming the damaged door. Another door closed and he knew Tom had gone outside.

Roger sat at the back door on his haunches, big tail wafting back and forth like a feather duster. Flynn glanced through the door to check that Tom had definitely gone, then ran back into the office to find Henry still propped up by the wall, his shirt unfastened to reveal the nasty-looking wound. He was touching it gingerly with dithering fingers as if it wasn't real.

He looked up at Flynn, ashen, shaking. 'I hope you've caught the bastard.'

'Done a runner out back. Got another gun, a pistol of some sort I think.'

'He seems pretty well armed.'

Callard, propped up on one arm, said, 'He is.'

'Is what?' Henry said.

'Well armed. That shotgun's his. He gave it to me. They made me go and try to kill Cain.'

'Ahh,' Henry gasped as his finger touched the injury.

Flynn squatted down by him. 'Phew – lucky.'

'This is lucky?'

'Two inches to the right and I'd be taking you to the butcher's.'

'Cheers . . . look, I think you need to find him . . . no, no, zap that. You don't have to put yourself in any more danger. Let him go and let's hope he goes to ground and not on a shooting spree. We'll get back-up tomorrow, whatever the weather.'

'I have a horrible feeling he'll be back.'

'Do you think you could get Alison back up here?'

'Yeah, good idea. I think I need her again.' He touched his ear that had been cut by the shotgun and rubbed the back of his neck where the muzzle had been skewered into his skin.

'I meant for me . . . and can you let Karl know what's going on?'

Flynn grinned, looked at Henry's shoulder, feigned an 'Ooh' of pain. 'Now do you believe me?'

'I'd shrug, only it hurts too much.' Henry winced. Sweat drizzled down his forehead; his face went a grey-blue shade.

'Whatever,' Flynn said and headed for the door, where he paused and turned to Callard. 'Thanks mate – you saved us all.'

'Unph,' he grunted. 'He'd've shot me too.'

'Oh, for definite.'

Flynn left the room and went back into the kitchen, slid the bolt across the outer door, dropped the blinds over the windows. Roger was still there, watching him with interest.

'If only you could talk,' he said. The dog responded with a deep bark and a wag of the tail. 'Maybe you can.' Flynn patted his head and made his way back into the hall to the front door. He opened it slowly, looking at the snow-encrusted vista, his eyes drawn to Tom's VW Golf behind Cathy's Shogun on the drive. The inner light was on.

Then he saw the bob of a head just before the light went out.

'He's made it to his car,' he yelled for Henry's benefit, before bolting out. The Golf's engine screamed as Tom reversed down the drive, slewing backwards, glancing off the back of Flynn's hired car that Henry had parked on the road.

Flynn ran through the snow, unsure of what to do. Leap on the bonnet? Or the roof? The Golf slithered to a stop at an acute angle, then Tom slammed it into first, revved the engine and let out the clutch. The front wheels spun, tried to grip, sending a shower of slush up against the mudguards. The car veered forward as Flynn skated down the driveway and came alongside the car.

Tom raised the pistol and fired. The window shattered but the bullet missed, though only because a split second before Tom pulled the trigger, Flynn had completely lost his footing and smashed down on to his backside in the snow. He was sitting there, his jeans getting soaked, as he watched the Golf eventually get some grip and speed off. He sat there, watching the rear of the car, his mouth popping like Toad of Toad Hall.

He swore and clambered to his feet, brushing himself down in disgust, his eyes on the car as it gathered speed. Too much speed.

He was heading towards a mild right-hand twist in the road. Under normal circumstances it was nothing more than a kink, hardly even noticeable. But in the present weather conditions, combined with travelling too quickly, not concentrating properly as a result of all the other things that must have been swirling through Tom James's mind, he yanked the steering wheel down, expecting the car to go where instructed. It did no such thing. So he slammed on and exacerbated the situation.

The car mounted the kerb with a sickening thud and smashed head first into the lamp post on that ever-so-slight curve.

Actually, he wasn't travelling that quickly, maybe had got up to twenty-five miles per hour, but as he wasn't wearing a seat belt, was only holding the wheel with one hand, a gun in the other, he could not even brace himself firmly for impact.

He was tossed forward in his seat and his lower face impacted on the rim of the steering wheel.

Then the crash was over.

Flynn made his way carefully to the car, approaching the last few yards at a crouch, coming in behind Tom's right shoulder. Tom was slumped over, but moving, and just before Flynn got there, he opened the door and swung his legs out of the car. He saw Flynn, raised the gun, before his whole being turned to mush. He sagged, sank to his knees, still waving the gun, which he then dropped.

Blood oozed from a cut around his chin. He spat out a gobful of it on to the white snow.

'I'm hurt,' he said plaintively.

'Tough,' Flynn responded. He kicked the gun away into the snow, grabbed Tom's bloodied shirtfront and pulled him roughly to his feet, then frogmarched him back to the house.

*   *   *

As Henry sat miserably on the side of the bath, stripped to the waist and shaking, Alison dabbed his wounded shoulder, squeezing out the disinfected cloth into the bloodstained water in the wash basin. Henry tensed himself for each touch, but the pain was less than it had been, thanks to some powerful, quick-acting analgesics Alison had produced from the medical kit she had liberated from Dr Lott.

Most of the time, Henry had his eyes closed. He didn't mind the sight of blood, unless it was his own. Since first checking the wound he'd studiously avoided looking at it.

Alison had hurried back to the house on receiving a phone call from Flynn and had gasped when she'd seen Henry slumped by the wall in the office, blood running down his chest, splattered on the wall behind him. He'd tried to give her one of his famous – at least to himself – lopsided grins and tried to act brave, but it was a thin veneer. She had helped him up to the bathroom, where she had cleaned the wound after administering the painkillers.

She did a last wipe with an antiseptic pad and stood back. The pellet holes wept and seeped blood like a series of mini-taps, but it didn't look as bad as at first. He could still move his shoulder and it seemed that the shot may have only entered the fleshy part and not penetrated the joint. It was not serious – at the moment – but still required proper hospital treatment, as at least half a dozen pieces of shot were embedded in him and Alison had no way of removing them. She was about to bandage the shoulder.

'The sooner you get to a hospital the better,' she told Henry. 'There's a real chance of infection and one way or another, you need to get there in the morning at the latest.'

'Weather dependent.'

'Stuff the weather,' she said.

'Yeah, OK. Thanks,' he said pathetically.

'It's a good job Dr Lott was still in the pub. I was just about to shout last orders and clear the place when Steve phoned.'

'Why didn't he come, Dr Lott that is?'

'It's his weekly inebriation. He's fit for nothing except dealing drugs. He just handed his whole kit over.' She started to bandage the wound.

'You've seen worse than this, then? Ow!'

'Much. This is nothing, so stop being a baby.'

'OK, nurse. What's happening down at the pub, by the way?'

'I've left Ginny to lock up, et cetera. She'll be all right, she's done it before.'

'And Karl?'

'Sent to bed. He wanted to come, but he's really ill. He needs more TLC than you.'

'And your guests, the ones in my rooms?'

'Causing no trouble at all.' She pulled the bandage tight, Henry juddered. 'There, how does that feel?'

He gave her sad, puppy-dog eyes, although the pathos of his expression was tempered with the heavy bags of an old bloodhound, which probably spoiled the overall effect. She pecked him on the cheek, stood back and looked tenderly into his eyes, then with an even sadder inflection said, 'I wish,' and sighed.

Henry swallowed – which actually hurt. He hadn't realized that his throat had a direct connection to his shoulder.

Flynn barged in, holding a tea towel to his ear. 'What's your plan of action, Henry?' he demanded, then his face fell as he realized he had stepped into a moment. He said nothing, but his demeanour changed.

Henry inhaled deeply. A shiver of pain arced through his shoulder. He tried to ignore it, and applied his mind to more pressing matters.

Alison busied herself by swilling out the blood-splashed wash basin.

Henry wanted to go to bed, too. Instead of admitting that, he got up stiffly and reached for a clean shirt Alison had liberated from Tom's wardrobe, easily big enough to fit Henry. He carefully slipped his arms through the sleeves.

'First things first. I need to tell Tom formally that he's under arrest for the attempted murder of you and me. Then I'm going to break the news to him about Cathy, although I suspect he knows we've found her. I'll arrest him on suspicion of that.' He turned to Alison. 'We'll need a statement from Ginny, by the way, saying she saw Cathy and Tom drive past, then only Tom came back.' Alison nodded. Henry went on to Flynn, 'I want to start a custody record, too.'

'Locked up in his own home,' Flynn quipped.

'You've heard of house arrest, haven't you?'

'The cells are certainly filling up. Then what?'

'Hold on to him until the cavalry arrives. I won't be questioning

him, or Callard. They've got some connection over the shotgun, if
what Callard says is true about Tom giving him the gun . . .'

'Which also connects Tom to Jonny Cain?'

'It hadn't escaped me.'

'Let me talk to him,' Flynn suggested.

'Talk or torture? Anyway, you're not a cop now.'

'I never tortured anyone, not even close.'

'Let's not go there, eh?' Henry buttoned up his shirt.

'What's that supposed to mean?' Flynn said.

'Forget it.' Henry tried to walk past him, his legs unsteady. But
Flynn didn't budge, blocked the way threateningly.

'I said . . .'

'Steve,' Henry said tiredly, 'when I investigated you, I turned over
lots of stones.' He arched his eyebrows pointedly. Flynn's lower lip
tightened. 'OK,' Henry relented, and glanced over to Alison, who
was transfixed by the interaction. 'The broken jaw of a witness against
you in Rossendale?' Henry held Flynn's stare. 'The drug dealer held
over a balcony in Morecambe?' Still they remained eye to eye. 'A
sock full of pennies on the guy in Preston . . . need I go on?'

Flynn's expression changed subtly. His eyes dropped and,
defeated, he stood aside for Henry to pass.

'Now then, let's have speaks with Tom James, soon to be
ex-detective of this parish.'

As he was a man of action, being debilitated was driving Karl
Donaldson crazy, especially with all the excitement going on at the
police house. It was almost destroying him that he hadn't been there
in amongst the thick of it backing up Henry who, he had come to
realize over the years, usually needed all the help he could get. He
hoped that Steve Flynn was as handy as he appeared to be.

But Donaldson was more exhausted than he'd ever been in his
life. Even when he'd been recovering from the gunshot he'd taken
from a terrorist, he'd had more energy to deal with things. It had
taken every ounce of his will power to put on the tough-guy act
behind Henry when he'd been challenging Jonny Cain and his
assorted rag-tags.

Now all he could do was think of sleeping.

The combination of food poisoning – an affliction intense and
fatiguing like nothing else he had experienced – and the sprained
ankle that had ballooned to double its normal size, had simply

floored him. That, plus the ill-conceived walk across the moors through conditions that would have been a test even in the rudest of health.

He did have a lot to thank Henry for, however, although his friend's reading of the weather could have been a mite more accurate.

'This is my room.' Ginny, Alison's teenage stepdaughter, led him down the corridor towards the living room and stopped in front of a door.

'Look, honey,' Donaldson drawled, 'I'm happy to crash out on the sofa. I don't really want to put you to any trouble.'

'Honestly, it's not a problem. My mum has a huge bed and I've slept with her before, on girlie nights.'

'If you're sure . . .'

'Course – and thanks for, y'know, flattening that arsehole. He deserved it.' Ginny opened the bedroom door, revealing a sumptuous room in various shades of pink, with a very inviting three-quarter width bed. There was an en suite off to one side, and lots of teddies. She stepped in and Donaldson followed. 'Well, this is it,' she said shyly.

'It's great,' he said enthusiastically. 'Thanks.'

She paused at the door before leaving. 'Those men,' she said, 'they're dangerous, aren't they?'

Donaldson nodded.

'Mm, thanks again.' She collected her PJs and left Donaldson in the room. He tossed his rucksack on to the bed, then sat on it himself, feeling his bottom sink into its softness.

'Ooh, nice.' He eased off his trainers, swung up his legs and, still fully clothed, closed his eyes. Within moments he'd drifted off.

Tom had been put in the main bedroom across the landing from the bathroom. He sat on the edge of the wide bed, hunched sullenly over, his cable-tied wrists between his legs. He glowered grimly at Henry as he came into the room, blood from the gash he'd received in the car accident smearing his face, some drops on the light-coloured carpet.

The two men stared at each other, judging, until Tom looked away.

Flynn stood behind Henry, filling the door with his big frame.

'This is shit,' Tom said.

Henry did not bother with any preamble. He told Tom he was under arrest on suspicion of murdering Cathy James, plus various offences including the attempted murder of himself and Steve Flynn. He cautioned Tom and asked him if he understood what had been said.

'No – how can I have murdered her?'

'We've found her body, Tom.' Henry waited for the reaction, but all he got was a subtle change in facial expression.

'And you didn't tell me? You didn't tell me about my wife?'

'I didn't, but now I have.'

'And you think I shot her?'

'How do you know she was shot?'

'Assumption,' Tom said quickly.

As much as Henry would have liked to pick up on that little error, and what Tom had let slip when he was threatening him and Flynn with the shotgun, he knew this was not the time or place. Tom had to be taken to a proper cop shop and processed scrupulously by the book.

'What's happens now?' Tom asked.

'You're under arrest and you won't be going anywhere, and you won't be dealt with until I can get you into a custody office. I won't be questioning you, so we're all going to have to sit tight until the weather clears and we can get out of the village.'

'What a joke. Suppose I just get up and walk?'

'You won't,' Henry promised him.

'I want a phone call.'

'Who to?'

'A friend.'

'Which friend?'

'Just a friend.'

'Denied,' Henry said.

'I want a doctor.'

'Alison will take a look at you.'

'I said a doctor.'

'She'll have to do.'

'And I want a brief.'

'Who would that be?'

'Jacobson in Lancaster.'

'I'll find the number for you.'

'And I want a shower. I need to clean off this blood.'

'That can be arranged.'

'I want it now,' Tom insisted and held up his connected wrists. 'Cut these things off, please. I can't shower with them on.'

Henry, Flynn and Alison were on the landing. Henry was weak and woozy, the pain in his shoulder severe. Tom had been allowed to use the shower in the en suite off the main bedroom, which was where he presently was. They could hear the sound of the shower running, hear the combi gas boiler firing up to heat the water. Henry leaned against the wall and glanced at his shoulder. Little flowering spots of red were blossoming through the clean shirt like tiny flowers as the peppered wound continued to seep.

'Are you going to hang around and help out?' The question was directed at Flynn. 'Once I know, then I can plan a bit better.'

'I'm staying,' Flynn said. 'He killed my friend.'

'OK, but no rough stuff. I think he'll continue to be a handful, but I don't want any OTT reactions. Everything measured, everything justified. I want to hit him as much as you.'

'Fine.'

'Right . . . what I need to do is call all this in and bring control room up to speed, see what the latest weather forecast is and find out how soon we can get assistance. Then I think it'll probably be easier to get Tom downstairs, cuff him to a chair in the office and keep an eye on both men in one location. Even though I'd like to keep them apart, it'll be easier for us.'

'I'll have that,' Flynn agreed.

'Alison.' Henry turned to her. 'If you'd be good enough to dress Tom's cut face, that'd be great. Then you can head back down to the pub. You don't have to stay here and I imagine you'd rather be down there with Ginny anyway. You've done more than enough. Thanks.'

'Are you saying you don't want me?' she said, mock offended.

'Not at all.'

'I'll see. I'll phone Ginny after I've seen to Tom.'

'OK.' To Flynn, Henry said, 'Can you stay up here with one foot in the bedroom? When he's finished showering, have him get dressed, then bring him down to the office.'

'Will do.'

'And thanks,' Henry said genuinely.

Flynn shrugged modestly. He glanced at Henry and Alison, sensing something between them, which meant he didn't stand a chance with her. He shrugged mentally as Alison smiled at him.

The two went down the stairs, leaving Flynn at the bedroom door.

In the hallway, Henry paused and turned to her. 'I hope this doesn't sound sexist, but I could really do with a coffee. Would you mind seeing if you could rustle something up in the kitchen? I know I sound a bit pathetic, but I need a shot.'

'Not a problem.'

Henry glanced into the office and saw Callard on the floor by the radiator. After all the action, he had fallen asleep again and was snoring. Something else caught Henry's eye, but before he could even begin to realize its significance, there was a knock on the front door.

He opened the door.

On the front doorstep stood a young woman, no hat, the snow covering her head and shoulders. She looked forlorn, lost and unsure. Henry thought there was something familiar about her, but could not quite place her. At the same time, his mind was elsewhere, nagging him about what he had seen in the office, and even as the girl was on the step in front of him, he knew he wasn't giving her his full attention.

'Yes?' he asked sharply.

'I'm sorry to bother you,' she said apologetically.

'Is there a problem?'

'Are you a policeman?' Her eyes took in his appearance, widening as they saw his blood-speckled shoulder.

'Yes.'

'Please can I come in?'

'Er, yeah, sure, sorry.'

She stepped into the hallway and stomped the snow off her boots. Henry put her at about twenty years old. She had a pretty face, spoilt slightly by an angular chin and a harsh look in her eyes.

'What can I do for you?' Henry asked, hoping it was nothing. He glanced distractedly into the office again, frowning.

'My name's Laura Binney.'

Henry forced his attention back to her. 'I'm Detective Superintendent Christie.' Then he pointed at her and exclaimed, 'You've been sat in the pub all day.'

'Yeah.'

'What's the problem?'

'I'm looking for my boyfriend.'

'Right . . . and?' A domestic situation was the last thing Henry needed. He estimated it would only be a few more seconds before he was propelling her back out the door. 'Look,' he said apologetically, 'I'm just a bit busy right now. Can it wait?'

Her eyes moistened and searched Henry's face. Her mouth quivered. 'No.'

'I'm afraid it might have to.'

Without further warning, she burst into tears with a loud wail, surprising Henry. 'Hey, what's up? Surely it can't be that bad. You had an argument with him.'

'It is bad,' she blubbered through a torrent of tears. 'I think he's dead, I think he's been murdered.'

The words, important as they were, desperately as they had been spoken, did not really register in Henry's distracted mind. The thing that had caught his eye in the office suddenly made sense to his worn-out brain.

'Shit – sorry love, hang on one second.' He held up his right hand, palm out, in an 'I'll be back' gesture, and rushed into the office. There was a cordless telephone on a base on the desk and a tiny red light on the base unit was flashing – blink, blink – indicating the line was in use somewhere else in the house. 'Sugar,' Henry uttered, thundered back out of the office, past the emotional and bewildered young woman, who watched him slack-jawed.

Alison came to the kitchen door, a puzzled expression on her face. 'What is it, Henry?'

'He's got a phone up there,' he said, then yelled upstairs, 'Flynn – he's got a phone in there.' He started to leg it up, jarring his injured shoulder painfully with each footfall.

By the time he reached the bedroom door, Flynn was already at the door of the en suite, trying the handle. 'Locked,' he said.

'Boot it down,' Henry ordered, crossing to him and glancing at the bedside cabinets, noticing the empty base of a cordless phone on one of them. Somehow Tom had managed to sneak the phone into the shower room.

Flynn stepped back. He had kicked down lots of doors in the past, loved doing it. Something he missed. He lined himself up and flat-footed the door by the gold-plated handle. It was a flimsy interior door and splintered spectacularly as it disintegrated and crashed back on its hinges, which only just stayed screwed to the frame.

Henry pushed his way past and found Tom, who had not even stepped into the shower, though he had turned it on in order to fool Henry. He had the cordless phone in his hand and his thumb was frantically pressing buttons. Henry strode to him.

'Give me the fucking phone,' he demanded and tried to snatch it.

Tom jerked it away, thumbed the last button, the phone beeped, and then he handed it calmly to Henry, with a sly grin of triumph.

'Who've you phoned?' Henry asked.

Tom simply gave a weak shrug. 'Just exercising my legal right,' he said smugly.

Nine weapons were laid out on the table. Four pistols, four machine pistols. They varied in make, origin and quality. They had however been oiled, cleaned and loaded with ammunition that had been home produced in a back-street industrial unit in Manchester. Each gun had two spare magazines that had been emptied and reloaded so there was certainty that they were full, even if the quality of the bullets was occasionally suspect.

The ninth weapon was a five-shot sawn-off pump action shotgun, made in China, but with professionally produced cartridges.

Jack Vincent put down the phone. He looked at the other two men, Henderson and Shannon. 'We're one down, guys,' he announced gravely. The men said nothing, their faces impassive. 'But it makes no odds. We're still going in because that fool Callard couldn't do a simple thing, and then we'll have another job to tack on immediately afterwards.'

'And that would be?' Henderson asked laconically.

'To get the boss out of jail.'

EIGHTEEN

Henry scowled at the cordless handset with infuriation stemming from his stupidity in allowing Tom to sneak the damn thing into the shower with him. He kicked himself inwardly. He was fuming for letting himself be lax, for not doing everything he would have done normally with a prisoner, for being seduced into believing that because Tom was a cop he would play by the rules. Cops, he should have known by now, know how to break the rules. But above all, for not sticking to the motto he had adhered to for the last thirty years: trust no fucker.

'He managed to delete the number he dialled, too,' Henry said bitterly. 'That means it's not recorded on this handset and it won't even redial the number . . . bastard!'

'I don't like this,' Flynn said.

The men were sitting on the double bed. Henry had decided to allow Tom to have the shower anyway, but had insisted on making him strip in front of him, then go into the shower and leave the cubicle door open and the en suite door too, whilst he washed himself off. Tom had complied by removing his clothes slowly, dropping them on to a pile in front of Henry, then doing a twirl and making a disgusting remark about not having anything else on him, or would Henry like to have a feel up his arse? It was pretty standard prisoner fare, so Henry held his tongue and watched Tom get into the shower.

He collected the clothing and deposited it on the landing. He knew he was taking an evidential chance by allowing Tom to shower, but he was prepared to take it. Some evidence might get washed away, but in terms of the evidence Henry was slowly amassing, Tom was in a very bad place as it built up. Once Tom was in a proper cell, the work would begin in earnest. At the moment Henry was just making the best of a bad job.

'I'm not keen either,' Henry agreed. 'He makes a call and deletes the number. What does that say?'

'Come and help me?' Flynn suggested.

Henry nodded. 'It's not exactly Colditz, is it? Tell you what, go and recover that gun from the car, will you, and lock the car up if you can. Then get back here and have a root around.'

'For what?'

'He must have had that pistol stashed somewhere, as well as the extra cartridges for the shotgun. Somewhere not too far away. Kitchen, probably. I'll look after him until you're back.'

'Then what?'

'Handcuffed downstairs, as I said, then batten down the hatches for the night and hope it stops snowing. We need a bit of help here, I'd say.'

'There's a lot of we's in that. I could just piss off and leave you to it.'

Henry could not be bothered to get into this dispute again. 'You do what you have to do. If you want to go, go. I can't stop you. I've had enough of being wound up.'

The griping pain came again just as Donaldson was falling properly asleep in Ginny's comfortable girly bed. It was as bad as ever and he sat bolt upright, cursing for even thinking the worst was over. Now he realized he should have starved himself and foregone the wonderful meal provided by Alison.

He gasped, sat up, and hoped it would pass. It did not, then suddenly there was an urgency to visit the toilet.

'Damn.'

He crossed over to the en suite toilet and seated himself on the loo as the gripe creased him again. Never had he felt so ill and miserable.

Henry stood at the bedroom window and watched Flynn trudge back through the snow, a plastic bag in his hand which, Henry assumed, contained the pistol Tom had used. Flynn saw him, gave a wave and, raising the bag, made a gun shape out of his fingers and pointed at Henry. Having had to face too many guns that day, Henry almost ducked.

'Henry,' a voice came from behind. Alison was at the bedroom door, a mug of steaming coffee in her hand. She held it aloft for him and he went to her, took it with grateful thanks and sipped it. 'Very nice,' he complimented.

'They have nice coffee in their kitchen. In fact, they have very nice everything. The kitchen must have cost an absolute fortune. It's one of those German ones. Twenty thousand at least.'

'Lucky them – but no more.'

'No . . . how are you?'

Henry cocked his head and said, 'Let me think about that . . . Mmm . . . stressed, tired, hurt and extremely worried that there's more to come.' She touched his cheek with her fingertips. 'Other than that, hunky dory,' he said brightly.

'What about that young lady downstairs? I told her to sit in the living room, incidentally.'

'Almost forgotten her . . . the one who thinks her boyfriend has been murdered? What the hell goes on in this village? She was in the Owl earlier. Do you know her?'

'She was, and I don't. She turned up today. I don't think she's local.'

'I'll speak to her once I've fastened Tom to a lamp post or something. I don't really think I've time to deal with a domestic dispute, which is what it sounds like.' The shower turned off, Alison backed out of the bedroom. 'Thanks for the coffee . . . much needed.'

'Pleasure.'

Henry stood at the door to the en suite as Tom stepped naked out of the shower and started to towel himself down.

Flynn recovered the pistol from the front passenger footwell of Tom's Golf. He did a quick search of the rest of the car, found nothing of interest, so locked it up and left it embedded in the lamp post with hazard lights flashing. Another thing that would have to wait until the morning, or when the snow had eased and a recovery vehicle could get through. He handled the pistol carefully, made it safe, and placed it in a plastic bag he'd brought along, one he'd found in the kitchen. Flynn knew guns, having been in the army at sixteen, the Marines at eighteen and the cops at twenty-four. He had spent some time as an authorized firearms officer in the late eighties before gravitating to the drugs branch. He wrapped the bag around the gun and made his way back to the police house.

He spotted Henry observing him from the bedroom window, acknowledged him but grumbled – again – at the thought of the man who he blamed for basically forcing him out of the force. Back then, Flynn had even been to see a solicitor who specialized in employment law, and the guy had been eager to take on the case and sue the constabulary for constructive dismissal. Flynn had backed off at the last moment, a nagging feeling of doubt at the back of his mind. Henry's earlier revelation about uncovering some real dirt about his past suddenly made Flynn realize in hindsight that it had been a good move not to take the organization to court. At least all those sleazy things had been kept under the carpet and the cloud he'd left under wasn't actually a hurricane, as it could have been. Although it was bad enough to have been suspected of nicking a million pounds' worth of drug dealer's money.

Perhaps Henry wasn't completely to blame after all.

Not that it made him feel warmer to him. He still disliked him intensely.

Flynn banged the snow off his feet and entered the house. He checked to see if Callard was still attached to the plumbing – yes – and noticed the young lady with the missing boyfriend now sitting primly in the lounge with a coffee in one hand and Roger's sloppy head on her lap, as she stroked the old dog.

He also noticed Henry and Alison sharing quiet words at the bedroom door.

Muttering something uncomplimentary about them both under his breath, he went into the kitchen, placed the pistol on the worktop next to the sawn-off shotgun and poured himself a coffee from the filter machine. He leaned with his back to the fridge, sipped the brew, eyes roving the room, wondering if Henry was correct.

Tom had been disarmed of the shotgun in the living room. He had then legged it into the kitchen, but Flynn hadn't been right on his tail. He estimated that Tom may well have had a good thirty seconds or more alone in the kitchen before Flynn entered. So if Tom hadn't had the pistol to start with – and Flynn was sure he hadn't – he'd used that half-minute to get his hands on it. Therefore it must have been hidden within fairly easy reach.

Trouble was, a lot of places were in easy reach. Flynn scanned the room and tried to visualize in his mind's eye what Tom might have been doing in those precious seconds. Flynn decided on a quick, structured, systematic search instead of trying to second-guess what had happened. Coffee still in hand he walked back to the open kitchen door and began a lazy search, one drawer, one cupboard, at a time; under the sink, in the tiny closet, and on top of the cupboards by climbing on to a chair and peering over the rim. He found nothing, frustratingly. He pursed his lips and placed his coffee down. This time he went through everything more thoroughly, taking his time, going down on his knees and actually moving stuff sideways, removing items to see properly. But then he thought, no. If Tom had managed to get a gun in those few seconds, he wouldn't have had time to move pots and pans out of the way. He would have put his hand straight on it.

Flynn ran it all back in his mind, then started searching again, but now believing there was nothing to find.

Would he be so stupid as to have a weapon in the kitchen?

Especially being married to a sharp-witted woman cop like Cathy, who had obviously stumbled on to something.

Flynn tried to put himself in Tom's position.

'If I had an illegal firearm, where would I hide it?' he muttered out loud.

'In plain sight?' suggested a voice behind him. Alison was standing at the door. 'Maybe somewhere a lady wouldn't usually look?'

'Such as?'

'Have you checked the fuse box?' She pointed to a rectangular box on the wall by the back door with a pull-up lid. Flynn had glanced at it, recognized it for what it was, but thought no more. The box was maybe eighteen inches long, a foot high and protruded about four inches from the wall.

Unimpressed, he lifted the lid, the hinges on the top so it opened upwards, and yes, there was the fuse panel. 'Too small,' he said, and added, 'but your theory isn't a bad one.' He shot Alison a look, as something caught his eye at ground level – the bottom panel of a cabinet that abutted the skirting board at right angles. It was slightly misaligned with the next panel along. Flynn tapped one end of the panel with his toe and it moved. He bent low and dug his fingertips into the end of the panel and pulled. It scraped out and revealed a cavity underneath the base of the cabinet and the floor.

'Henry, you brilliant bastard,' he said begrudgingly. He dropped even lower, to mouse eyeline, stared into the darkness, gave a short laugh and reached inside.

Henry tossed a pair of tracksuit bottoms and a T-shirt at Tom. He had found them in a wardrobe.

'Not exactly a zoot suit, eh?' Tom smirked, turning his back to Henry, bending down and pulling up the pants. He was referring to the forensic paper suits given to prisoners when their own clothing had been taken for scientific analysis.

'It'll do. I imagine you were wearing something different when you killed Cathy.'

Tom turned slowly, putting his arms in the T-shirt. 'Is this an interview? Is that an allegation? I don't see my brief present, do you, Detective Superintendent? In fact, I don't see much in the way of any police procedure so far, do you?' He sounded cocky and self-assured.

'Things will work out for the best, you mark my words,' Henry smiled.

Outside, a large lorry went past the house, one of the few vehicles that had driven past. Tom turned and watched it, then looked back at Henry and slitted his eyes. 'Best hope you don't nod off tonight, eh?' he taunted.

Henry held up a cable tie. 'Time to fasten up.'

Tom approached Henry with arms outstretched, inner wrists touching. 'Something else not quite right, eh?'

'The handcuffs?' Henry looped the plastic around the wrists and crimped them up. 'Violent and unpredictable prisoners get them.'

Tom simply raised his eyebrows. 'Not too tight. You wouldn't want me to lodge a formal complaint about excessive force, would you?'

'Be my guest,' Henry said. And with each passing second and each interaction, Henry was more and more convinced that Tom James was a corrupt and dangerous individual. He gave a flick of the thumb and Tom went out of the room ahead of him. A sudden shock of pain in Henry's shoulder made him scrunch up his face.

Flynn withdrew his hand, his fingers wrapped around the barrel of a Skorpion machine pistol, black, ugly, dangerous looking, a twenty-round curved magazine slotted in it. He placed it carefully on the kitchen floor and slid his hand back inside the secret compartment.

'If there's any spiders in here, I'll scream.'

'You've already found a scorpion,' Alison said.

'You know your guns,' he said.

'Afghanistan does that to a girl.'

Next he withdrew a semi-automatic pistol, indeterminate make and origin, but probably Chinese, Flynn guessed. He placed this next to the Skorpion and went searching again, pulling out a box containing shotgun cartridges of the exact type used in the sawn-off shotgun taken first from Callard and then from Tom. The next handful was a medium-sized plastic food bag stuffed with 9mm calibre rounds of ammunition. Another foray produced a tight roll of twenty-pound Bank of England notes, causing him to give a whistle of appreciation. The last find was a bag of white powder, about as big as a kid's pencil case.

'That's it,' he said, pushing himself on to his knees and smiling at Alison's astonished face. 'Welcome to the land of the corrupt cop.'

Tom reached the bottom of the steps ahead of Henry. Flynn stood in the hallway by the kitchen door and he and Tom exchanged venomous looks. Henry came down the last step and pushed Tom gently ahead of him towards the office door.

'Do you want to see what I've found?' Flynn asked Henry.

'Is it interesting?'

'Very.'

'Does he need to see it?' Henry nodded at Tom.

'You probably need to see his reaction.'

Tom said, 'What's this, another set-up by my wife's lover?'

'Let's look anyway,' Henry said and gripped Tom's elbow. He walked him along the hall to the kitchen. Flynn backed into the room, Alison already standing at the back door, then revealed all: the two weapons, the ammunition, the roll of cash, the white powder, all still on the floor next to the panel that plugged the hidey-hole underneath the cupboard.

Henry took in the find, then looked at Tom. 'Let me remind you, you're under caution. Anything to say at this moment?'

'Yeah – this is all bollocks and I'm being set up by this twat here.'

'And I did it all from Gran Canaria,' Flynn said.

Henry said to Alison, 'Can you back this up? Can you be a witness to what Steve found and how he found it?' She nodded. Henry, who had not released Tom's elbow, tightened the grip and pulled him back out of the room and steered him towards the office. They walked past the open living-room door in which the young woman with the missing boyfriend still sat, hunched up, looking wretched on the settee, Roger's head still in her lap.

Tom spotted her. She saw him at exactly the same moment. The expressions on both their faces changed dramatically. But then they passed and Henry edged Tom into the office, sat him down in a chair.

'Some big questions coming your way, Tom,' Henry warned him. He made no reply.

'Sir, excuse me.'

The young woman was now standing at the office door, a fearful look on her face, her eyes darting from Henry to Tom and back again.

'I'm sorry, love,' Henry said. 'I had some things to do. I'll be with you as soon as I can. Sit down, just give me a few more minutes.'

'No – you don't understand. Him!' Her forefinger pointed accusingly at Tom. 'It's him . . . he's one of them.'

'What do you mean?'

'My boyfriend,' she blabbed, trying to find her words, but everything in her mind was obviously jumbled.

'You need to think very carefully about what you're going to say, darlin',' Tom said. There was more than an undercurrent of menace in his voice, accompanied by a pointed, meaningful look.

'Shut it,' Henry growled. 'This man's your boyfriend?' Henry asked.

'No, no . . . last time I saw my boyfriend,' she tried to explain, 'he was with *him*, he was one of them . . .'

'One of who?'

'One of the ones that came for him, to take him away.' She got a grip on herself and said clearly, 'Last time I saw my boyfriend, he was with this man.' She jabbed her finger at Tom again. 'And I've never seen or heard from him since.'

'And what's your boyfriend called?' Henry asked.

'Massey,' she said, her lips quivering, 'Wayne Massey.'

NINETEEN

On the morning of his death Massey had woken up heavy-headed from the previous night's excess. He had disturbed his girlfriend when he jumped quickly out of bed and teetered to the toilet, where he vomited noisily and copiously. After swilling out his mouth, he came back to bed, sat on the edge, head in hands, making soft moaning noises. He looked around at her when she reached across and touched his naked back with her fingertips.

'You OK, babe?'

'Yuh,' he answered. They had been together a couple of months now, much to everyone's surprise. Laura Binney was a quiet, reserved girl who had pretty much avoided the pitfalls that came with an upbringing on one of Lancaster's most deprived council estates. She was not the most intellectual of girls but could see beyond the prospect of living on benefits, like her older sister Linda, or getting a dead-end job on a supermarket till. A streak of stubbornness inside her got her work in administration with the local council. It wasn't the greatest job in the world, but there was the possibility of advancement and it provided enough money for her to rent a little flat on St George's Quay by the River Lune. Cash was tight – only occasionally did she allow herself a blast night out with the girls – but strict budgeting ensured she survived.

She had known Wayne Massey for a while. He had gone out with Linda, a short tempestuous relationship that ended acrimoniously when she accused him, justly, of stealing cash from her.

From the sidelines, Laura secretly fancied him. He was a known drug dealer in the city, a hard man, even though he was only twenty-three, and he possessed a mysterious, dangerous aura that fascinated Laura, even though it went against her sense of sanity.

It was on a girlie night out with Linda and others that she bumped into Massey in a club where, it was rumoured, he controlled the drug trade.

He had a stand-up squabble with Linda over their failed relationship and she flounced off, carrying her high heels. But Massey caught Laura's eye and the bottle of champagne he sent over fuelled a feeling of naughtiness. She had just broken up with her own feckless boyfriend and was on the lookout for a physical encounter just for the hell of it.

The champers got them chatting. And at three that morning they were fucking like there was no tomorrow in her flat by the river. It was the beginning of an intense relationship for Laura, who found herself inexplicably obsessed by Massey and the way he threw himself around the city like he owned it. Pretty soon she thought she was in love, as he seemed to offer excitement she had never before experienced.

Despite a stark warning from Linda – 'He's a dangerous, unpredictable fuckwit and knocks about with dangerous people and he'll screw every penny out of you' – Laura was certain that once she got her hooks into him, she could change and mould him.

When Massey disappeared for a couple of days once without contacting her, she became worried, but he returned haggard-looking on the doorstep. He refused to tell her where he'd been, but did promise her he had not cheated on her, all she needed to hear. He screwed her dispassionately that day, a cold, clinical fuck, and just once she caught him looking at her in a way she did not quite understand. But it was only a fleeting glance, a moment of uncertainty, before they climaxed together.

Post coitus, she lay tucked into him, her head on his chest, her hand holding him gently, willing him to become hard again.

'Babe?' he said.

'Yes, what is it?'

'Yeah, look, I need to borrow some money. I hope that's OK.'

'From me? I don't have anything.'

He chortled. 'I need a few grand to tide me over.'

'What for?'

'Just a bit overstretched.' It was a complete understatement.

'I haven't got that sort of money. You know that.'

He took her hand from him and pushed her away as he sat up. He took hold of her chin in the V of his right hand, where his thumb and forefinger connected. 'Don't fucking lie.'

She jerked herself away. 'I'm not lying.'

'Honey – some very bad men think I did the dirty on them, y'know, short changed them. If I don't pay back, I'm going to suffer.' She blinked. 'And I know you've got money in a building society account.'

'You've been through my things,' she accused him.

'Yeah – and you've got three big ones stashed away. I need it.'

'Honey, it's my money. I've been saving it for years.'

'Do you want me to get my head kicked in?'

'No, but . . .'

'Then trot down to the building society and draw it out.' His voice softened. 'I'll pay you back, you know I will.'

Laura was now sitting on the edge of the bed, her mind tortured, but knowing she would do as asked. She withdrew the money later and handed him the cash.

'I need it back,' she said.

'Trust me,' he said, reassuringly.

The money was never mentioned and their love life returned to normal, until that morning three days ago. The day on which he would die.

Massey had been out the previous night, without Laura, having returned very drunk to her flat at 3 a.m. He stumbled into bed and slept with his mouth agape, snoring horribly, ensuring that Laura got no sleep for the remaining hours in bed.

When he returned to bed from vomiting, she had touched him and asked if he was OK. He had just uttered the words, 'Yeah, yeah,' when she heard the first crash at the door. A massive smashing sound that initially puzzled her. It was followed by another.

Massey, however, seemed to know exactly what was happening. He screamed an obscenity, fell to his knees by the bed, forced his hand between the mattress and bedstead, frantically searching for something.

In the short hallway there was another crash.

'What's going on?' Laura demanded. By this time she was on her feet, wide eyed, terrified, the duvet clasped around her.

'Where is it, where is it?' he chuntered, his voice rising, his right hand still groping under the mattress.

'What's going on, what are you after?'

Massey extracted a snub-nosed revolver from its hiding place, spun around with it as the bedroom door was kicked off its hinges and two men, followed by a third, burst into the room. The first pair were carrying baseball bats and as Massey swung the gun towards them, shouting something incomprehensible, they were on him. A bat smashed down on his wrist and the gun dropped from his fingers. The second man kicked it out of reach and the third stepped forward as Laura watched the spectacle, horrified.

This man carried a semi-automatic pistol and as the first two men hauled the cowering Massey to his feet between them, the weapon was ground into Massey's cheek, and the man's face leered into Massey's.

'Time to face the music,' said the man she later identified to Henry as Tom James.

The story had been told falteringly, with certain parts omitted, to Henry Christie in the living room of Tom James's house in the snowbound village of Kendleton in north Lancashire. Tom himself was handcuffed in the office across the hallway, watched by Steve Flynn, whilst Henry listened to the tale behind a closed door.

'You're sure it was Tom James? The guy in there?'

She nodded. 'I didn't know his name, or who he was, but that is him. Yeah, he got Wayne to get dressed and then the other two men walked him out between them, and that's the last I saw of him.'

'Three days ago?'

'Yes.'

'Did you contact the police?'

Laura dropped her eyes. 'I was too frightened. I knew this was a gangland thing.'

Henry ruminated a moment. 'What brought you here?'

'I did make some enquiries,' she said defiantly. 'I asked questions of the people I'd seen Wayne with in the clubs. No one wanted to say much, really, but a guy eventually told me that Wayne was selling drugs for a guy called Jack Vincent. Then someone else told me the rumour was that Wayne had skimmed loads of money and drugs from a deal and that this Vincent guy was after his blood. He was in serious trouble. I think that's why he borrowed from me, to pay Vincent back, so I can't understand why Vincent kidnapped him. Surely he must have paid him with my money, otherwise . . .' A dawn of realization crossed Laura's young, innocent face. 'Unless he blew it, and didn't pay them off, otherwise why would they have . . .?' she said. All Henry could think was, you poor deluded woman. Men like Wayne Massey have self-destruct buttons where money is concerned.

Henry doubted two things. First that she would ever see her money again, that was long gone. Second that she would see Massey again.

'I heard something else, too,' she said meekly. Henry waited. 'That Jack Vincent owns a leopard or mountain lion or something – and he feeds people to it.'

Henry stared at her, his initial disbelief replaced by a shiver running down his spine as he recalled the ghostly shape behind the fencing on the hill and the effect it had on Roger, the German shepherd dog. He laughed it off. 'Sounds rubbish that,' he said, but his voice didn't even convince himself.

After a second urgent visit to the toilet, Donaldson curled up in Ginny's comfortable bed, certain the worst was over, that his insides were completely evacuated. The pains had all but gone, a faint twinge now and then. His ankle continued to throb, but the elastic tube bandage that Alison had found for him held it firmly, yet gently.

He tapped off the bedside light and snuggled into his favourite position, sleeping mode as he called it, on his right-hand side, left leg drawn up, right extending, hands palm to palm underneath his face.

A few things whirled through his mind. The day's terrible walk, Ken's infected chicken, his wife and the baby growing in her tummy, the evening's events and whether Henry was coping without him. But his meanderings circled back to his future child, sex still unknown. That was going to be a surprise for both of them. He started to drift off, working through lists of names.

He came awake with a start at the sound of a click. His whole body tensed as he listened, his brow furrowing, certain he had heard something. The click, then a creak. Then a footstep – soft, but definitely a footstep. Donaldson held his breath. Someone, he was positive, had entered the bedroom. Ginny, he wondered. Forgotten something? Not wanting to disturb him?

He was facing away from the door, so opening his eyes didn't help.

Another shuffle, then he was aware of a presence by the bed. He heard a rasping breath, then smelled cigarette smoke and body odour and he knew this was an intruder, someone who should not have been there.

'Now then, you foxy bitch, I'm going to continue what I started,' the voice croaked.

Donaldson relaxed, a smile spreading across his face, and what little light there was in the room caught the mischievous twinkle in his eye.

'You are going to get it,' the man said huskily. A smell of alcohol joined the other fine aromas. 'And you're gonna like it.'

Donaldson allowed himself to emit a slight squeak of air from his lungs, hoping it would sound like the sort of noise a girl might make. He snuggled down deeper under the duvet, aware of the figure leaning over and a hint of warm breath, garlic laden, wafting across. He must have had the garlic mushrooms as a starter, Donaldson thought.

'I'm gonna shag you silly, you little bitch.'

It was at that point that Donaldson felt enough was enough.

Although he was sick and injured, the sugar-rush of adrenalin ensured that these disabilities were sidelined.

He moved fast and hard and violently, all his training kicking in – particularly the offensive tactics he had learned and continued to practise to perfection over the years.

The duvet went down. The back of his left hand, bunched into an iron fist, arced upwards and slammed directly into Danny Bispham's face. It was a perfect landing and even as he continued to move, Donaldson patted himself mentally on the back for this excellent blow. It may only have travelled less than two feet, but the power of the punch was tremendous, rather like being hit by a flat iron.

Donaldson felt the gristle crack, the septum snap, and the resultant mush get forced back into Bispham's face. The second punch he had received in more or less the same spot that evening.

He fell backwards, the combination of the blow and its surprise knocking him back against the bedroom door. His senses reeled, the pain was intense, the shock overwhelming. He sank down on to his backside, uncomprehendingly holding his face.

By which time Donaldson was out of bed, giving the intruder no respite, dragging him to his feet, driven by that terrible combination of rage and precision. Rage at the gall of the man to think he could continue what he had started in the restaurant by putting his hand up Ginny's skirt; precision in the way he clinically proceeded to beat the man senseless. The assault lasted less than a minute, though to Bispham it felt more like a month, until he was curled up in a ball, whining for mercy, sobbing.

Towering over him, Donaldson growled, 'Still want to screw me?'

Tom James had been stuffed down into one corner of the office with firm orders not to move. He sat wedged there, knees drawn up, his cable-tied hands resting on his knees, watching everything that was going on. Callard was still asleep.

Flynn stood in the open doorway, one eye always on Tom, whilst he talked in whispers to Henry. 'It's going to be a long night,' Flynn said. It was approaching midnight now and both men felt as though they had lived three lifetimes that day. 'Good news is the snow seems to have eased off.'

'Now it looks like it's starting to freeze.' Henry was in the hall, looking past Flynn into the office, angled so he could see Tom and

Callard's outstretched legs. 'At least if it's clear, they'll be able to get the helicopter out to us at first light . . . some relief.'

'Don't bank on it.'

Both men exhaled simultaneously, caught each other doing it and grinned.

'You know I didn't take that million, or have anything to do with it,' Flynn said, and added, 'apropos nothing.'

'We'll have to see what your ex-partner says about it, won't we? If he ever gets caught. And anyway, why are you so bothered? Do you crave for my, I dunno, stamp of approval or something?'

'Just want you to see the truth . . . I don't like clouds hanging over me.'

Henry gave him a scornful look. 'I've got clouds queuing up to hang over me.'

'But you're still in the job.'

'Yes, I am,' he said tiredly and rolled his injured shoulder, which was stiffening up painfully, still weeping blood.

Behind them, the living-room door opened and Alison stepped out.

'How is she?' Henry asked.

'OK – tired, wants to sleep.'

'I don't suppose you could . . .?' Henry's voice trailed off.

'Put her up? I'm afraid we're full at the inn,' Alison said biblically.

'She'll have to bed down here, then. There's a guest bedroom made up. Not ideal, but we need to keep hold of her.'

They were talking in hushed tones, but not quietly enough it seemed.

Tom piped up. 'This is my house. You are taking liberties. This is an invasion of my civil liberties . . . you cannot do this.'

All three heads turned to him, the withering expression on all three faces identical, though Henry's suddenly morphed into something much more serious. He stalked over to Tom, who scowled.

'Henry fucking Christie,' Tom sneered. 'I know all about your chequered past, all about your very dicey history of bad judgement calls. I know you've been suspended before . . . you're a freakin' legend, mate . . . and this is all bollocks, it'll be the icing on your cake.'

'And yet here you are in handcuffs and I'm a superintendent.'

'Only because you're up the chief constable's arsehole. Everybody knows – everybody!'

'And yet you're the one in handcuffs,' Henry repeated, 'suspected of murdering your wife, consorting with known OC targets . . . and much, much more. When the dawn comes, you'll be fucked and facing justice, Tom. You'll be going down for life and you'll never set foot outside again for at least what, thirty years?' Henry grinned. 'By which time I'll be in my dotage, bouncing great-grand-kids on my knees.'

Tom laughed. 'Don't think so, Henry,' he said smugly. 'You just don't know who you're dealing with here.'

'And plainly, nor do you.'

Henry felt someone grip his arm and squeeze gently. It was Flynn. 'Henry,' he said, and did not need to speak another word. Flynn had watched him get sucked into a fruitless confrontation, a tit-for-tat argument, the only winner of which would be Tom because he had nothing to lose.

Henry nodded and withdrew from the room. In the hallway, this time definitely out of Tom's earshot, he said, 'Got my goat. I'm just tired and irritable.'

'Oh I know that, but you know what worries me most?'

'What?'

'His confidence.'

'Mm,' Henry mused. 'That phone call.'

For good measure, Donaldson bashed Bispham's head against the door frame, a blow that caught the edge of his temple against the right angle of the door jamb and instantly split the skin. There was a slight delay, then blood poured out down the side of his face.

Bispham was thin and wiry, built like a scrapyard dog, all bones and bollocks, and he was light enough for Donaldson – much bigger and stronger and fitter – to manage easily. He forced one arm up his back, trapping the hand between his shoulder blades. Donaldson twisted the man's ponytail around his other fist and could easily have torn it out of his skull by the roots.

Holding him thus, like a Roman shield, he manoeuvred him out of the door into the corridor. Directly opposite was the door to Alison's bedroom and Ginny, disturbed by the commotion, had emerged sleepily in her jim-jams, her face falling with shock at the sight of Donaldson coming out of her room carrying Bispham in front of him.

'Night-time visitor,' Donaldson said, turning left and marching him along the corridor, Bispham's toes hardly touching the floor. He led him to the door that opened out to the bar and noticed the splintered wood around the lock, answering a question in Donaldson's head. Bispham had jemmied his way into the living accommodation, naughty man. Donaldson pinned him to the wall and toed the door open. He said, 'Gonna be a cold, cold night for you, buddy boy.'

The man's bloodied face was crushed up to the wall and he could not respond. Then, as the door opened, Donaldson reaffirmed his grip on the ponytail and the hand, and pushed him out of the door so they emerged into the pub, the bar to their left.

It was fortunate for the American that he was holding Bispham up like a shield because he was faced with three masked and armed men who, in turn, were surprised by his sudden appearance.

The men were in a V-shaped formation. The lead man, the point of the V, was armed with a pump-action shotgun and he swung it around and pointed it at Donaldson's writhing captive, who had also seen what was in front of him.

Donaldson had little time to react. Just enough for him to take in the situation – the weapon coming around in his direction – so he drew himself in as tightly as he could behind Bispham and held him forward like an offering.

And the shotgun was discharged from a distance of about ten feet, not giving the cartridge load the space to spread before it slammed into Bispham's chest, right on the sternum, blowing a fist-shaped hole in him.

Donaldson held on, even though the force of the blast waved through his arms, and Bispham suddenly went limp. Dead.

He heard the cartridge being ejected, the weapon being racked as a new round slid into the breech. He held Bispham slightly to one side, now literally a dead weight, and saw the man racking the shotgun was blocking the way of the other two, causing them to hesitate unless they shot their colleague by mistake.

Using Bispham like a battering ram, Donaldson emitted a warlike roar and charged the intruders, driving the dead man into the shotgun guy before he could fire the next round, then barged on, using all his power to force him backwards, before with one last heave he threw Bispham ahead of him like a demented zombie.

Donaldson knew he had only seconds.

The element of surprise, both ways, had gone.

He turned, moving quickly, and before the men could regroup and work out what had hit them, he threw himself back through the door into the living accommodation, slammed it shut and slid the three big old bolts across.

Ginny was standing in the corridor.

'Get down,' he screamed, gesticulating wildly – but she was affixed to the spot, still did not know what had happened. He ran towards her, keeping low, and, being as gentle as he could about it, tackled her and carried her through into her bedroom. The door behind them seemed to explode as two shotgun cartridges ripped into it. But the door was almost as old as the pub, constructed over a hundred years before of thick oak and fitted together by craftsman-made joints and pride. It held well against the shotgun blast and the bolts made the thing virtually impregnable.

He gave Ginny a 'shush' gesture and on his belly he wriggled into the hallway and along to the door, keeping to the edge of the corridor, moving like a lizard, or maybe a crocodile.

At the door he stopped, listened hard, but could hear nothing and he knew why.

The intruders were not remotely interested in anything on this side of the door. They had not broken in for him or Ginny.

TWENTY

Entering the Tawny Owl had been easy, simply because the front door next to the revolving door had been left unlocked unwittingly by Danny Bispham, whose mind had been on other things. They had parked their vehicles down the road and run silently through the snow, each of the three men in black, ski masks pulled down over their features, had gone in through the front door and into the bar which was in darkness, other than for the faint glow of some low-level security lighting. The bar itself was secured by a roll-down metal mesh, and all the chairs had been upended on to tables for cleaning purposes.

The men halted just inside the pub, allowing their vision to become accustomed to the relative darkness and the geography of the place.

Jack Vincent was lead, shotgun ready, fingertip laid across the trigger. He also had a semi-automatic pistol tucked into the waistband at the back of his black jeans.

'OK guys,' he said and began to move them forwards to the door which led up to the first floor accommodation. That was when the staff-only door had been flung open and the blood-soaked figure of Danny Bispham came out, dancing like a drugged-up raver. Vincent's mind didn't fully compute what it was seeing, the fact that Bispham was being held by someone else, but he reacted in the only way he could, by pulling the trigger and blowing a hole in Bispham's chest.

Bispham's absence was only noticed by Sim Riddick when he sat up on the double bed in urgent need of a piss.

The pair of them, Riddick and Bispham, were sharing one of the bedrooms that the group had muscled into and intimidated the landlady into allocating to them. Napier and the boss, Jonny Cain, were using the other – sort of. Cain had instructed his men in no uncertain terms that they had to keep awake and alert just in case Jack Vincent should try anything else. Napier had been posted outside Cain's bedroom to keep guard on his boss. Out there in the corridor, miserable, Napier had slithered down the wall, knees drawn up and his forehead wedged on them. He'd had too much to drink to be much use as a watchman, as they all had, and he had fallen quickly asleep, annoyed by the thought of Cain lording it in comfort in the double bed. 'Boss's privilege,' he muttered. The gun wedged in his waistband caused him discomfort but did not prevent his eyes from shutting, and he quickly nodded off.

In the other bedroom, Cain had ordered at least one of the men to keep watch from the window which overlooked the front of the pub, whilst the other crashed out. So long as one of them kept nicks, it didn't matter if the other was snoring. They worked it out between them: Bispham would take the first couple of hours and Riddick could get some sleep.

All four men had been anticipating action that night, but Cain had knocked any thought of reprisals on the head because of the presence of the cop, Christie. Cain decided that his revenge could wait another day and take place in another arena, but he couldn't say the same for Jack Vincent, which was why he ordered his men to keep on guard.

Bispham had pulled a chair to the window and lit up, despite the no smoking rule of the premises. He opened the window a crack and blew his smoke out of it in order not to activate the ceiling-mounted alarm and rouse the whole establishment.

He was also fuming internally. His humiliation at the hands of the big fucking American who had knocked him on to his arse and almost broken his nose was making him seethe with fury. Most people he met and had confrontations with either backed down with their tails between their legs, or he took them on and beat them mercilessly. Despite his stature – he wasn't a big man – he had an evil temperament coupled with an innate joy at inflicting violence and had often pounded people to the ground, smashing them down, making them beg. He especially enjoyed abusing women.

But even Bispham knew he'd met his match with the Yank. Not only was he a very big guy, but he had a look about him and the eyes of a killer. Bispham realized he would get no revenge on him . . . but the girl, well, she was another matter.

His eyes glazed over lustfully and he stroked his ponytail and touched his throbbing face as he considered the ways in which he would assault her. *That* would be his revenge on the American – revenge by proxy.

Jonny Cain's orders meant nothing to him sitting at that window, his rage smouldering. OK, Jack Vincent may well have sent some ludicrous drunk to have a pop, but the chances of anything else happening that night were slim to zero, especially with the weather being like it was, killing everything. Cain was the main man, Vincent and his pathetic cronies mere nothings. They wouldn't dare try anything.

And that was how Bispham justified his decision. He flicked his cigarette out of the window, checked on Riddick who was spread-eagled on the bed, pants unzipped, already asleep. He was in a sequence of breathing that would lead to snoring.

Bispham stood up quietly, walked past the bed to the door, stepping out and stopping when he clocked Napier in the corridor, expelled from Cain's room. He was also asleep. He trod quietly down towards the steps and came out on the ground floor in the bar area. To the left was the door leading to the living quarters.

He went outside to the Range Rover and got the tyre lever from the boot. Coming back into the pub he hadn't even thought about locking the outside door. He then went to work on the inner door, prising it open around the keypad lock using the tyre lever as a jemmy. He'd broken through tougher doors in his past, and in a moment he was through into the corridor.

Already, in his excitement, the blood pulsed in his groin. He walked silently along the carpet, wondering how he would find the room he wanted. The sign on it, 'Ginny Sleeps Here,' was just a bit of a giveaway.

A growl came to the back of his throat. He opened the door and saw her all nicely cuddled up in bed, all warm, safe and ready for him.

Too many beers woke Sim Riddick. He sat up quickly, dreaming he had been urinating, but thankfully it was a dream. He swung out of the bed, groggy, then saw that Bispham had gone AWOL. Riddick guessed that his mate would be paying the waitress a midnight visit.

'Tosser,' Riddick murmured and went into the en suite to pee. Relieved, he came back into the bedroom, glanced out of the door and saw Napier asleep in the corridor. He padded over to the bedroom window where Bispham had been sitting, drew back the curtain and looked sleepily at the whitewashed view. At which point his heart nearly stopped.

The three masked figures, each carrying a weapon, running at speed up the road made him discharge an anguished cry of terror.

'Oh fuck, fuck, fuck,' he gabbled, fastening his pants, stumbling around to find his shirt and shoes, then falling out of the room into the corridor. He booted Napier in the backside, then pounded desperately on Cain's door, before barging through and yelling, 'They're here, for fuck's sake, they're here. And they're tooled up.'

Cain sat up dazedly. Napier stood behind Riddick, a stupid expression on his face.

'Get the guns,' Cain said calmly after shaking his head.

'What you reckon, boss?' Henderson asked, his voice muffled by the ski mask that had slipped slightly askew and now covered part of his mouth.

'That guy's not one of 'em,' Vincent said breathlessly, now hyper after shooting Bispham. He was referring to the man who had chucked the unfortunate Bispham at them, then retreated behind the thick door and locked it. 'We've got one down, only three to go.' His eyes shone wild and evil from underneath the ski mask slits.

'The element of surprise has gone down the shitter,' Henderson mumbled.

'In that case, we move fast and hard, but remember, try not to kill Cain. He's cat food.' Vincent trotted to the door that opened to the narrow flight of stairs leading up to the first floor rooms. He pinned himself to the wall, opened it cautiously, then spun in and arced the shotgun through the tight angle in front of him. 'Clear,' he called and led the way, taking the stairs two at a time.

He emerged warily on to the landing, the corridor ahead, off which were the two guest bedrooms on the left side, about thirty feet from where he stood. Henderson and Shannon were lined up behind him, flattened to the wall.

But before they moved, the second bedroom door along opened and a man – Riddick – stepped out incautiously, saw the three of them and yelled something, caught completely by surprise.

Vincent fired the shotgun instinctively, catching Riddick in the right shoulder and spinning him away from the door across the corridor like a top. As Vincent racked the shotgun again, Henderson stepped out of line and fired a short burst at Riddick from the machine pistol he was brandishing. Even though they were badly aimed, a diagonal line of bullets sprayed across Riddick's body.

Suddenly Napier contorted out of the bedroom and loosed a couple of rounds off with the heavy pistol in his hand, somehow catching Shannon at the back of the line, one bullet grazing along his forearm. Napier managed to duck back into the room before Vincent could fire the shotgun again, which he did, splintering off a chunk of door frame.

Shannon fell back with a scream, clutching his arm. 'He fucking shot me!'

Vincent ignored him, ran on low, then pivoted as he passed the bedroom, catching Napier completely by surprise, not expecting such a fast and aggressive move. He had only stepped back a couple of feet into the bedroom, working up the courage to lean out again and have another couple of shots.

The shotgun was aimed low and the blast smacked into Napier's lower belly and groin, hitting him like a steam hammer. The blast doubled him over and sent him back across the room where he sat on the edge of the bed for a moment, looking down at his wound with disbelief. This was replaced by agony and he fell back, screaming and writhing in agony, his hands covering his guts.

Vincent's momentum carried him on past the door, almost tripping over Riddick's convulsing body. He stopped, flattened himself against the wall next to the bedroom door. Henderson took up a position on the other side of the door, with Shannon still on his backside, desperately holding his wounded arm.

'You want us to come in, Jonny?' Vincent shouted.

'Go fuck,' Cain said from the bedroom.

'You want to know what happened to H. Diller and Haltenorth? I stuck 'em in a crusher, now they're in the foundations of a motorway bridge.'

'That's supposed to make me want to come out?' Cain said. He was on one knee behind the bed. Napier was rolling and moaning back and forth across the bed, spreading vast amounts of blood across the sheets and calling for his mother.

'If you come out, we can talk.'

'About what? You owe me money, end of. I want it back.'

'You're not going to get it.'

'Figured that. So what's to talk about?'

'Not much, I guess. Other than to tell you you're out of business and we're taking over.'

'We?'

'Yeah, me and Tom.'

'Your tame cop?'

'Whatever – anyway, the choice is yours. You can walk out of there alive if you want and then walk away, or we'll just come in on the count of three and blast fuck out of you. You won't even get the chance of a lucky shot.' As he was talking, Vincent was expertly reloading the shotgun – back to a full load of five in the magazine and one in the breech.

'I'll walk out of this alive?' Cain said. In front of him, Napier stopped rolling. His agony had passed now. He was dead.

'It'll make our takeover easier.'

'Maybe I don't want you to take over . . . and whatever happens here, pal, you're dead men anyway.'

'OK, fine,' Vincent said, not really taking in the meaning of Cain's words. 'I'm going to start counting now, Jonny. I don't do small talk. You get up now and throw your shooter down and come out and you'll live. That's it, chatter over . . . One . . . two . . .' Vincent eyed Henderson, who was obviously ready.

Cain shouted, 'I'm coming out.'

Vincent backed away from the door, stepped a third of the way across the width of the corridor, and trained the shotgun on the open door. Henderson mirrored his actions, so the two of them had weapons aimed diagonally at the open door.

Cain came to the door, hands clasped behind his head.

'Face away from me,' Vincent ordered.

With no fear in his face, Cain turned around. Vincent stepped smartly up behind him and smashed the butt of the shotgun on to the back of Cain's closely cropped head, splitting the skin and sending him straight down to his knees. He followed this with another blow which pivoted Cain on to his face, but still did not knock him unconscious. The next four blows managed to accomplish this feat.

Another strong coffee in hand, two more painkillers down his throat, Henry sat on the dining chair that Flynn had positioned for him in the office doorway. The coffee was in a mug resting on his thigh and tasted wonderful, but even the caffeine wasn't having the desired effect of keeping him alert. It worked for a moment, giving him a quick energy burst, but then his overwhelming tiredness cut in and rushed through him, unstoppable.

His head fell. He jerked it up with a mumble and tried to keep his eyes open, and glanced at Tom James who was watching him carefully. Tom hadn't dozed, but seemed to be waiting for Henry to do so.

Henry was suddenly envious of Karl Donaldson, who he imagined to be curled up in Ginny's comfortable warm bed, snoring contentedly.

'You can't afford to drop off,' Tom warned him.

'Don't intend to.'

'Neither does the car driver who falls asleep at the wheel. Then look what happens – a fatal.'

Henry sighed deeply and masked a yawn. The sudden inrush of oxygen brought him round a little, but he knew what Tom said was true. The way things were going he'd be asleep before he knew it, although the excruciating pain in his shoulder did help to keep him awake.

'Top up?'

Alison had returned from the kitchen with a jug of newly filtered coffee. Henry downed what was left in the mug and held it up for a refill. She poured carefully, holding the cup in place, giving Henry a hidden smile.

'Thanks.' It was hot and strong. 'Where's Flynn?' he asked quietly. Alison gestured with an upward spiralling movement of her head – upstairs.

'He thinks we're under siege,' she said.

'It sort of feels that way for some reason.'

Alison took the coffee back to the kitchen and returned with another chair, placing it next to Henry but out of line of sight of Tom.

'You look whacked,' she said, keeping her voice low.

Henry angled slightly towards her and their knees brushed gently. 'I have never been so utterly knackered in my life.'

'How's the shoulder?'

'Stiffening up. Getting sore, despite the drugs. Hurts.'

Alison leaned forward to check on Tom, whose forehead was now resting on his up-pulled knees. This meant she was touching Henry and their faces were just millimetres apart. She stayed in the position longer than necessary and Henry could smell the aroma of her hair, which almost touched his face. He could see the skin of her neck and feel the softness of her breast just touching him. His heart missed a whole bar of beats, but at least the contact brought him wide awake again as probably the last shot of adrenalin left in his system spurted out.

She sat back up. 'I don't throw myself at men,' she whispered. 'But after this is over, do you think we could meet for a coffee somewhere?'

'I'll have to come back for statements.'

'Good,' she smiled – and Henry suddenly felt very stupid. He knew there was no chance of anything going anywhere with her. He was happily married, second time around to the same woman, and he was going to do nothing to spoil that. But there was something in him that found it very hard to say no, something still quite juvenile and reckless. He harangued himself internally for even thinking about kissing another woman than his wife.

His thoughts were interrupted when from upstairs there was a crash of a door slamming shut and the sound of Flynn's heavy footsteps. Tom raised his head, a sly, knowing look on his face. Flynn thundered down the stairs.

'Henry, problem. Two guys approaching, blacked up, weapons,' he said urgently, then explained, 'I've been watching from an upstairs window.'

A bleary-eyed Laura Binney appeared at the top of the stairs, squinting as though she had just woken up. Roger was at her legs.

The phone in the office started to ring.

'You sure?' Henry said.

'I know men in black carrying guns when I see them.'

Henry stood up, crossed to the office desk and snatched up the phone. Before he could say his name, Tom James sneered, 'And so the fun begins.'

Donaldson dressed quickly, ignoring the recurring stomach cramps and ankle pain, then after instructing Ginny to stay well back, he approached the door leading out to the bar. He listened hard, but could hear nothing, being aware that the thickness of the doors and walls in this old pub meant hearing anything happening in any other part of the building was virtually impossible.

He drew the bolts back slowly, opened it a crack. He turned back to Ginny, who was peering fearfully out of her mother's bedroom, and mouthed, 'Lock it behind me.' Holding his breath, he stepped out into the bar where the body of Danny Bispham still lay, but was not now twitching. The three masked men had gone but the door up to the first floor was ajar and he could hear voices and thumping noises, the sound of people coming back down the steps.

He did not panic, but stepped across into the darkness of the dining room and flattened himself against the wall in a position where he could see, but not be seen.

They came downstairs seconds later. Two of them dragged the semi-comatose Jonny Cain between them, their arms scooped under his armpits. The third guy followed at Cain's outstretched feet, one of his arms held across his chest. Donaldson could see the man had been injured.

At the front door, one of the men holding Cain said, 'Hang fire.' He pulled his arm free, took a couple of steps towards the bar and raised the shotgun he was carrying. He fired four holes into the security mesh, the shot spraying out and shattering optics and glasses on shelves behind the bar. Then he turned back, grabbed Cain again and dragged him through the door.

Donaldson came out of the shadow, walked across to the front window and watched Cain being hauled through the snow of the car park. They dragged him to the back of his Range Rover, opened the back door and lifted him in. Two of them got into the Range Rover, the third, injured man jogged down the main street to a heavy goods vehicle parked a short distance away.

Donaldson stepped back over Bispham, then climbed the stairs to the first floor and walked along the corridor, sniffing the cordite from the shotgun discharges, noting bullet holes in the ceiling and the door frame splintered by the shotgun blast.

And, of course, Riddick's body twisted and bloody at the far end of the corridor. Steeling himself, Donaldson looked into what had been Cain's bedroom where he saw Napier's body splayed across the bed, lying in vast amounts of dark blood, his guts blown out.

'Oh my God!'

Donaldson spun, found Ginny behind him. He steered her away from the carnage, knowing there was nothing he could do for these men.

'Got to call Henry,' he said.

Henry listened as Donaldson succinctly described the events at the pub, his eyes flitting from Alison to Flynn and back. He had come out of the office with the phone to his ear and mee-mawed for Flynn to watch Tom whilst he spoke to the American.

'Right – thanks, pal.' He pressed the end call button and stared at Alison.

'You got a problem, Henry?' Tom shouted with delight.

'Not as big as yours,' Henry quipped.

Flynn had been standing close to Tom, peering through the Venetian blinds that he had closed after switching off the lights. 'Behind the hedge now,' he reported. 'What was the call about?'

Even though he didn't want to talk in front of Tom, Henry did not have much choice. 'They've already paid a visit to the pub . . . no, it's OK,' he said, reacting to Alison's gasp of horror. 'Ginny's all right . . . but three of Cain's men aren't and they've abducted Cain himself.'

'I need to get back immediately,' Alison said.

'No, not yet,' Henry snapped, 'we need to see what's happening here.' He flicked off the hall light and went into the office to join Flynn at the window. Both men peered out through the crack. Flynn pointed out two black figures kneeling by the low hedge that formed the boundary of the garden. 'I see them,' Henry said tightly.

'Henry, they've come for me,' Tom explained. He began to get to his feet, but Henry slammed him back to the floor.

'Stay there and keep quiet.' Henry pointed a fairly meaningless finger at him.

Tom looked sadly at him. 'Henry, this is too big for the likes of you. You need to let me go.' He held up his wrists. 'Let me go and no one else gets hurt – promise.'

'You're going nowhere, pal. Remember what I said about facing justice? Still applies.'

'In that case, they'll come by force, and people will get hurt. People like her.' He jabbed a finger at Alison. 'Do you want that to happen?'

Flynn took Henry by the uninjured arm and pushed him out into the hallway, stepping over Tom's outstretched legs, giving the prisoner an aside as he passed. 'Don't give me a reason to rip your fucking lungs out, you bastard.'

Tom laughed.

In the hall Flynn whispered urgently. 'Let's get tooled up. Use the guns I found.' He gestured to the kitchen. 'We might need them and it'll all be reasonable and justified if it all goes shit-shaped. If we have him covered, they might back off.'

Panic – that he tried to suppress – rose like bile in Henry and his overriding thought was that this was a real shitty end to a shitty day. 'OK,' he said heavily. Already his mind was a whirl of inquests, trials, cross-examinations, internal discipline boards, plus newspaper headlines, family crises and an uncomfortable future. 'Make sure the guns are loaded, but they are a last resort, Steve, you know? Way down the line.'

'I hear you – but it's going to be a short line.'

Then there was a huge crash as something hit the front door, a rock, brick or stone, making everyone jump and duck, for it also sounded like a gunshot. Flynn dashed back to the front-room blinds.

One of the crouching figures was now standing in the driveway, holding up his hands to show he was unarmed. He was shouting something. Flynn relayed this latest scenario to Henry, who opened the front door an inch, then snaked past Henry to the kitchen to sort out the guns.

'What?' Henry called.

The figure was Jack Vincent. He cupped his hands around his

mouth to amplify his voice. 'Just let Tom go, will you? That'll be the end of this and we'll be out of here, no probs.'

'Not an option,' Henry called back through the gap. 'I suggest you back off now and start running so you can put some distance between you and the law. Give yourself a head start. That's all I can offer you.'

'Not good enough. If you don't hand him over, we'll just come and get him, then it'll turn nasty.'

'Why do you want him so badly?'

'Because I like him.' Vincent dropped his hands. 'Look pal, just open the door and push him out.'

Flynn came up behind Henry. He fully opened the door and stood shoulder to shoulder with him, the very menacing-looking Skorpion machine pistol held across his chest. Henry saw it and quivered.

Vincent snorted and made a dismissive gesture. 'Guys, if that's the way you want it . . .'

He backed away and ducked out of sight behind the hedge.

Henry and Flynn reversed into the hall, closed and locked the door.

To Alison, Henry said, 'You and Laura get into the dining room at the back of the house. I know you want to get back to the pub, but there's no way you can go safely at the moment. Karl will look after Ginny – *he will*,' he emphasized. 'I'd trust him with my life.'

She nodded reluctantly and took Laura to the back of the house.

Henry got on the phone and called the FIM to bring him up to speed. As he was talking, the phone was ripped from the FIM's hand and another voice came on the line, one Henry recognized instantly – the Chief Constable, Robert Fanshaw-Bayley. This was the man Henry had had a hate-hate relationship with for over twenty-five years. Normally Henry's heart would have sunk without trace, but there was something reassuring in the gruff, unpleasant tones of FB, as he was known. He had obviously seen fit to turn out for this incident.

'Henry, what the hell have you done this time?' he demanded.

'I'd argue nothing.'

'Likely story. Look, you just keep calm. I've got a firearms team, a support unit serial, ambulance and fire service and the helicopter all en route to you. As far as they can go, that is. As soon as the council get off their fucking arse and get the snowploughs through, we'll be with you.'

'Thanks boss.'

'In the meantime, keep a lid on it and tell that twat Tom James I'm going to have his guts when I get hold of him.'

'I will.' The call ended. Henry said to Tom, 'The chief sends his regards.' Tom scowled.

'Did he have a message for me?' Flynn asked.

'Yeah, says you're a twat.'

'Ahh, I love him too.'

There was a noise. A noise that crept up on them from the background, building up. A vehicle. Getting louder as it got nearer. A big vehicle. Henry and Flynn frowned at each other. Flynn stepped over Tom's legs again. Callard, still sleeping through everything, grunted something. Flynn looked out of the window.

'Oh hell,' he said, 'remember that HGV that drove past?' Henry recalled it. He joined Flynn at the window. 'Well, it's coming back.'

And there it was, bearing down on the house. Having turned off the road, it demolished the low garden wall and lumbered across the front lawn at the bay window of the lounge. It was the lorry that Vincent and his men had driven down to the village earlier. It came like a tank. At the wheel was Vincent's injured man, Shannon, driving the huge machine easily despite his wound.

At the window, both men watched mesmerized as the lorry drove right into the bay window.

Vincent had taken up a position at the bottom of the drive, a machine pistol held at hip level. He pulled the trigger and sprayed the office window with a stream of bullets.

Henry pushed Flynn, who landed on Callard, as a line of bullets splattered through the window and thudded into the back wall.

The huge lorry plunged into the bay window with a crunching, cracking, grinding and howling engine noise, and that whole section of the house crumbled around the front of the vehicle like a pack of cards combined with a matchstick model.

Henry and Flynn untangled themselves, keeping down and scampering on all fours around the desk, only to see Tom's legs and bottom as he did the same thing, but ahead of them. Taking advantage of the distraction, he'd crawled away. Henry lunged for him and got his fingers around an ankle. He held on, but Tom flicked himself over and kicked out repeatedly, one blow connecting hard with Henry's wounded shoulder. He screamed and had to let go.

Flynn came up, trying to get the Skorpion ready for use.

Shannon slammed the lorry into reverse, and with another terrible crunching and tearing noise the vehicle backed out, leaving a huge hole in the front of the house as bits of concrete, stone, bricks and the PVC window frame crashed down.

In the hall, Tom rolled up on to his feet and threw himself at the living-room door, but he hadn't accounted for Alison who had emerged from the dining room, terrified but needing to know what was going on. Behind her, the diminutive figure of Laura hovered. Alison had seen Tom kick Henry, then come to his feet and go to the door. She ran towards him and started to hammer punches on him.

At the same time, Vincent fired another burst from his gun, and bullet holes perforated a diagonal line across the front door. They were high and missed Alison, but one caught Laura and knocked her back into the dining room.

Alison automatically turned at Laura's scream. Tom almost casually slid his cable-tied hands over Alison's head, twisted with her, kicked open the lounge door, pulled her through behind him so she formed a shield then took her across the devastated lounge and out through the gap, ducking as a brick fell. She struggled, but Tom was big, strong and desperate.

Shannon had dropped out of the lorry, drawn a pistol and fired a couple of unaimed shots into the house, covering Tom as he backed away with Alison. 'Come on, bitch, come on,' he was saying into her ear.

Henry had seen her attempt to have a go at Tom, seen her distracted by Laura's scream, but then had to drop to the ground instinctively as the bullets came through the front door, by which time Tom had taken Alison as a hostage.

Flynn came up behind Henry, crouched low.

Vincent put another half-magazine into the front of the house.

And then there was silence, followed by the sound of another vehicle drawing up.

'Henry. Henry Christie,' Tom shouted. 'You can look – we won't shoot.'

'I don't think so.'

'Whatever . . . don't fucking come for us, yeah? You haven't got the manpower anyway – but if you do, Alison's dead. Leave it twelve hours, then do what you have to do. Until then, if I see anything I don't like, she's dead, and I've seen how much you like her.'

A car door slammed, an engine revved.

From the back dining room, Laura screamed, 'Oh God, oh God . . . help me.'

Flynn, still positioned on his haunches behind Henry, said, 'You know she's dead, don't you? Whatever we do or don't do – she's dead.'

Callard, who had woken properly at last, raised his head and said, 'He's right.'

TWENTY-ONE

Flynn stalked the room like a caged tiger, rage simmering. Callard, now fully awake, but still bleary-eyed and smelling, watched him nervously.

Henry leaned on the desk, the phone on loudspeaker, in hurried discussion with FB, the chief constable. Sweat poured down him and he felt faint, his injured shoulder now causing him agony, and after the last burst of activity, he wondered if he was going into some sort of delayed shock. Whatever it was, he was feeling very ill all of a sudden and it was a massive effort to keep going, pushing himself on.

'You're saying you don't even know where they've taken her?' FB said.

'Not for sure, but Mallowdale House is the best bet. They're as trapped as we are . . .' Henry ended the sentence thoughtfully, 'But they've managed to steal Jonny Cain's Range Rover and we know they have other four-wheel-drive vehicles at their disposal. Might possibly try to make it through.'

'Henry, even the snowploughs can't get through,' FB pointed out.

'I know – just thinking . . . Vincent knows the hills, the quarries.'

'And you have no idea of their intentions?'

'No.' He sighed, and as he did so pain shimmered through him. 'They took her at gunpoint and drove off, using her as a bargaining chip maybe . . . but I'm very concerned about her welfare.'

'That's putting it mildly,' Flynn interjected angrily, still pacing.

'Who was that?' FB asked.

'Steve Flynn.'

'Oh,' he said dubiously.

Henry waved Flynn to zip it. 'Also we have a wounded girl in the back room here. It doesn't look life threatening, but she's going into shock and I'm worried about her. I've turned out the drunken doctor, but she needs to get to hospital ASAP.'

'As I said, our helicopter's on standby, as is the air ambulance, but the weather—'

'I know, I know,' Henry said shortly. 'And we've three dead bodies down at the pub, and Cain's been kidnapped too and not been seen since. He could be in a ditch with a bullet in his brain by now.'

'Not that we care,' Flynn interrupted again.

'Steve – you're not helping here,' Henry said.

Flynn abruptly stopped his stalking and planted his hands on the desk. 'We need some action here,' he said. 'All this chitter-chatter isn't getting us anywhere.'

'Flynn again, I assume,' FB said. 'All very well, but you're not the SAS or a police firearms unit and we don't want any other lives lost by doing something completely stupid.'

'We've got the firepower – those guns in the kitchen.'

Henry rolled his eyes. He did not want to admit it to Flynn, but if he had been uninjured, then his instinct would have been to go for it. He, too, was a man of action and he knew he would be devastated for the rest of his life if Alison came to serious harm because he'd done nothing to try and prevent it. But he also knew it was plain nuts to go charging in. It wasn't as though they even knew for certain where she was. 'We don't even know the provenance of those guns,' he said to Flynn. 'They could've been used in murders or robberies.'

'And they're all we've got, so who gives a shit?'

'Look, I want her back safe and sound just as much as you do. I also want Tom James's collar and every other bugger in this blood-soaked village who's committed a crime – but we're screwed.'

'Henry,' FB interjected from the safety and warmth of the control room some thirty miles away. His voice was firm. 'You're on the ground, you have to make the decisions, I'm afraid. Whatever you decide, as long as it's thought out and justified and reasonable, then I'll back you one hundred per cent.'

'Can I have that in writing?'

'No – just do not get yourself or anyone else killed.'

'OK boss, thanks.'

The front door of the police house opened. Karl Donaldson entered, accompanied by Ginny and a very frazzled-looking Dr Lott, who was clearly wearing his thick pyjamas underneath his clothes.

'Keep me informed,' FB said. 'And good luck.'

The line went dead. Henry examined the faces now surrounding him: Flynn, Donaldson, Ginny, Dr Lott and Callard.

'Well, I hate to say it,' Flynn commented, 'but you're the boss and bosses make decisions.'

After giving Flynn a snappy sardonic look, Henry said, 'We don't know anything for certain. We don't know what they think they'll achieve by taking Alison' – Ginny had been told of her stepmother's predicament, and here he caught her look of anguish – 'and even if they have taken her to Mallowdale. It's a bloody big place with huge grounds, and there are the quarries nearby, operational and non-operational. They might have some way of getting out of the area. But' – he changed the subject quickly and turned to Dr Lott – 'you have a patient in the dining room who needs medical attention.'

The doctor, trying his best not to be too drunk, nodded and left.

Henry's eyes moved to Callard. 'You know your way around Mallowdale House and the surrounding area, don't you?' It wasn't really a question, more a statement of fact – and hope.

'Eh, me? I'm not getting involved.'

'Oh, you are.' Henry turned to Flynn and Donaldson, then a feeling of nausea came over him and he had to take a deep breath and started shivering. He fought it, pulled himself together. 'I'm sorry to admit it, but I'm struggling here, guys. Even if we decided to go in, there'd only really be you fit.' He pointed to Flynn.

'And me,' Donaldson claimed. 'I've just overdosed on Imodium and some mega-strong painkillers, so I reckon I've got a good hour to give you.'

Dr Lott bustled back into the office, now very definitely sober. 'This girl needs a hospital immediately. She's gone into deep shock and without proper care, her body's going to close down. The wound isn't that serious, but there is a good chance of losing her.'

'Treat her as best you can,' Henry said. 'Hospital isn't an option just yet. What about your surgery? Would it be worth getting her there?'

'I'm not sure I want to move her,' he said thoughtfully. 'I'll try and see if I can get one of the practice nurses in to come and help. There's one who lives in walking distance – but I need a phone that works.'

Henry handed him the office phone. To Ginny he said, 'Can you help him? Keep yourself busy? I know it's a big ask.' She said she would, so Henry looked at Flynn and Donaldson. 'Go check the guns and see if they're all likely to work – just in case.' Next he turned to Callard and said, 'Right matey, what do you know?'

Taking Alison had been an instinctive thing, a desperate act by a man who wanted nothing other than to escape in any way possible. Tom had thrown her into the back footwell of the Range Rover, wedged painfully behind the front seats. He jumped in and stamped his feet on her, keeping her pressed down like a sardine on the journey back up to Mallowdale House. In the luggage area behind the rear seats was Jonny Cain, unconscious and badly beaten, his body forced into the space in such a way that his head was tilted upwards and he was breathing blood down into his throat and lungs. He was making a sickening gurgling sound.

Henderson was at the wheel, Vincent in the front passenger seat and Shannon was alongside Tom in the back seat, cradling his wounded arm. His feet were also pressed on to Alison.

The Range Rover moved easily through the multitude of rutted snow tracks up towards the house.

'Plans?' Vincent asked, looking at Tom.

'Get back to the house, pack up and go.' Tom sounded cool and in control. 'We can outfox these numb bastards for ever,' he said dismissively.

'But we're stuck here,' Henderson pointed out.

'We can get out through the quarries, even in this weather,' Tom said. 'The Shoguns will get us across the hill.'

'What about Cain?' Vincent said. 'I thought he could feed Kitty.'

'Don't think we have time,' Tom said. He leaned over the back seat and looked at Cain for a second. Then he leaned forward and waggled his fingers at Vincent and said, 'Gimme.' Vincent handed him the pistol he'd been using. Tom twisted round and fired two shots into Cain's head. 'Too much like a problem,' he said. 'How much d'you reckon we've got?' he asked Vincent.

'Four mill, give or take. Same in gear,' Vincent said.

Tom nodded, thought for a moment, then quickly placed the gun against Shannon's temple and pulled the trigger twice more, jerking him against the side window, blood spraying out across the glass.

'Fuck, Tom!' Vincent shouted.

'Three of us is enough,' he explained. 'Give us a good start, that money – South America, yeah? Just a suggestion.'

Shannon's body slumped down, his dead eyes inches above Alison's upturned face, blood gushing out of his head wound over her.

'They're good to go,' Flynn announced with certainty.

'Let's see.' Donaldson inspected the weapons, checked each one with an expert eye and touch.

'What the hell do you know about guns?' Flynn asked.

Donaldson gave him a quick glance and Henry blanched. Even he didn't know the answer to that one for sure, but he had a damned good idea that the American knew far more than Flynn about weapons.

'Bit of FBI training,' Donaldson said modestly, his lips curling into a tight smile.

Flynn watched him carefully, trying to read the expression but failing, even though he did get the impression that Donaldson had a greater, more dangerous depth than the slightly dim Yank he portrayed himself as.

Henry backed out of the kitchen and tried to hold himself together physically and mentally, going into the dining room where Laura was being tended by Dr Lott and Ginny. The patient had been covered by a quilt, the wound had been dressed and she'd been drugged up. But she was the colour of puce, trembled and moaned frighteningly.

'This isn't good,' Lott said. 'The practice nurse is on her way up here on foot, via the surgery. I don't want to take the chance of moving her, but at least I'll be able to get a drip into her and other medication. But what she needs—'

'Yeah, a hospital,' Henry finished. 'I know. Ginny – you holding up?' The young girl looked stressed beyond measure.

'I'm worried about Mum.'

'Yeah, yeah,' Henry said inadequately. He wanted to promise that she would be OK, but didn't dare. Fortunately the office phone rang again and Henry went to answer it.

'Henry, it's me.' Henry immediately recognized the voice of DC

Jerry Tope, the intelligence analyst who Henry often used to good effect, and who was also beholden to Flynn. Tope was the last person Henry had expected to hear from.

'Jerry, nice to hear from you.' Henry sat down weakly at the desk, trying to roll his ever-tightening shoulder, which radiated pain. 'I'm just a tad busy right now – y'know, bullets and broads and all that.'

'So I hear,' Tope said, unimpressed. 'And I've been dragged out of my pit by FB to do some digging around the archives for you.' He sounded desolate. 'FB asked me, no – fucking ordered me – to look into Jack Vincent, Tom James and Jonny Cain. Thought the background might be of some use to you.'

'Is it?'

'Take it or leave it, but from an initial sweep, I've come up with some connections, and I know you love connections.'

'Fire away.'

'Six years ago, as a uniformed PC, Tom James arrested an up-and-coming drug dealer and haulage contractor by the name of Jack Vincent for various vehicle licensing offences and tax disc fraud – but no charges were ever brought. The custody record was marked off as not enough evidence . . . one interesting connection, yeah?'

'Their first link, maybe?'

'Additionally, at that time, Tom was massively in debt – horses, usual shit. According to some credit ratings databases I've accessed, not long after that arrest the debts had vanished.'

'OK, he's connected to Jack Vincent. I get it. Keep digging, mate, and if I survive the night, I'll give you a pat on the back.'

'There's more. After that arrest, Tom's arrest record suddenly went through the roof. He could do no wrong, got transferred on to CID on the strength of it . . . coincidence? My view is that Vincent was feeding him stuff, whilst Vincent himself managed to keep lily-white, if I'm allowed to say that.'

'So they scratched each other's backs?'

'There's more. Jonny Cain – he was up for murder, the one he was acquitted of, and you'll remember that the investigation was overseen by your old mate Dave Anger.'

'Yes,' Henry said. Dave Anger, a name to conjure with. Anger had been a detective chief superintendent, a sworn enemy of Henry Christie, and was eventually toppled after Henry uncovered some very nasty things about him. That said, Henry was pretty sure that Anger's investigation into the murder allegation against Jonny Cain was above board. The trial had only collapsed after Cain ordered the hit on Felix Deakin and the other witnesses suddenly lost their memories.

'Tom James was a DC on the murder squad. He was part of the intelligence and financial analysis team, which gave him a very interesting insight into Jonny Cain's activities. In other words, he knew virtually everything about Cain, how much he was worth, how much he was making, where the money went, everything.'

Henry put his head in his hands, still with the phone to his ear. 'And he and Jack Vincent maybe decided they wanted Jonny's pile?'

'I dunno – that's for you to find out. Something else, too. Jack Vincent became a National Crime Squad target. I've been doing a bit of delving into Tom James's work computer and found out he's been accessing NCS files on Vincent by a very clever route.' Tope paused, obviously wanting Henry to say, 'Not clever enough for you, though.' He went on. 'He knows about ongoing and proposed operations concerning Vincent, and strangely enough Mr Vincent hasn't been caught or convicted of anything for many a year now.'

Henry took all this in and said, 'And then Tom married Cathy, who must have discovered all this somehow . . . thanks, Jerry. Speak later.' Henry was about to hang up, but before he could, Tope said quickly, 'Be careful, boss – you might have a tiger by the tail here.' Henry suppressed a giggle at the irony of that and ended the call, turned to see Flynn leaning on the office door watching him. He lifted up the phone and said, 'Your mate Jerry Tope.' He knew Flynn and Tope were old friends. 'Tom and Vincent go way back, and it transpires that Tom knows just about everything there is to know about Jonny Cain's operation.'

'I gathered – I eavesdropped.'

Henry slumped back in the chair, his shoulder feeling as though it was being squeezed by six tiny vices. He gasped.

'You OK?' Flynn asked. Henry shook his head. Then, in the hallway, Donaldson hurried past clutching his stomach and ran upstairs, saying, 'You know I said I had an hour? So wrong.'

Flynn's head went from one man to the other in disbelief.

Donaldson came downstairs a few minutes later, shaking his head despondently, entered the office and said, 'Hell, I thought I had that beat.'

Henry, who had been sitting at the desk with his eyes closed, trying his best to deal with the pain, the feeling of sickness and dizziness, also shook his head.

'We're not going to be much use,' he admitted.

'No,' Donaldson agreed, 'so where do we go from here?'

Henry's whole body deflated, a feeling of defeat overpowering him, something he had rarely experienced. One thing he always did was keep going to the bitter end, never gave up. Being shot in the shoulder shook that up somewhat. 'Where's Steve?' he groaned. 'We need a conflab.'

'Kitchen, I guess.' Donaldson walked down the hallway, peered into the dining room at the worried faces of Dr Lott and Ginny, still tending Laura, who looked very ill, but was now awake and talking. He went into the kitchen saying, 'Steve . . . we need to— Shit,' he said as he saw that the Skorpion machine pistol and the Chinese-made semi-automatic pistol had gone, as well as the bag of ammunition. Nor was there any sign of Flynn.

TWENTY-TWO

It was tough going. The snow was deep, and trudging through it in jeans and trainers was energy-sapping and unpleasant. Flynn followed the tyre tracks up the road until they veered off and disappeared underneath the gates at the end of the driveway leading up to Mallowdale House. The high, wooden electronically controlled gates were closed. Flynn surveyed them for a moment, then looked up at the CCTV camera with which he'd had a conversation about a million years before.

He knew assumptions were bad things to make, but he guessed that under the present circumstances it would be unlikely that the security system was on and the CCTV was being monitored. Tom and Jack Vincent, plus cronies, would be scurrying around like rats to get out of the place. They were hardly going to settle down and bust open a bottle in celebration. They had to get moving soon, although Flynn didn't quite see what their plans for escape might be. But that wasn't his problem. They'd made the play, killed people, shot cops, destroyed a house, sprung a man from lawful custody and the rest. They'd opened that particular door and had to accept whatever it was that came charging through.

In this case, Steve Flynn. A man driven by the fact that one of his best friends of the last twenty-odd years had been murdered and he did not wish to see the murderer get away. If Tom did escape somehow, then there would be no chance of Flynn ever coming face to face with him again, which would be a tragedy. Flynn wanted to get his hands on him now, not have to sit back whilst the cops carried out a manhunt that would probably be a shambles. People like Tom and Jack Vincent, Flynn suspected, knew how to evade the police and it was highly likely they would be out of the country within hours.

He stood in front of the gate, then unslung the Skorpion he'd snaffled and flung it over. He scrambled up and over and dropped untidily on to the other side, where he crouched in the shadows, getting some of his breath back and brushing the snow off the machine pistol.

He'd thought of using Alison's four-wheel drive to get him up to Mallowdale House, but decided it would be more trouble than it was worth. Although it was a fair distance from the police house to the gates, he thought approaching on foot would give him the greater advantage.

First, if he had used the car it would have alerted Henry Christie instantly. As it was, with Donaldson firmly rooted to the toilet and Henry half-comatose from the shotgun wound, sneaking off on foot probably gave him the lead he wouldn't otherwise have had. Also, if he turned up in a car, it might have alerted Tom straight away. As tiring as it was on foot in the snow, to Flynn this seemed the better option all round and he knew his fitness would see him through.

So far, so good. He was on Mallowdale House property and hadn't yet been spotted, he hoped. But he did have a slightly queasy feeling about the big cat that had cropped up in conversation a few times, the one Jack Vincent was supposed to own. Did it really exist? If so, where the hell did he keep it? Did he allow it to roam free? Flynn doubted it was real, sounded like a local myth. And if it was a mountain lion, that didn't bother him too much anyway. He knew they were cowardly cats where humans were concerned . . . but if it was some other species . . . He dismissed the thought.

He cut into the trees by the driveway and made his way slowly and carefully to the house, a distance of about two hundred metres, following the snaking drive like a river. Then the tree line stopped and the drive cut through a wide lawn, opening out into a semicircular gravel-covered parking area at the front of the house.

Flynn crouched, keeping cover. There were external lights on the house walls which would normally have illuminated the building, but they were all switched off and the house was a big black shadow. As Flynn's eyes adjusted and took in the light available, he could make out the features of the building, and the fact that Jonny Cain's Range Rover was parked directly between himself and the front door, which provided some cover for his approach to the house.

He remained perfectly still for a minute, watching, listening. There was no movement, nothing to hear, just his heart pounding against the wall of his chest, the throbbing pulse in his temple.

He thought he heard a swish of movement behind him. Gritting his teeth and not allowing any sound to pass from him, he turned slowly, the hairs on the back of his neck rising. There it was again, up in the branches. A large, dark shape, and he relaxed and exhaled. An owl.

Stop it, he told himself.

He took another moment to control his breathing and get ready. The Skorpion was slung across his chest at an angle, the iffy Chinese pistol tucked down the waistband of his jeans at the small of his back. Keeping very low, he emerged from the cover of the tree line and ran towards the Range Rover, maybe fifty yards away from him. He ran quickly, scrunching the gravel underneath the snow, then dropped by the vehicle, twisted and leaned against it, once more catching his breath. He'd only come a short distance, but it had felt like a quarter of a mile, exposed, and fully expecting to be picked off by a sniper at one of the house windows, or brought down by a fucking lion.

Scratch the cat crap from your brain, he ordered himself. He could not resist checking the tree line, though, to see if there was movement other than a barn owl. Or a pair of feline eyes watching him.

Satisfied there was nothing, he looked at the house through the rear passenger windows of the Range Rover, except that the view was obliterated by something smudged and smeared across the nearside window.

For a moment, Flynn could not work it out, then it clicked. The inside of the window was covered in blood and for a horrible moment he thought it was Alison's. He rose a little higher so he could see inside the car, making out the figure in the back seat, slumped over. Not Alison, but the bigger shape of a man – one of their own guys.

Flynn came up even higher, knees still bent, but getting a better view inside. Yes, definitely a man, he reassured himself, his head lolling between his legs. Flynn swallowed and suddenly realized how reckless he was in coming here alone. Thinking he could take on these men, when clearly they had no hesitation in killing members of their own gang. They would simply be conditioned to put him down. But on a lighter note, the odds had improved slightly. Now three to one.

He came up almost to his full height, still using the cover provided by the rear offside of the car, his head ducking in and out, checking the front door, the windows – and then something else caught his eye. The second body in the vehicle, Jonny Cain stuffed into the luggage space behind the back seats.

Flynn dropped down again and ran a hand across his face, then over his hair to flick off the snow.

Jonny Cain. According to Donaldson he had been kidnapped alive. Obviously they would have had some reason for that, some purpose – then they must have had a change of mind and killed him. Too much of an encumbrance under the circumstances, Flynn guessed. No time for anything fancy with him – like torture – so let's kill him.

Which begged the question – what about Alison?

Flynn could not come up with one good response to that. They had taken a hostage to facilitate their escape, now what use could she be? If none, he knew he would find her dead.

He took firm hold of the Skorpion, a gun he'd been introduced to during weapons training all those years ago in the Marines. He knew about it, how to handle it, knew its capabilities, though he'd never fired it in anger, just down a range. That was over twenty-five years ago, when he'd been nothing but a lad. Bracing himself, he bent low and ran to the front door of the house, flattening himself next to it, one hand reaching out to the handle and turning it slowly. It had to be locked, he told himself. Surely they wouldn't have . . . There was a click and Flynn's insides tightened . . . it was open.

Now – fast or slow? High impact or sneakiness?

He opened it slowly, took the chance, sidled in and found himself in a huge deserted hallway. A staircase ran up to the first floor just to his right and at ground level there were five doors off it. Lounge, dining room, kitchen, another lounge perhaps, he guessed, not knowing the layout of the place.

He took a few paces, his senses working at full tilt. He could hear the sound of muffled voices from behind one of the doors. He swallowed dryly, held his breath, moved forward again, bringing the Skorpion down into a firing position, concentrating on the origin of the voices. Not from behind the first door, nor the second . . . the third. Was this the kitchen? It was certainly a room at the back of the house. Then he cursed himself for not being cautious enough, spun around and saw the huge figure of Ox Henderson hurtling towards him silently, but powerfully and terrifyingly.

Even then, Flynn knew that if Henderson could not be taken down instantly, soundlessly, the little adventure would be over and nothing would have been achieved. The only advantage Flynn had was that Henderson had not shouted a warning or war cry.

He bore down, a murderous look on his face, reminding Flynn of a James Bond baddie – but without the humorous side.

It had to be done perfectly. Flynn had only one chance, one blow. He stood his ground, a mock-horror look on his face, hoping it would lull the big man into subconsciously believing that this would be easy. Which it was – until the very last moment. Flynn stepped aside with the agility of a ballerina, a skill honed by years of balancing on a sportfishing boat. Henderson grabbed nothing but fresh air and Flynn crashed the butt of the Skorpion into the side of his unprotected head. It was a hard blow, perfectly aimed, another skill perfected on a fishing boat when using the gaff to hook a deadly shark in the gills, waiting for exactly the right moment. Henderson's head was as hard as a rock, but the shockwave stunned him.

Flynn thought he had hit hard enough, but realized how wrong he was when Henderson staggered sideways, shook his head like a bull – flicking the blood from the newly acquired cut – and launched himself at Flynn again. Flynn did a neat sidestep and, using the Skorpion once more, smashed it across Henderson's head, successfully putting him down. His legs went to jelly and he dropped. Not out cold, but well out of it.

At which point the kitchen door opened. Tom stepped out and saw Flynn standing over the big man.

There was a moment as both men computed their predicament.

Tom's right hand came up, the pistol in it coughing twice, but Flynn was already moving away, readjusting his grip on the Skorpion as he leapt, firing in mid-air. The gun kicked hard, but he was expecting it. A burst of slugs sliced through the air, then the gun jammed. They were badly aimed, but one caught Tom and he fell backwards into the kitchen. There was a female scream from behind him.

Flynn threw the Skorpion away in disgust and pulled the pistol out of his waistband.

Tom's feet were sticking out of the door, moving as though he was trying to propel himself backwards. Flynn flattened himself against the wall by the kitchen door, pistol in both hands, pointing downwards.

'Vincent,' he called. 'Vincent.' There was no reply. He called the name again and added, 'It's over, this stupid game is finished.'

Tom moaned, 'Oh God, I'm shot.' His legs continued to kick out.

In the hallway, Henderson moved.

Flynn shouted again. 'Vincent, Jack Vincent.'

'Flynnie,' came Alison's weak voice.

'Alison?'

'He's gone, out the back door.'

'You sure?'

'Yes.'

Flynn licked his lips, exhaled. He ensured he was holding the pistol correctly – in the right hand, fingertip resting on the trigger, left hand cupped underneath, supporting – then he inhaled and pivoted into the doorway, coming into a combat stance. Legs shoulder-width apart, bouncing down slightly on his knees and the gun at the point of the isosceles triangle formed by his arms. The gun covered the room, top to bottom, side to side, and unless Vincent was behind the door – and Flynn did check through the gap – he had gone.

Alison, battered and bedraggled, with blood smeared over her face and around the neck of her jumper, was sitting on the floor by the cooker, knees drawn up, arms clasped tightly, shaking.

'He's gone?' Flynn said. She nodded. Flynn cautiously lowered the weapon, reversed into the hallway and went to Henderson, who was just about to push himself up on to all fours, blood dripping on to the tiled floor. Flynn callously cracked him hard with the pistol on the back of his head and he went down like a squashed insect, his arms splayed, face down in his own blood. Flynn waist-banded the gun, pulled Henderson's arms around his back and cuffed them with the cable ties he had snaffled from the desk in front of Henry.

Next he crossed to Tom and kicked away the pistol. He was laid out at an angle on the kitchen floor, the bullet from the Skorpion having torn apart his upper right biceps. He bent over him and they locked eyes. 'She found you out, didn't she?'

Injured though he was, his defiance remained. 'Fuck you,' he gasped nastily.

With a sneer of contempt and a complete disregard for the wounds, Flynn kicked Tom over, pulled back his hands and cable-tied them together, ignoring his screams of pain. This done, he stood up and pulled out the gun again.

'How are you?' he asked Alison. 'Is this your blood?' He wiped away some from her cheek with his thumb.

'I'm OK,' she nodded. 'Not good really. Where's Henry?'

'Getting forty winks, I think. Look, I'm going after Vincent.'

'Let him go,' Alison pleaded.

Flynn pretended to think about this for a second, but said, 'Nah.' He went to the outside kitchen door, opened it and looked out. Parked there were two long-wheelbase Shoguns, both with their hatchbacks open. Foot trails in the snow led from the kitchen to the cars and back. Flynn stepped out and a security light came on, bathing the whole area with brightness.

Instinctively he bobbed down beside one of the cars, then glanced in the back of it and saw a stack of several half-brick sized blocks made of polythene and wound with gaffer tape. He assumed they were drugs, probably cocaine, and next to them was a cardboard box filled with bound wads of Bank of England notes. Although Henry Christie would probably never believe him, Flynn had never seen so much money. He thought there could be in excess of a million.

'Now then, my old cocker.'

Flynn froze. The cold hard muzzle of a gun had been pressed into the back of his head. An arm reached around and wrenched the pistol out of his grip.

'Didn't think I'd actually do a runner, did you?' Jack Vincent sneered, dropped back a stride and glanced at the gun he'd taken from Flynn. In his right hand he was pointing a similar handgun at Flynn, who had turned slowly to face him. He waggled the gun. 'I imported fifty of these two years ago . . . very fucking iffy guns, always jamming. Like those fucking Skorpions, useless shit.' He tossed the gun away into the snow. 'I really don't know who the fuck you are,' Vincent said, 'but you're a real handy guy. Flynn, is it?'

Flynn kept his mouth tight shut, incensed at himself for dropping his guard. Who the hell would leave money and drugs like that behind? Certainly not Jack Vincent. Should have known he wouldn't be far away.

'By yourself, though, eh?' Vincent said. 'Silly chap.'

'Not for long,' Flynn said.

'Long enough – walk that way, boyo.' Vincent gestured with the gun and Flynn looked into the darkness beyond the pool of light.

'Why don't you just shoot me here?'

'Cat food . . . now move away from the car and start walking. It's not far.'

Flynn did as instructed. As Vincent walked past the car, he reached in and grabbed a big torch which he thumbed on. 'Don't try to be stupid, or I will just shoot you in the back . . . at least this way you'll have a chance.'

Flynn stumbled on and Vincent shone the torch on to a path. 'Down there.'

'So you do have a big cat?'

'Oh yes. Be sorry to leave him, but needs must. I'm sure you'll give him a bit of sport. The last guy didn't . . . mind you, he was dead . . . The one before that, he was alive but shit scared. You'll be fun for him.'

'I presume you have a licence? Get into trouble if you don't.'

'Hey, funny guy – keep going.'

They walked another twenty yards and suddenly there was a high, steel mesh fence in front of them with an integral gate.

'The enclosure – runs right up the hillside,' Vincent said. 'Walk right up to it, Mr Flynn, put your nose up to it.' To assist, Vincent pushed him violently and held Flynn's face against the mesh with his left hand, digging the gun into his back with the other hand. Vincent kicked the fence, making it rattle, and shouted, 'Kitty, Kitty.'

'You're out of your tree,' Flynn said through his misshapen face.

Vincent leaned into Flynn, still holding his head hard, still digging the gun into his lower back. 'No one fucks with me, Flynn.' He kicked the fence again and shouted, 'Kitty – come here.'

Suddenly there was movement on the other side of the fence. A shadowy figure in the darkness, lit by the broken beam of Vincent's torch as it shone through the mesh. Inches away from Flynn, separated only by the thin fence. Flynn, with his head pinned, saw a beautiful, muscular beast, prowling back and forth along the fence, growling with each step it took, its eyes occasionally catching the light. The odour of it was overpowering and terrifying.

'Jesus,' he hissed in awe, 'what is it?'

'You like him?' Vincent was still leaning on Flynn, trapping him against the fence. 'Just a leopard, nothing fancy.'

'You sick bastard.'

Vincent laughed, then pulled Flynn away from the fence and across to the gate, which was secured by two bolts, top and bottom.

'I'd thought of feeding Jonny Cain to him, but changed my mind. You'll do. Go on, open up and step inside – then fucking run!'

'I don't think so.' Flynn was eyeing the angles, working out his chance of disarming Vincent, but he'd stepped right back beyond reach and the gun hovered threateningly.

'I'll kill you if you don't, I don't give a shit.'

The torch played on the fence, picking up the cat beyond, pacing, growling impatiently, wanting to eat, wanting to hunt. Vincent pushed Flynn against the gate, which rattled, surprising the cat. It reacted with a howl and the torch caught the ears pinned back, the long, pointed incisors revealed in their full glory.

'See, he likes you – now open up, step inside. I need to get going.'

Flynn reached for the upper bolt and slid it back. Then he bent down for the lower one, images in his mind of having to outrun, outmanoeuvre an animal designed to bring down and kill others. A supremely designed killing machine.

Vincent was standing about ten feet behind Flynn, who therefore did not see it happen. He was holding the gun and the torch on Flynn, an evil, leering smile on his face which disintegrated spectacularly as the soft-nosed bullet struck his right temple, fragmented as it passed through the bone, made mincemeat of the brain tissue, then exited through the left temple, removing that whole side of his head.

Four days later

Henry Christie looked pale and unwell. He'd had to have a minor operation – under full anaesthetic – on his shoulder to dig out several shotgun pellets from the flesh. He was on the mend, but it still hurt like hell. He could easily have been on sick leave, but insisted on being at work. Not through any great altruistic or professional motive. He just did not want to miss anything.

He was in his office at police headquarters at Hutton, near Preston. There was a cup of coffee in one hand, a handful of tablets in the other, which he slapped into his mouth and swallowed down with a swig of coffee.

The office, although reasonably sized, was easily filled, as it was that moment. Henry was at his desk and in an arc opposite him, from left to right, were Steve Flynn, Karl Donaldson and the Chief Constable, FB.

Henry had just put the phone down on Rik Dean.

'He's at crown court with Calcutt, who's due to be sentenced today. He's been to see him in the holding cell. Apparently he's reverted to type and is saying nothing more. He gave us the heads-up about a hit man being recruited by the same person who recruited him to take out Felix Deakin, and we know – although we still can't prove it – that it was Jonny Cain. Looks like he got someone to take out Jack Vincent over some disagreement they were having . . . fortunately for you,' Henry said, looking at Flynn, who made a gesture of agreement. 'It's to be wondered if he got paid, bearing in mind what happened to Cain.'

'At that level, it's usually half upfront. He won't starve,' FB said.

'Seems a shame that we even have to try and catch him,' Henry said, 'but we will. I'll use the same team that caught Calcutt.'

There was a pause.

Flynn said, 'Where do I stand?' He had spent two days being interviewed and giving a long, detailed statement to detectives. He still wasn't sure if he was going to be arrested or not.

'I'll put it all in to the CPS,' Henry said.

'With what recommendation?'

'That everything you did was reasonable and justified. There's a lot of negotiating to do with them and Tom's making a lot of noises about excessive force.'

'That's a joke!' Flynn blurted. 'He shot you. And killed his wife.'

'He's not admitting that yet, though. However, Callard can't stop talking,' Henry said. 'Lots of stories about feeding people into crushers and such like.'

FB leaned forward and looked along at Flynn. 'You have nothing to worry about, Steve, we'll see to it – won't we, Henry?'

Henry bobbed his head, a bit shamefaced. 'Yeah.'

'You will be required for any trial, though, whenever this all gets sorted out,' FB went on.

'That's fine . . . does that mean I can go home?'

'Home being?'

'You know, where I live and work. It's no problem to get back here, especially on witness expenses.' He pushed himself up. 'So, can I go?'

Henry nodded. 'Yeah, I need to get on. Things to do, not least of which is try and find a good home for an arthritic ex-police dog and a zoo insane enough to take in a man-eating leopard.'

Outside Flynn breathed the cold air. Flecks of snow drifted down from the leaden sky. As he walked across to the car park, his plan was to get to the nearest library, log on to the Internet and book the first available flight back to Gran Canaria, no matter the cost. That was where he belonged, where he wanted to be. There was nothing to keep him here. As he reached his hire car Flynn pulled out his mobile phone and made a call.

'Alison, it's Steve, yeah. You still OK? Look,' he said, checking over his shoulder to ensure no one was in earshot. 'They're certain Vincent was killed by a hit man hired by Jonny Cain . . . so everything's fine. Yeah, please don't worry. What you did was the right thing and it would have made life unbearably complicated for you if we'd told them what really happened . . . yeah, do not worry. You saved my life. You know you did right and having to justify it before a court could lead to all sorts of complications. Just hang tight, stick to the story and it'll be fine. I will, if you will. Yeah, OK, good. Speak soon.' He ended the call, breathed out, and leaned on his car roof, jumping almost out of his skin at the voice behind, thinking no one was near.

It was Karl Donaldson, who had somehow come right up to Flynn without him noticing.

Donaldson held out a hand. 'It was nice to meet you, pal.' They shook hands. 'You seem a handy guy . . . but just a word to the wise.'

'What would that be?'

'Don't underestimate Henry Christie. He was the first detective on the scene and whilst he may have been shot and injured and exhausted, he was still sharp as a knife.' Donaldson looked knowingly at Flynn. 'He's a man who knows.' Donaldson tapped his nose, turned and limped away without a backward glance. 'And if you'll excuse me, I need to see a man about a chicken.'

Flynn watched the American, mouth open, wondering just who the guy really was. His mobile phone rang, interrupting his thoughts. No number was displayed.

'Steve? It's me, Adam Castle.'

'Boss, I was just thinking about you.'

'Well, good – I need your arse back here as soon as,' Castle said.

'Why?'

'We have a charter arriving in two days from Germany, that bunch of businessmen you took out last year. Two weeks, paid upfront – and they asked for you. Can you make it?'

'Already on my way.'